TACTICAL SUBMISSION

A Windsor Club Story

ADA MARIA SOTO

ROOKERY

Cover designed by Tiferet Design

Rookery Publishing
rookerypublishing.com

Written in New Zealand

First Printing: November 2017
Second Printing: February 2019

ISBN-13 978-1-9732139-0-1

❀ Created with Vellum

CONTENTS

Author's notes   v
Acknowledgments   vii

Chapter 1   1
Chapter 2   16
Chapter 3   21
Chapter 4   36
Chapter 5   40
Chapter 6   50
Chapter 7   65
Chapter 8   83
Chapter 9   89
Chapter 10   96
Chapter 11   102
Chapter 12   120
Chapter 13   129
Chapter 14   134
Chapter 15   138
Chapter 16   144
Chapter 17   152
Chapter 18   165
Chapter 19   172
Chapter 20   188
Chapter 21   198
Chapter 22   209
Chapter 23   217
Chapter 24   223
Chapter 25   229
Chapter 26   236
Chapter 27   244
Chapter 28   251

Chapter 29   257
Chapter 30   264
Chapter 31   278

About the Author   293
Also by Ada Maria Soto   295

AUTHOR'S NOTES

Please note this story contains an act of domestic terrorism on a civic building. It's not overly graphic and our heroes are fine, but it does happen. The sequence all takes place in Chapter 30 if you feel the need to skip it.

This story also contains spanking, rope bondage, floggers, riding crops, forced orgasms, mild CBT, anal toys, hand feeding, book shelving, and a lot of sex.

Feel free to contact the author if you have questions about content before reading.

ACKNOWLEDGMENTS

With huge thanks to Cooper West, my evil enabler. Moya, who said 'too much sex'. Tina, who wrangled the commas. And as always, my love to Nick for giving me the space and time to do this.

CHAPTER 1

I *f you haven't read the Author's Notes please go back and do so.*
Seriously.

THE DEEP CHAIRS OF THE WINDSOR CLUB SPOKE OF WEALTH AND
civility for those who knew how to listen. Doctor Isaac Bard
leaned back, closing his eyes, breathing in the smell of leather
and wood polish. The air was warm, a soothing contrast to the
cold, antiseptic, fridge where he spent his days.

Around him the soft flow of indistinct voices acted as a sort
of white noise only adding to the relaxed atmosphere. He
considered ordering a meal from the top-flight kitchen or a glass
from the extensive wine cellar but there were a hundred places
where he could get a good meal or a glass of wine. He was at the
Windsor Club for something different.

He scanned the faces on the far side of the room where the
unattached boys congregated, each hoping to catch the eye of
one of the club's more dominant members. There was nothing
flamboyant about any of them, the Windsor didn't do flamboy-

ant, but there were subtle flutters of eyes and particular twists of shoulders and hips, lips lingering on the edges of crystal tumblers. There were a few Isaac had spent time with in the past. They tilted their heads in his direction. He glanced at them, but work and responsibilities had kept him from the Windsor Club for months and he was in the mood for something new.

The common room door opened and a large man stepped in. Isaac took a quick glance, looked away then looked back. He knew he sometimes had difficulty recognizing faces out of context, and tried not to mingle his life inside the Windsor with his life out, but the face of the man was familiar and it itched at him. He was tall with broad shoulders and light brown hair. He looked like he should be on an army recruitment poster or hocking aftershave. A slight haze of nerves surrounded him. His gaze darted around the room before he sat himself at an empty table near the other submissives. Isaac sipped his water. Even if he was imagining the recognition, it was unusual to see particularly large men spending time on that side of the room. He could simply be looking at a new member who hadn't yet learned the subtleties of the common room.

A waiter offered the newcomer a glass of water which he hunched over as if he could make himself look smaller. Isaac frowned. He'd seen large submissives try that regularly. The man had to be six foot three if he was an inch. There was no way he was ever going to pass as a five seven twink. And six three with broad shoulders was exactly Isaac's type, at least on a physical level. He wondered if it was less recognition and more simple desire.

That thought was still niggling at him when Hugh Lancing stepped into the common room. That soured Isaac's mood. There was a smoothness to the man that was closer to slimy. He moved in a way that made his thousand-dollar tailored suit look like something from a 70's swingers party. The little he knew about Lancing's techniques in the bedroom did nothing to improve his image of the man. And what he suspected but could never prove, made it unpleasant to even be in the same building as him. Isaac figured at some point he would slip up enough to have his membership revoked but it hadn't happened yet.

Lancing paused for only a second to scan the crowd before heading toward the new boy. He leaned against the table and the boy looked up at him. Isaac didn't need to hear to guess at the slightly condescending ooze that must have been coming from Lancing. The boy shied away, not saying much. Lancing leaned in closer to whisper something.

That was the moment recognition clicked in Isaac's head. Jack Burnside, leader of one of the county's top SWAT teams. As a forensic pathologist, their paths had crossed a few times, mostly in the courtroom, but he had a memorable look to him. Isaac glanced around the room looking for anyone else who might be law enforcement. He could be undercover but the Windsor Club was known for extensively screening its members. Even hearing about it meant you already moved in certain circles. Jack didn't seem like the type to move in those circles, but then he didn't seem the submissive type at all. Isaac was usually pretty good at spotting people with those leanings.

Despite a tight curl in his shoulders, Jack looked like he might go with Lancing.

Like hell. Isaac took long strides across the room. A few of the other subs tried to catch his eye as he approached but he was centered in on Jack.

He stopped next to Jack and rested a hand on his shoulder. It was bad form to touch without invitation, even something as casual as that, but he was not going to let Lancing anywhere near Jack. He tried to put forth an air of calm and control while something primal in him growled.

Jack turned and looked at him while Lancing all but snarled. He frowned, then his eyes went wide. Isaac tipped his head acknowledging the recognition and Jack went pale, even under the club's warm lights. Within seconds his lips became chalky and his hands trembled. Isaac might not be a regularly practicing doctor but he could still spot shock. He squeezed Jack's shoulder in what he hoped was a reassuring manner.

"Hello," Isaac said calmly and softly before tilting his head away from the table and Lancing.

Jack dropped his eyes and stood, ignoring Lancing who was scowling at Isaac. Fortunately, fights were forbidden in the Windsor Club or he was sure he'd have one on his hands.

At well over six feet Jack towered over Isaac's five foot seven but he'd learned early on that being a Dom had nothing to do with height and everything to do with frame of mind. He turned to the discreet side door off the club's main room and collected a key from the maitre d'. He led Jack down the well-lit and thickly carpeted hall, until he reached room twelve and gestured him in.

⚘

SHIT, WAS THE ONLY WORD RUNNING THROUGH JACK'S HEAD WHILE his stomach churned and his hands shook. He swallowed hard desperately trying not to throw up. He'd heard rumors of the Windsor Club. It took him over a year to find, and nearly another year to get in. He picked it because he assumed the chance of someone he knew being there was almost none. Almost wasn't the same as zero.

He'd seen Doctor Bard giving testimony as a Forensic Pathologist, at trials where SWAT had also been involved. He was on the short side, with well slicked dark curls, and he carried the intelligent authority of a doctor. He certainly didn't seem like someone who'd be a member of the Windsor Club. But people would probably say the same about him.

"Why don't you sit down, Jack?"

It was phrased as a question but the doctor's voice was smooth and calm with firmness under it. The room had two plush antique looking chairs to go with the four-post bed carved out of heavy wood. He felt his face flush and took a seat. This was not how the night was supposed to go. Being recognized was not part of the plan.

"It's good to see color in your cheeks. If you went any paler I was going to have you lay down with your feet up so you didn't pass out from shock."

Jack didn't reply. There was still a churning in his stomach. He'd had his membership for two months, before he worked up the nerve to come to the Windsor Club. It wasn't the first time he'd gone looking for a quick fix for the desires he shouldn't have, but it had been a while and he'd been nervous as all hell. Rightfully so it seemed.

"I'd ask what you are doing here but that is blatantly obvious." Jack nodded but didn't want to speak. Speaking had not been part of the plan either. The plan had been to find someone who would take him down and use him enough to fry out the tangled mess of desire and stress his mind had become.

There was a knock on the door. Jack jumped but he didn't stand. He hadn't been told to stand. Was the club being raided? That was stupid. He knew from experience that police raids don't politely knock. Had Dr. Bard invited someone else? That other guy who was talking to him? The doctor stood and opened the door only half way then closed it again. Now he carried a tray with a teapot and two cups.

"My standing order." He placed the tray on the small table beside his chair. "Jasmin green tea. Would you like a cup?" Jack shook his head. He wasn't sure if his stomach could handle something even that simple. Dr. Bard poured a cup and the smell took him back to late lunches with his mother at The Golden Palace Chinese Restaurant and Tea Shop when he was a teenager.

"You would be more comfortable kneeling right now."

He hadn't taken his eyes off Dr. Bard but now he dropped them. It wasn't a question but a statement of truth. That was what he had come here for, for someone who'd tell him to kneel.

"Come here." Dr. Bard gestured to a spot beside his chair. Jack didn't move. Yes, this was what he wanted when he followed Dr. Bard into the room, but still he hesitated. He always hesitated, his desires fighting with his rational mind telling him it was stupid.

He tried to breathe, tried to keep calm but the thread of panic that was telling him to run; screaming that the world was about to know his secret, was fighting with the part of him that was desperate to let the night happen.

Dr. Bard didn't ask again, he simply sipped his tea with a patient air. Jack stood and took the three steps to the spot by the chair. Dr. Bard gestured to the floor and Jack knelt. His breath came out of him in a rush as his body relaxed while his heart was still racing. With his eyes down, as was proper, he strained his hearing trying to anticipate what might be next.

He felt Dr. Bard lace his fingers into his hair, petting him softly before gently guiding his head down until his forehead was resting on the doctor's knee.

"There we go." He pressed two fingers against Jack's throat. Jack started. He didn't like hands or anything else touching his neck. "Easy, I want to check your pulse. May I?"

Jack nodded but squeezed his eyes as two fingers were pressed against the side of his neck.

"Take deep breaths. I *did* become a doctor working on living people. I want to make sure you're okay."

Jack was not okay

"Your pulse is too fast. I'm not sure if that's fear or arousal but I'll bet fear." He went back to stroking Jack's head. "Let's start with what I'm sure you want to hear. I'm not going to speak about this to anyone so you don't need to worry. Aside from being against the club's bylaws it would be both hypocritical and petty, and while I am capable of both of those things in certain situations, this is not one of them."

Jack nodded against his knee. "Thank you," he whispered.

"I would have left you alone all together but that man who was talking to you is... notoriously sleazy and unpleasant, and that is about as polite as I'm willing to be. I cannot work out how he still has his membership."

Jack hadn't been getting a great vibe off him, but he'd encountered several Doms over the years who didn't take him seriously as a submissive. He'd gotten used to taking what attention he could get.

"Now I would like to ask a couple of questions, if you don't mind?"

Jack nodded again. There were usually questions. At least at the better places.

"Have you done this before?" Jack nodded. He had enough experience to please most people.

"How long has it been?"

"Fifteen months," he answered quickly. He didn't have to think about it. He knew almost to the hour how long it had been.

Dr. Bard's hand stilled for a second before he returned to his petting. "Why have you waited so long?"

Jack shrugged.

"I'll make you a deal right now, honesty is important in these situations. Don't lie to me and I'll never lie to you." Jack nodded. "Now, why have you waited so long?"

It was a question no one had ever asked him and in truth he didn't want to answer. "I shouldn't... I shouldn't be the type—" He was losing words and his heart sped up again. The calm that had begun to settle in broke. "I'm too..." He spread his arms but kept his head down.

"Big manly macho SWAT commanders shouldn't enjoy kneeling at the feet of another man, waiting for orders."

Jack grit his teeth. It was a blow to his already queasy stomach hearing it laid out so plainly.

"I promise you, you're not the largest to kneel in front of me and you are very much my type."

That surprised Jack. He didn't think he was much of anyone's type.

"In an ideal world, how often would you want to spend time like this?"

Jack's mind rushed to the two extremes, one part screaming never while the other moaned always.

"More often," he managed to get out. "Something regular."

"I see. Something regular requires a more regular person however." Jack nodded. "And a regular person would have to be someone aware of what you do, and have an understanding of things like 'on call' and 'triple overtime'."

"Yes."

"That can be a tall order."

Jack shrugged, more of a twitch. He had never tried to find someone regular, a Dom or even a boyfriend. It seemed like too impossible a goal.

"Do you have any questions for me?"

From the corner of his eye Jack could see Dr. Bard's other hand resting on his knee. A simple gold band was on his ring finger. He wasn't sure if he should say something. It might only serve to make Dr. Bard mad and send him away. But it sounded like he was feeling out the possibility of a repeat arrangement. Better to ask now than later.

"That ring?"

"I'm married, and my wife knows exactly where I am tonight and has a good idea of what I'm doing. Heck, she practically kicked me out the front door. Said I was getting cranky. And I know where she is this evening and that is with her other partner of many years. A very nice person whom I am quite fond of and I personally think should be getting more commitment than they are getting, but it has been pointed out to me that I don't actually get a say on that." Jack smiled at Dr. Bard's ramble, relaxing some. "I have certain tastes that she is unable or uninterested in fulfilling and she has tastes that I am unable or unwilling to fulfill. We decided long before we even got married that there was no reason we should deny ourselves our pleasures. You can have more than one flavor of ice cream in the fridge."

Jack let out a small chuckle of relief at the analogy. There were several things he didn't particularly like about himself and he didn't want to add home-wrecker to the list. Of course, Dr. Bard could be lying. He certainly wouldn't be the first, but then why not simply take off the ring.

"We do have rules," Dr. Bard continued. "If either of us wants to take on someone long term or bring someone else into our home we have to discuss it, but that might be getting ahead of ourselves." Jack nodded but didn't say anything else. Dr. Bard continued to stroke his head. It was distracting but he didn't want it to stop. It wasn't what he'd come looking for but it had been fifteen months since he'd had physical contact with someone in a non-professional situation. He curled his back up and raised his head, craving a firmer touch.

"Do you have anything else you'd like to ask me?" Jack didn't, already fading from the sensation of Dr. Bard's fingers running along his scalp. Dr. Bard lifted his hand. "There are other questions you should be asking me."

Jack tried to focus. Other questions? He didn't think they were that far in. Had he missed some steps? Everyone took things at a different pace. He supposed it was fine. This was what he was there for. Dr. Bard seemed comfortable and sure, which was more than Jack could say for himself. Hell, he was already on his knees. He straightened his back but kept his eyes down. "How may I please you, sir?"

There was no answer. He felt time slow as he waited. He wished he could hear a clock. He tried to track time with his pulse but it was speeding up. He kept still. The temptation to look up was strong but Dr. Bard's silence could well be a test. Finally, he heard the clink of a tea cup lifted from the tray, the sound of a sip, and the cup being placed back down. Then Dr. Bard's hand was on his head again guiding it back to his knee. "You haven't done this in fifteen months. Have you had any sexual contact with another person? Even a date?"

"No, sir."

Dr. Bard sighed and Jack wondered what was wrong. He knew he wasn't hugely experienced but he was pretty good with the basics and learned quickly. "Let's hold off on the sirs for now, okay?"

Jack nodded. Sir was usually a good default if he hadn't been given detailed instructions. "Yes, Dr. Bard."

"How about just Isaac to start? If you weren't into certain things you wouldn't be here, but those things fall under a very wide umbrella and your things might not match up with my things, though I am quite open to negotiation. Now, you are obviously open to kneeling and you seem to enjoy a good petting, I'm worried you're simply touch starved there."

Jack jerked back at those words.

"And there would be the first nerve." Isaac said softly.

He continued to stroke Jack's head. "How about if I ask you a few more questions and you chime in with yours when they come up?"

Jack nodded but despite the fingers in his hair he was starting to feel uneasy. He had come looking to find someone to shut down the bad neighborhood spinning of his brain, not to talk.

"What do you want? What are you looking for here tonight?"

He didn't answer. No one had ever asked, not really. They'd ask for safe words sometimes or if he was clean but he wasn't sure how to answer this. He'd heard Isaac answer cross examinations on the stand and knew he was fiendishly intelligent. He'd left some of the best defense attorneys in town stuttering messes. What was he supposed to say that didn't make him sound like a needy idiot?

"My brain gets loud. I get tired."

Stupid! Could you sound any more like a dumb jock?

"I understand. It's not uncommon for men in positions of authority. Taking orders instead of giving them means you don't have to think for a bit. Let go of the Ego, indulge the Id. Shed the weight of responsibility. Give yourself some peace."

Peace.

"Yes."

"Your knees must be getting tired. Do you think you could sit in the chair now without the urge to run screaming into the night?"

He hesitated. His knees were sore but not that bad. Certainly, nothing he couldn't handle. Pain was part of it after all. Some discomfort at the start then a chance to move beyond it. And if he stood, Isaac would stop rubbing his head. He'd seen those boys dressed up as leather dogs getting petted. It wasn't his thing but Isaac was right, it was perhaps too long since he'd been touched at all.

Isaac stood. "How about if we stretch out on the bed?"

That perked him up. He leaned forward onto all fours but was there for not even a second before he felt Isaac's hand on his upper arm guiding him to his feet. He had a pinched expression as he looked up at Jack but Jack wasn't sure why. He was acutely aware of their height difference.

Isaac turned away and strode to the bed taking a seat near the head of it, toeing off his shoes as he did. Jack followed but as he got there he wasn't sure what to do. The whole night was proving far more frustrating and confusing than he'd planned. He berated himself for not going back to the Dog Box Bar or maybe Club Steel. Quick, nearly anonymous, and no one asking him to be introspective.

Isaac patted the bed next to him and he sat. Once there he started to push and pull Jack around until Isaac was propped up against the headboard with Jack stretched out at a diagonal, his head resting on Isaac's thigh. Isaac began carding his fingers through his hair again and Jack sighed into it.

"Tell me," he began as Jack was feeling himself begin to drift. "Do you enjoy pain when you do this or is it the submission you want?"

Jack shook his head. Isaac's hand stilled. "Is that a no to the pain or the no to the submission? I'll need a few words here."

"Everything. I'm okay with it."

"Being okay is not the same as enjoying."

The frustration was creeping back into the nice place he'd been drifting to. He wasn't sure what Isaac wanted him to say. He started to sit up but Isaac placed his hand on Jack's forehead.

"It's okay. I'm sorry. You don't need to think right now. Maybe we'll talk more later. May I touch you? I think you need it."

Jack nodded, trying to hold back the eager relief. "Yes."

"Stand up and take off your shirt."

He unbuttoned his shirt, neatly folded it, and placed it on top of the dresser.

"Very nice."

Jack looked down at himself. He tried to keep himself in shape. The job was physically demanding and he felt it was important. He didn't put particular effort into sculpting himself in strange ways though. He looked over Isaac in his black slacks and dark blue shirt. His arousal was obvious. Jack hoped that it was a sign that he'd get what he came for by the end. Things were certainly leaning in that direction.

"Thank you—" Jack barely managed to bite off the 'sir'.

"Lay down on your back."

Jack did. Isaac sat beside him and began sliding his fingers around the edges of his muscles. "Pre-med anatomy would have been so much more fun if I'd had a body like yours available as a learning tool. External oblique, internal oblique, transverse abdominal."

Jack pressed his body up into the touch. It wasn't exactly what he had been looking for but it felt nice. The faint tickle and occasional scratch from a blunt nail. One of those nails scratched along his right nipple. It wasn't even enough to cause pain but he still jumped. It was like a sharp static shock had been sent directly down his spine. He'd been turned on for some time, once the initial panic wore off, but the arousal went from background noise to nearly painful with that single small touch. Normally it took a crop or lash to send a feeling like that through him. Isaac did it again, and again used hardly more than the lightest touch, but he whimpered.

"May I take off the rest of your clothes?" Jack nodded and reached for his fly but Isaac pushed his hands away. "I'll do it."

He bit his lip but kept his hands at his side while Isaac efficiently undressed him, dropping his pants at the side of the bed. Then he went back to touching Jack. He ran his hands up and down Jack's body in broad flat strokes, avoiding his cock and even his nipples, occasionally naming muscle groups as he did. He tried to raise his body into the touch. His head was spinning and his breath was hard and fast. He knew he was on the verge of cumming without even having his cock touched. Then Isaac stopped and Jack recognized the pathetic whimper that filled the room as his own.

"Even if we never do this again don't let yourself go this long without being touched. It's not healthy, and a body like yours is made for it. So responsive. Keep your eyes closed and feel this." Then Isaac's hand was on his cock and he felt like he was burning. His strokes were slow and even, strong yet teasing. Jack pressed his hips up trying to fuck Isaac's hand but Isaac kept his rhythm steady.

When he felt on the verge of going mad two words managed to fight their way through the fog of his mind and fall from his lips. "Please, sir."

Isaac switched his strokes to hard and fast and within five seconds a wave of fire raced its way up his spine and exploded behind his eyes.

ISAAC AIMED JACK'S COCK SO HE CAME ACROSS HIS OWN STOMACH. It looked lovely and obscene. He frowned as Jack's body went limp. He didn't completely pass out but he looked close to it. There was so much wrong with the situation yet there was so much potential for it to be amazingly right. Denying himself for so long was certainly a sign of a tangled-up head and there were obvious issues. Nothing Isaac hadn't encountered before. He had a fondness for large strong subs. It was rare they didn't come to him weighed down with preconceptions about what people should be and should want. Being a five foot seven Dom had gotten him slapped with the word 'should' more than once as well. He hated the word should.

Jack had also started to crawl. He found that to be the finger-prints of an amateur or an undeserved ego. Not on Jack's part but on the part of whomever he'd hooked up with in the past. But then Isaac had been told on more than one occasion that he was a snob about those sorts of things. The fact that he couldn't seem to sort out the difference between pain and submission, or even what he truly wanted reeked of quick encounters with people who didn't care enough or possibly at all.

But then there was the glorious opportunity. He had much the same problem as Jack when it came to a long-term arrange-ment with a dedicated partner. Working for the Coroner's Office meant he got called in at weird hours if something major happened. He couldn't talk about much of his work since it was often tied up in investigations, and he came home smelling of death, latex, and hand sanitizer. There were not many subs that would put up with that on a regular basis. Throw in being married and there was the opportunity for total disaster, which had in fact happened in the past. But Jack was law enforcement. He understood what being on call meant and that a good shower could get the smell of a bad day off your skin, but sometimes it required something more creative to get it out of your head.

Jack began to come back to himself. Isaac brushed a finger over his lips. They were dry but full from lust. He opened his eyes. "Thank you," he whispered.

"Thank you for letting me do that. You are quite impressive." Jack glanced away. "I think we need to talk some more, but not tonight. Tonight, you need to rest." He combed his fingers through Jack's hair. His eyes began to shut again.

"Yes, sir."

CHAPTER 2

It was close to four in the morning when Amalie crawled into bed next to Isaac. He'd been home since one. He'd let Jack sleep, and dozed himself before cleaning him up and sending him on his way. He didn't make Jack answer any more questions but did talk him into another night at the Windsor Club the next weekend. Isaac really hoped he kept the date and didn't have some sort of freak out.

"How was your night?" Isaac mumbled still half asleep.

"It was good."

He could smell a sweet floral scent on his wife. "Lydia changed perfumes again."

"You've got a good nose." She gave him a light kiss. "How was your night?"

"Interesting. We should talk."

"That interesting?"

"In the morning." He wrapped his arms around Amalie's waist and pulled her close. "Sleep now."

"Definitely sleep now."

AMALIE SLEPT UNTIL ALMOST NOON ON SUNDAY GIVING ISAAC plenty of time to stare blankly at a paper on capillary disruptions and think about Jack. The more he considered it the more Jack seemed ideal, as long as their proclivities roughly lined up. He had reasonably broad tastes, though medical school had thoroughly put him off some. Jack didn't seem to know what his tastes were. That itself could be fun, if Jack was willing. And there was the lure of having someone regular. Isaac had long since admitted to himself that he got twitchy if he didn't let his dominant side out for a run regularly. Amalie called it being his whole self.

He heard her stirring upstairs and flipped the coffeepot back on. Neither of them had gotten over their university days' caffeine habit and felt no reason to. They both refused however to embrace the weird, hyper-sugared, chemically questionable energy drinks the kids chugged these days. There was nothing wrong with good old $C_8H_{10}N_4O_2$ as far as he was concerned. Amelie stumbled into the kitchen in a worn green bathrobe. He handed her a cup of coffee and a slice of toast. She sat down and leaned over her cup, her dark hair falling around her face, hiding it. She was about halfway down the cup when she finally gave Isaac a good look. "So, what did you want to talk to me about?"

"Jack Burnside."

She looked up at the ceiling, her face twisting up in thought. "Should I know that name?"

"No, but I do. He's a SWAT team leader. Big guy. Ten feet tall, built like a brick wall."

"Right, SWAT." She turned her focus back toward her coffee.

"We've crossed paths in court a few times, anyway I ran into him at The Windsor last night."

"Really?"

"Yep. And he wasn't sitting on my side of the room."

"*Really?*" Amelie was aware of his broader tastes just as he was of hers. "So, you had a good night."

"I had an interesting night. When he recognized me he went into shock, and I'm not exaggerating here. I got him into a private room, pulse too fast, dead pale, I didn't have my kit with me but I'll bet anything his blood pressure was through the floor."

"Closet case panic."

"Big time. And yet—"

Amelie grinned. "Now *here's* where things get interesting."

"I don't know where he's been or who he's been with, but I'll bet anything it's a list of amateurs and assholes. He isn't even entirely sure what he likes, total mess but—"

"Is it a nice butt?" Amelie interrupted.

"It is a very nice butt. *But* the two of us have similar problems when it comes to finding someone more long term, job, schedule."

"You found a stray and you want to bring him home."

"I'd be lying if I said it didn't cross my mind pretty quick."

"You know that's how we got this fur ball." Amelie pointed to Murrcat, their once half-starved kitten, now a fifteen-pound ball of fluff and fangs, who jumped up on the kitchen table and tried to lick butter off the uneaten toast. Amelie rescued her toast and shooed the cat back to the floor.

"You love Murrcat and you know it."

Her face became serious. "I understand where you're coming from. You know I do. You do have a history of rushing into things. And out of them. And there aren't many who can handle our life."

Isaac nodded. He still felt twists of both anger and shame remembering his last long term relationship with a sub. He and Ricky had not ended well to say the least. He and Amelie weren't even married yet at the time, and Isaac hit a bad patch that left him deeply questioning which direction his life should take. He tried not to let himself dwell on it too long. "I know. However, that was almost eight years ago, now. I like to think I'm older, wiser, and have learned from my mistakes. Also, Jack is *completely* different from Ricky and my life is different now as well. Despite the job, I'm much more settled. I think?"

"You are."

He looked into his own coffee. He'd had other repeat subs over the last eight years, some lasting multiple months, but none he'd considered taking home. He'd always kept them separate from the rest of his life. "When I asked him if he had any question for me, the very first thing he did was ask about this?" Isaac held up his hand with his wedding ring. "The vast majority of the boys don't. There's honesty in him."

"That in itself could be a problem."

"I know. Truthfully, I'm probably getting ahead of myself. We agreed to meet next week. Talk when he was not having a panic attack. He might not even show up. I just wanted to keep you in the loop."

"I'll consider myself looped in."

THERE WASN'T AN INCH OF JACK'S APARTMENT THAT DIDN'T sparkle. He wasn't sure if it was left over from his army days but he did his best thinking while cleaning, and he had quantities of thinking to do.

His first thought, the big one that hit him as soon as he woke, was that Isaac hadn't cum. He'd noticed the obvious bulge in Isaac's pants, but he hadn't once moved to touch himself or have Jack do it. He hadn't even taken his pants off. Instead he petted Jack until he came all over himself.

He had nearly passed out from that simple petting and all other thoughts had been burned from his mind, which was what he'd been looking for. He wondered if he should have asked or offered. If Isaac was expecting that, if it was some kind of a test, but it had slipped his mind after Isaac had stroked his head until he fell asleep. Maybe Isaac went home and had his wife take care of it? If that was his thing. Get turned on by some guy then go back home to his marriage bed.

Jack aggressively scrubbed the grout around the base of his toilet.

And then there were all the questions Isaac asked. He knew he should have better answers for them. What did he like, what did he want? Did Isaac even want to do the things he liked? The whole evening, he hadn't made a single gesture that could be considered aggressive or even physically strong. He had only talked, only made polite requests. He didn't even want to be called sir.

But you obeyed, Jack thought.

Yes, he had. Isaac had told him to kneel and he had, and it felt good. If he hadn't been mid panic, he would have quite possibly cum only from those words. And he had cum, eventually, with nothing more than the soft touch of hands on his body. It had been too long. Way too long.

And Isaac had asked him to come back and he had agreed. Without a thought, he had agreed. And he was pretty sure he *would* go back. He'd woken up with killer morning wood and the memories of hands caressing his body making it that much worse. He knew if he went back though, there would be questions again and this time Isaac would want answers, answers to questions he barely understood.

He stopped scrubbing. Any more and the grout would start coming up, and his building manager wasn't much of one for the little bits of maintenance. As long as it wasn't flooding or on fire, he didn't particularly care. He leaned back on his knees which only brought back memories of the previous night. He grit his teeth as his dick began to get hard.

Maybe it's time for a run.

CHAPTER 3

The rhythmic clink of the weights gave Jack something to focus on. They weren't loaded up overly heavy. It was bad form to get called out and be too tired to lift your weapon. Still, he'd spent the weekend scrubbing his apartment, running more than he had since Basic, and trying not to masturbate like a teenager. Now he was hoping to space out on the weight machine. He might be confused, distracted, and sexually frustrated but at least he was going to be in great shape at this pace.

"Jack, you missed the game on Saturday. We tried to call you."

Jack settled the weights down and looked behind him. Dan Lewis, the leader of SWAT team Alpha, was standing at the entrance to the gym in his workout clothes. "Yeah, sorry about that." Jack had completely forgotten that he'd been invited over to Dan's place with a couple of the other guys to watch a game. "I was a little under the weather after last week. Made it an early night."

"Under the weather. Sure. Well you missed a hell of a game."

Jack nodded, trying for an expression of mild remorse then

went back to his weights. He could not remember which team or even which sport he was supposed to be watching when he was actually getting stroked off by a forensic pathologist in a posh BDSM club.

Dan sat down at the weight machine next to Jack. "While we're on the topic of not going out, I met this girl on Friday night and she's got this girl friend—"

"Not interested." Dan was notorious for trying to set people up. It was his prime hobby as far as anyone could tell.

"She's also got this guy friend." Jack felt his heart stutter and he briefly lost the rhythm of his reps. He glanced over at Dan, trying to hide any reaction in his face but he might have failed at that already. "Hey, I've never seen you go out with anyone and it's the 21st century, I don't judge."

"I'm fine, thanks." Jack continued with his reps, hoping Dan would take the hint and go away.

"I'm not buying that. I think you are a lonely man, and I'm going to keep throwing people at you until someone sticks."

Jack fully believed that because he'd seen Dan do it to others. Yes, at least two marriages had come out of it but it was still disconcerting being in his line of fire. "I'm fine. I don't need you to throw anyone at me."

"Does that mean you've already got someone?"

Jack got up and moved over to the leg machine. "It's—"

"Complicated?"

You have no idea. Jack thought.

"Complicated means they're either married, not as interested as you wish they were, or they're into something really kinky and you are just desperate enough to consider trying it."

Jack rolled his eyes. He did wish he could run it all by Dan. Dan was probably his closest male friend and possibly his only friend on that side of the country. They'd been in a few tight spots together and hung out fairly regularly, but Jack had always played things close to his chest, even as a kid. And as an adult there were secrets in his life beyond his sexual tastes. It would be nice to simply blurt it all out.

Hey, you know that short kinda nerdy doctor with the Coroner's Office? Well I ran into him the other night at a really posh kink club and it turns out he's a total Dom, and good at it and I'm thinking about seeing him again next week.

"Look," Dan lowered his voice. "If it's the kink one, make sure you know what you're getting into. All about safe words, open communication. No means no. Stop means stop. Voice of experience here. You don't want to end up in the ER trying to explain—"

"Don't need to know," Jack cut in. "I'm fine."

"Okay, but I have a long list of all types that would be completely into you."

I doubt what I need is anywhere on your list.

THE GREEN TEA WAS SOOTHING IN ITS WARMTH AND JACK cradled the bone china cup that Isaac had handed him. He tried to use the heat soaking into his skin to ground himself. He was feeling rattled, and not only by the current situation. His morning involved exchanging gunfire, something that was never enjoyable and not as common as TV would have one believe. The adrenalin crash after was not pleasant either and he could still feel the ache in his muscles and the buzz in his head. He'd gotten to the club early hoping Isaac might be early as well. The man from the last time, Jack couldn't remember his name, had blatantly looked him over before starting a proposition. Fortunately, Isaac had shown up only seconds later. He could still feel the man's eyes on his skin. Oily.

Isaac sat in the opposite chair looking far more relaxed than Jack felt.

"I'll let you start this time," Isaac said. "What do you want to know about me?"

Jack took another sip of tea and held the warm liquid in his mouth. He'd spent most of the previous week trying to think up answers for the questions Isaac had posed to him. "What do you want?" He finally asked. "What do you want to do to me, or what should I be doing for you, I mean—" Jack felt a babble coming on and Isaac raised his hand. He fell silent and quickly took another sip of tea.

"There are a good many things I'd like to do with you, and to you. You have lovely skin. I'd love to spend more time exploring it. I'm not looking for a whipping boy, I can get one of those anywhere, but I am curious to see how you react to my hand firmly on you, or a crop across your legs, a flogger on your backside."

Jack felt his face burn.

"I'd like to see you tied up. I'd like to fuck you at some point, and you have beautiful lips. I'd also like to see you kneel. Just kneel. I'd like to watch you drift in that in-between place. Like I said I don't need a whipping boy. Ideally, I'd like to find someone whom I can share that very particular sense of peace with. I can go into more detail if you wish?"

Jack shook his head. That was plenty of detail, enough to paint a whole gallery of pictures in his mind's eye.

"May I ask you a question?" Jack nodded. "I don't think you fully know what you like and I think I know why but I'm not going to go there, yet. Let's take this from a different angle. What don't you like? What scares you or grosses you out? What do you never want to do again?"

"Umm..." Jack wondered if Isaac had studied interrogation techniques somewhere. He'd spent a week trying to think up answers to one set of questions, and now he was faced with the complete opposite. "Ah... Burns, fire, cigarettes." Isaac nodded, his face serious. "Blood. Most bodily fluids."

"Semen?"

"I don't mind that." Isaac nodded again and Jack continued quickly. "Needles. That's really just in general, I don't like needles." He looked into his nearly empty tea cup and watched the few leaves swirl around the bottom. "Gags," he said softly. That seemed to be the one that bothered most Doms he'd been with. "I can keep quiet but I don't... I need to be able to—"

"No gags," Isaac repeated.

"And collars, I don't like things touching my neck." He'd had multiple Doms balk at that, ones that had been eager to put a collar and leash around his throat. He looked up at Isaac who nodded at him.

"No calisthenics," he added quickly. "After the Academy, I swore I'd never do another jumping jack again."

Isaac grinned. "I still have nightmares involving gym teachers. I would get no pleasure subjecting someone else to that. I mean, I'm sure there is someone out there who finds push-ups arousing but I can't say it's my kink. Anything else major?" Jack shook his head. "That all seems perfectly reasonable. And we'll discuss anything new that comes up as we go along. Assuming you want to continue?"

This was one of the many things he'd spent the week considering. It was one thing to agree to come back and talk, quite another to come back and submit. He'd never had so little time between submissions. It was usually months, or even years. He wasn't sure how he'd handle it. And he'd never submitted to the same person more than twice. But this was what he'd been quietly looking for all these years, when he let himself think about it, since that first time in a motel room at barely twenty. The guy told him to kneel more as a joke but he had, and at that moment some band that had been wrapped around his chest snapped and for the first time he felt like he could breathe. The guy laughed and Jack laughed it off as a joke as well. That motel room smelled of cigarettes and the bedspread felt like sandpaper. This room smelled like green tea and jasmine. Jack drained the last of his tea.

He stood, took the few steps across the room and stopped in front of Isaac, then with a deep breath he sunk to his knees, clasped his hands behind his back, and lowered his eyes. He was pretty sure his heart was going to beat out of his chest. Isaac stroked his cheek. "Beautiful."

❂

THE BEAUTY OF JACK SINKING TO HIS KNEES WAS BREATHTAKING. Isaac hoped he would get to see this, Jack back on his knees, presenting a gift he probably didn't realize he was giving. In truth, he'd been worried that Jack might not show up at all but he had been there waiting in the common room when Isaac arrived, shaking his head at Hugh Lancing and looking uncomfortable. Isaac approached and Jack had stood to follow, Hugh giving them a cold look as they left. And now here was Jack on his knees. He stroked his cheek.

"I want to take your pulse. May I touch your neck?"

"Yes." Jack's voice was soft.

He trailed his fingers down to the carotid artery. Jack's pulse was rapid but strong and even.

"Tell me your safe word before we go any further and I want to know if you'll use it."

"ROWPU."

"Rowpoo?"

"Reverse Osmosis Water Purification Unit."

Isaac nodded. He'd heard some interesting safe words in his day but that one was new. "I see. Are you able to use it? If I take you too far can I trust you to say it?" Jack nodded but there was a moment of hesitation. Isaac growled to himself. Too many people were being told that using a safe word was some sign of failure. It was like being told that wearing a seatbelt made you a coward. "Good. Any time you need to stop, say that and we will stop. Or even just say stop. Understand?"

"Yes."

"Good." Isaac took one last sip of his own tea and stood, getting his game face on. He always tried to be at his best, but he wanted to impress Jack. Impress him and teach him. Show him what it's like to not be under amateurs and jerks. "I want you to stand now and get undressed. I didn't have a chance to properly look you over the other night. I want to see what I'm working with."

"Yes—" Jack stumbled.

"Sir will be fine."

"Yes, sir."

He stood and stripped. It wasn't a tease or meant to arouse. It was quick and efficient with his clothes neatly folded and tucked away. Then he stood in the middle of the room, feet spread, hands behind his back, dick hard, and eyes straight ahead.

Isaac licked his lips. "For me, the naked and the nude stand as wide apart as love from lies, or truth from art." Jack only blinked at the quote. He'd have to give him some Robert Graves to read at some point. He slowly walked around Jack. He kept his touch firm and clinical, something he was well versed at. Jack's muscles were defined if not sculpted and his skin was flawless and unadorned, except for a thin appendectomy scar that was faded to nearly nothing, and a dusting of pale freckles across his shoulders. He took Jack's balls in his hand, again keeping it clinical, and rolled them around checking for anything that shouldn't be there. Jack drew in a sharp breath but kept his body still.

"Very nice. Let's start with a few things you should know." They were things that Isaac would have gone over before they began but Jack jumped the gun again. "I never want to see you crawl. It does nothing for me and wastes time as far as I'm concerned. Direct disobedience, just to be contrary, will be punished promptly, failure however will not. If you fail at a task I set you, it will be because I have misjudged your abilities or skill level and most likely more practice will be required. I will not try to trick you or set you up to fail. I see no point in that. I will not mark you in any way that can't be easily covered and I will not do anything that will cause a distraction for you later. I know your job is dangerous and I respect that." Jack took another sharp breath and his cock twitched.

Wow. I wonder if I could get him off with just positive reinforcement.

"You will not cum without permission," Isaac continued. "You can call a halt to any activity any time you wish but I reserve the right to do the same. Do you understand all this?"

"Yes, sir." A bead of pre-cum worked its way to the tip of Jack's cock. Isaac took a swipe of it with his middle finger then pressed it to Jack's lips. He sucked at it, twirling his tongue around before Isaac slowly drew it out.

"We will certainly be making use of that." Isaac struggled to keep his voice steady, the urge to simply put Jack on his knees and shove his dick into his mouth was a strong one. Instead he drew his finger down Jack's body leaving a thin pink line starting between his nipples and stopping at the edge of his navel. "I have a feeling you have training and habits that need to be undone and you possibly need to work out where your limits actually are, so we're going to start with the absolute basics." Isaac slipped off his shoes and stripped off his pants, leaving his black boxer briefs in place. Then he sat on the bed leaning against the padded headboard. "Come here and lay yourself across my lap. I want to make sure I don't hurt you in the future by hurting you a little bit now."

Jack's face was unreadable as he walked across the room. Luckily, it was difficult to have a poker cock, and his was thick and twitching. He guided Jack until he was settled across his lap. Then Jack tensed up. Isaac ran his fingers through Jack's hair and took long slow strokes of his back. Jack tensed up harder. "I told you I'm not looking for a whipping boy, I want someone who can share the sense of peace with me and balance it. This doesn't however mean I don't fully appreciate a rosy red bottom from time to time, or a hard, dripping cock pressed against my thigh. So, take a deep breath. I'm not going to start until you relax. And I'm not going to start if I don't believe you want this."

Jack did as told, taking a deep breath and then a few more. Isaac scratched at his scalp and he finally melted across Isaac's lap. "That's better."

He kept the first spank light. It hardly made a sound and didn't so much as turn the skin pink. Jack still jumped. He matched the next few strokes in strength. Then slowly, almost imperceptibly, keeping a steady rhythm, he increased the force of his blows. He watched as Jack's skin shifted through gradients of pink. Between blows Jack ground his hips down into the sheets. As his skin shifted to properly red his body began to tremble and his shoulders tensed. His hips were jerking and his face was pressed hard into the bed. There was a rough cadence to his breath.

Isaac worked his left hand back into Jack's hair. He stopped the spanking, his own arm tired. "It's okay. Let go. There is no shame in your tears. You are taking this so well. I am very impressed. Such a good boy." Jack's whole body jerked. He reached between Jack's legs and wrapped his hand around his cock. "You've done very well, I'm very proud of you, now cum for me." Jack thrust into his hand only a few times, his body still shaking, before he came against Isaac's thigh.

Between the gasps of release, were choking sobs. Isaac rubbed his scalp and stroked his body. "Let it out," he whispered. "Let it all out."

JACK HAD BEEN QUIETLY DRIFTING IN THAT CALM SPACE BETWEEN pleasure, pain, and Isaac's words when the tears hit. Like an ambush, he had no idea where they came from. He tried to fight them back. He squeezed his eyes tight and clamped his jaw but Isaac had noticed, had told him it was okay, to let it out. He couldn't fight them after that. He couldn't remember the last time he had cried. Years perhaps, slowly built up and set free by Isaac's kind words. Too kind. He had lain himself across Isaac's lap and he wasn't sure what was praise worthy in that, but it had felt good. Warm and peaceful until the tears came.

He wasn't sure how long he cried, he had only been half aware as he came. With Isaac's gentle hands and soft voice a constant.

When the tears began to subside, Jack ordered him to his knees. He kept his head bowed and his eyes down until Isaac grasped his chin and raised it. "I have seen men take a lash until they were raw without so much as a tear, but turn into messes at a simple spanking." He produced a handkerchief from somewhere and wiped the tears from Jack's cheeks. "In truth, I'm surprised when it doesn't happen, especially the first time."

He nodded. "Yes, sir." His throat felt raw and his skin burned, not with lust but humiliation despite Isaac's words.

"Do you wish to continue?"

Jack nodded again. He wanted to show he could do this without turning into a blubbering mess. Something which had never happened before.

"Wait here." Jack stayed, his head dropping as soon as Isaac's hand left his chin. He returned with a large glass of water which he held to Jack's lips. Jack drank it down, the chill easing the raw burn of his throat and the tight knot in his chest. Isaac lifted his chin again and pressed the cold glass to his cheek.

"I think it's the intimacy of the action. Skin on skin, transfer of heat, even cells. No restraints, simply acceptance of what is happening in the moment."

He didn't reply, just closed his eyes and pushed himself against the glass. His head ached but he tried to focus on the cool slick of the water. Isaac ran it across his chest and pressed it to his cheek before holding it for him to drink the rest.

"Feel better?" Jack nodded despite a lingering burn of shame. Isaac leaned across the bed and ran his tongue along Jack's lips and up his cheek to the corner of his eyes.

A shiver ran through him, followed by a wave of renewed lust. He looked up at Isaac whose lips were turned in a smirk full of mischief.

"That's better. I think you look your best while wanton. Most people do. Now stand up at the end of the bed. Spread your legs as much as you can and try to touch the floor. I want an idea as to your level of flexibility."

Jack was sure his face was already pink but he felt the sensation of blushing across his entire torso. He stood at the end of the bed and tried to stretch. He always stretched before workouts but he wasn't into yoga or anything. He managed to get his feet past shoulder width and his fingers to the floor. He held that position while his calves and thighs began to burn. Isaac stepped behind him and ran a hand along his inner thigh. He began to lose balance and tip forward.

"Stand up." Jack jerked himself up before he landed on his face. "Flexibility is so often overlooked when people are trying to build muscle. Not much point in having all that muscle if you're too tight to move." He stood in front of Jack and teased his fingers over his cock without looking at it. "I want to tie you up now. Not much, nothing complicated. I just want to hold your arms in place. May I?"

"Yes, sir." Jack answered without thinking. It wasn't an order, there wasn't a hint of command in Isaac's smooth controlled voice, but the idea that he would say no felt like a ridiculous one.

"Thank you. Sit on the edge of the bed, arms at your sides."

Jack sat while Isaac went to the high, antique looking dresser that was against one wall. From the bottom drawer he pulled out two bundles of soft looking rope and a ball of leather twine. "One of the nice things about the Windsor is they keep each room stocked the same way. You never have to go looking for things. Arms out."

Jack held out his arms while Isaac looped the ropes around his wrists then the bedposts. He tied them off just above the mattress leaving Jack's arms angled down. Then he put an end of rope into each of Jack's hands. "You don't know me. Not really, not yet. And as much as you want someone to trust, a part of you is on guard. I can see it in your face. Pull on those and the knots on the bedposts release. No need to even use a safe word. One yank and you're free."

Jack felt insulted, like he couldn't choose his own partners or couldn't be trusted to stay where told, but there had been times when he needed out to get to a ringing phone or just out of a room and he'd had to wait, heart racing, while knots were untied or cut. He'd had to ask. "Thank you," he said softly.

Isaac brushed his cheek then picked up the ball of leather lacing. "Now for this," he said with a wicked grin before wrapping it around the base of Jack's cock, then between and around his balls. He had been half hard before but now it felt like his cock might burst. Isaac stroked his fingertips up and down Jack's cock, sending shivers along his body. "I'm going to tease you now. I'm going to drag this out and I will make you cum, but it won't be like usual." He grazed his thumb over the tip. "I'm going to make you cum again and again and again. You're not going to move a muscle but you'll think you ran a marathon."

Isaac drummed his fingers along Jack's cock. Each tap was light but they vibrated across his whole body like a plucked bass string. Isaac gripped his cock loosely and ran his thumb around the tip, slicked by the drops of pre-cum pushing their way out. He wanted to watch what Isaac was doing but he had a hard time opening his eyes or even keeping them focused. Only a couple minutes of the lightest touch and his head was swimming, his body straining with the need for release. He tried to push his hips up into Isaac's hand but Isaac simply let go leaving Jack thrusting into the air. He wrestled his body back under control whimpering as he did and Isaac started his gentle strokes again. Fingers trailing up and down and his thumb going around and round the tip. It was all Jack could focus on, those five finger tips touching him so lightly. When the orgasm did hit, it wasn't an explosion but rather the crash of a wave rolling up his body then retreating.

He pried opened his eyes and watched as a couple little spurts of cum, hardly more than drips, jumped from his cock. He didn't go soft, there was no soothing glow of release. He stayed hard, wrapped in the cords and he began to pull against the ropes. Isaac took the cum and smeared it into his cock, humming no particular tune, as he continued his little taps and feather light touches. Jack let his head roll back. It felt like too much effort to keep it up. Whimpers, moans and soft pleas for nothing in particular fell from his lips. The second orgasm was like a wave but this one was a storm crashing hard and taking his breath. His cock stayed hard even as his body tried desperately to squeeze out more cum. And again, that soft afterglow was denied him. Isaac murmured to him, soft words of praise, calling him a good boy, calling him beautiful. Jack's heart raced, beating against his ribs so hard he thought they might break, every muscle strained and every nerve burned. He attempted to choke out the word 'please'.

There was a quick tug and the cords binding his cock were gone. In seconds, pleasure burned through the pain and he was gone.

When he came back to awareness he was laying on his side. There were still ropes around his wrists but they were no longer tied to the bedposts. He wasn't sure if he'd pulled the ropes himself or if Isaac had.

"Next time I do that, I think I'll add some nipple clamps. Dividing your awareness should drag things out longer." Isaac was standing a few feet away holding another glass of water. He helped Jack sit up and gave him the water. Jack chugged it. He was sticky with cooling sweat and cum and he could remember few times he'd ever felt so thirsty. "That was glorious to watch, by the way. You look amazing in ropes but watching you cum like that..."

"Thank you, sir." Jack managed to croak out. He wasn't sure what else to say. He'd never had a night like this. Made to cum over and over when Isaac still hadn't touched himself as far as Jack could tell. He found himself staring at the bulge in Isaac's briefs, as Isaac removed the ropes from his wrists and placed them in a hamper.

"Now," Isaac stroked his cheek with the same soft touch that had driven him to the edge. "What would you like?"

It was unfair asking him to think, when his brain still felt like a shorted-out fuse box. "May I... may I see you, sir." He wasn't sure why he felt so embarrassed asking that, considering what they had been doing only minutes before. Isaac smiled though.

"Of course." He stepped out of his briefs sighing in pleasure as he did. His cock was dark and full. Not overly long but thick. Isaac stepped in close. "Touch it if you like."

Jack reached out and wrapped a hand around it. Hot and hard with soft skin, a wave of ease washed across him.

"If I told you to suck me off right now, would you?"

Jack leaned forward already licking his lips. He knew guys who only gave head as a sort of courtesy but Jack enjoyed it. Isaac pressed a hand to his forehead stopping him. "I said *if* I told you to suck me. But it's good to know you're eager." Isaac took a step back. "I know it's not really fair to ask you now, and I'll ask you again after you're showered and dressed, but would you be willing to do this again? I can see so much potential in you and I'd very much like the chance to bring it out."

Jack's head was still, swimming and he was drooling over cock which he hadn't tasted in far too long, but still he nodded. "Yes, sir."

Isaac smiled. "Thank you." Then he began to stroke himself. "I think I'm going to make you sucking me a treat for both of us. Next time."

CHAPTER 4

The birds chirped outside Isaac's office window, loud enough to be heard despite the thick industrial glass. They were dusty little urban chickadees, but they reminded him that outside was a bright pleasant summer day begging for his feet to go wandering, or at least his mind. He half daydreamed while filling out cause of death reports. There were far fewer grizzly serial killer murders than TV would lead someone to believe. He signed off on a dozen heart attacks and a half dozen strokes. When he signed the last one he closed his eyes and let his mind drift. It fell easily onto the previous Saturday night. In the end, he'd rubbed his own cum into Jack's skin then watched him shower it off. When they were both dressed, and seated across from each other, they talked and Jack had once more agreed to meet with him. Isaac thanked him for that but inside he'd been crowing. He'd done his best to treat the night like an audition, giving Jack a peak at what he could do.

It would be a few weeks though, both of them, with a bit of embarrassment, had pulled out their phones to double check work schedules and other social commitments. But that they hadn't needed to explain 'multiday inter-department training' or 'weekend shift' to each other, showed what an ideal arrangement they could possibly have. They'd found a day when neither he nor Jack was rostered and Amalie had her own date. He hoped that Jack wouldn't change his mind but he also hoped that Jack would take some time to think, really go through his own experiences and develop a better idea of what he enjoyed versus what he tolerated or *thought* he was supposed to enjoy. He was all for taking his time exploring but it would be nice to have a list of things Jack was already comfortable with, so that he could have some place to start.

Physically Jack was his ideal male, especially for a sub. He also liked intelligence with a sense of humor.

There was a knock on his door. One of his autopsy technicians popped his head in and waved a thick binder before Isaac could respond. "Official hard copy of the department efficiency report is in."

That was a quick way of killing the warm little mental buzz Isaac had been building up in his thoughts. "Are we digging around dead bodies efficiently enough for the efficiency consultants?"

"Haven't read it." His assistant dropped it on his desk. "Thought you'd like it first."

Isaac forced a smile, cursing the intrusion of the real world into his dirty little daydreams. "Thanks."

THERE WAS THE SHARP CRACK OF CHEAP WOOD SPLINTERING, AS the battering ram drove the lock out of a front door in what had once been a pleasant suburb. Jack rushed in, first in line, with his team fanning out behind him searching the house. The house was quiet. No shrieks of surprise or shouts of anger. No gun shots. One room after another was called clear. He had a bad feeling. He pushed through the back door of the kitchen into what should have been a utility room. Hardly through the door he froze. The sun coming through a dirty window glinted off rows of beakers.

Shit.

"Everybody out!" he yelled over his radio. "We've got a lab back here." Like Jack, many of the guys on SWAT had some military experience and prided themselves on being bad-ass with balls of steel, never backing down, never running. Except from meth labs. He had never personally seen one blow and had no desire to. If the explosion didn't kill you, a lungful of caustic, half cooked drugs could lay you out.

The team retreated behind their van, Jack doing a head-count of his people while others called in for specialist teams to come out and deal with the lab. He'd been told they were busting an ecstasy distributer. He'd have been fine with that. Party drugs usually didn't blow up and the dealers weren't known for being quick on the draw. He was going to find someone to chew out about that piece of misinformation.

An old lady walking an antique looking poodle came up the street, stopped, looked at them huddled behind the van then looked at the house they'd broken down the door to. She gave Jack a sharp nod then dragged her dog back the way she'd come.

By one, Jack was covered in sweat from the sun beating down on the layers of black body armor he was wearing. He honestly wasn't sure why his team was being made to hang around. The suspects obviously weren't there, had probably been tipped off somehow, and weren't coming back. The lady with the poodle had come back, thanked them for taking down the house as it was well known in the neighborhood what had been going on, and brought them several bottles of water and iced tea. It was technically against policy to take anything from a civilian but he would have had a small revolt on his hands if he'd refused.

It was after four before he was back in the locker room stripping out of his gear with the rest of his team. Isaac had been good with the ropes. What little marking there had been on his wrists had vanished by the next morning. He hadn't managed to get a look at his own ass though. He generously waved everyone else ahead of him into the showers and waited until he could score a private one.

That would be an issue if he continued things with Isaac. Isaac had said he wasn't looking for a whipping boy, but he'd felt Isaac's cock hard under him while he was being spanked. And as loath as Jack was to admit it, he did enjoy a certain amount of pain. Not as much as some. He'd seen guys nearly split open by whips and loving every second of it. That wasn't him.

When he was only letting himself spend time with a Dom every year or so, he could schedule it for the start of long weekends or vacation time. Time for anything to heal or at least fade to something less noticeable. But if it was every month or even more often than that, he'd need to find some way to hide it or talk to Isaac about things that would heal fast. He was a doctor after all, even if it was an FP.

Despite his worries, his dick had gotten hard thinking of what Isaac could potentially do to him or with him. There was no way of silently jacking off in the echoing shower room. Even in a private stall the sound of hand on flesh would travel. Instead he slowly turned the shower to cold and tried to think of exploding meth houses.

CHAPTER 5

The twitch in his head had built over the weeks. Jack
scheduled his next night at the Windsor Club into
his phone as Ball Game. The little corner of his
mind that had never grown past fourteen snickered at that, but
the more logical part pointed out that anyone looking at his
phone would assume he'd be watching or be involved in a
sporting event. Not that anyone was looking at his phone. He
hadn't been this nervous the previous time. Maybe because he
hadn't been entirely sure what he was getting into. Maybe he
hadn't thought it through enough, or thought it through too
much as the weeks ticked by. They had not arranged to have
any contact with each other. Maybe they should have. He
could have easily gotten ahold of Isaac, knowing perfectly well
where he worked but there would have been questions. What
is a SWAT grunt doing calling the Coroner's Office? Another
layer of secrets. He could have probably even found out what
Isaac's cell number was, but he wasn't sure if that was stepping
over a line. Isaac was married, and yes he said his wife was
cool with it but he could have been lying or massaging the
truth. The only way to truly know would be to ask Isaac's wife

directly and that was not a conversation he felt he was in any position to have.

All that was rolling through his head as he stared into a glass of water in the common room of the Windsor Club, waiting for Isaac to arrive.

His head snapped up as someone sat across from him. It wasn't Isaac. It was the man that had approached him both the first and second time he'd been in the club. The one Isaac dragged him away from. Hugh?

"Waiting for someone?" His voice was smooth in a way that made Jack's skin crawl.

He raised his chin. "Yes, I am." Out in what he considered the real world, he had no problem telling people to fuck off but here his voice was not as strong as he would have hoped.

"Waiting for the dissecting doctor. He was quite rude interrupting our first conversation, and he doesn't seem like your type."

Jack wanted to defend Isaac, but the way Hugh looked at him managed to rob him of reasonable words.

"A boy like you certainly needs a stronger hand, someone who can bring you to heel."

Suddenly Isaac was there, leaning in, his face inches from Hugh's. "Whatever he needs," Isaac hissed. "It's not you. No one needs you."

With no other comment, he took a step away from the table. Jack rose and followed.

THERE WAS ALREADY TEA WAITING WHEN THEY GOT TO THEIR private room. Jack went to his chair but didn't sit. He felt the need to pace.

"I'm sorry I wasn't here earlier. No one should have to spend so much as ten seconds face to face with Hugh.

"He was only there a minute. I'm fine."

"That's a full minute too long. I apologize." There was a heavy formality to Isaac's voice. "What else is wrong?"

"Nothing," Jack replied instantly.

"I thought we agreed not to lie to each other. You've got waves of nerves coming off you. Sit down, have some tea, and tell me what is wrong. I don't want to go into anything with you in this state."

Jack hesitated to sit, his body rejecting the idea of stillness. Isaac poured a cup of tea and held it out. He took it and finally sat, his leg jiggling up and down.

Isaac sipped delicately from his own cup and watched him. His face was calm and there was precision in his small movements.

"I want a way to contact you," Jack blurted out. He'd never asked for that before. Half the time he'd never gotten his partner's full name.

"Of course. I should have given you my number after last time, in case you wanted to cancel or had questions. That was an oversight on my part." Isaac took his wallet from his coat pocket and pulled out a standard issue county business card. He pulled a pen from another pocket and scribbled on the back. "Here we go."

He handed it to Jack who looked at the number written on the back. "Thank you. Is that a seven or a nine?"

"Nine. And yes, in med school there is an entire class on how to make your handwriting completely illegible."

Jack couldn't stop his smile at the small joke but became a good deal calmer just for having that number.

"Now, what else is tangling your head?"

"I was in the shower, after this raid we did. I need to be careful about marks. More than I used to be if... If this is more regular then—"

"Nothing that won't be at least well faded by Monday morning or can't be written off as something else. Nothing you can't at least hide under a t-shirt."

"Yes," Jack answered mostly to his teacup.

"That's understandable and acceptable."

"Thank you."

"Don't thank me for accepting your limits. My acceptance should be a given." There was a strength behind Isaac's words that sent a burning flush across Jack's body and caused a throbbing in his cock, which had been mostly indifferent to the proceedings until now. He kept his focus on his tea. "Is there anything else?"

He shook his head.

"Have you given more thought into what it is that you really enjoy? As opposed to what you think you're supposed to enjoy."

Jack had given it some thought. It hadn't been easy. He'd done his best to clinically analyze his past experiences. He knew he needed a therapist as much as a Dom, but listening to some shrink would probably not be nearly as much fun.

Let's try not to sound like an idiot this time.

"I like being exhausted. I like getting to where I can't think and I don't have to think, and I like just... drifting. I don't mind a bit of pain but I don't think I need much, not as much..." Jack trailed off.

"Not as much as has been used on you in the past."

"Yes."

"I think I can think up some ways of wearing you down that'll be fun for the both of us."

Isaac put his empty cup aside. "Are you feeling better now?"

"Yes."

"Do you want to continue?"

That was the question of the hour. Jack couldn't honestly say he *wanted* this part of himself any more than he wanted his blue eyes or slight obsessive tendencies, though he could blame those last things on his parents. For as much as he didn't want, he did *need*. Every attempt to deny it had landed him in a bad place, physically, mentally, or both. And Isaac was about as ideal a partner as he was going to get. Local, discreet, understanding of the nature of his work and the limitations that came with it.

And no one has grayed you out that fast or made you cum that hard.

"Yes."

Isaac smiled. "Good. In that case, when you're ready, get undressed and kneel in the middle of the room."

Jack took no time standing and stripping off his clothes. Isaac took a pillow from the bed and dropped it in the middle of the room. Jack knelt on it and clasped his hands behind his back.

"Very nice." Isaac walked around him a few times skimming his fingers along Jack's face and through his hair. Jack took deep, slow breaths wanting to drop into the right headspace as quickly as possible after weeks of spinning himself around. "I'm going to blindfold you first. I won't leave the room and I won't bind your hands. You can remove it whenever you need."

"Yes, sir."

Behind him he heard a drawer open and close before a mask of soft leather went over his eyes and was clasped at the back of his head. Then there was nothing. There was no shuffling of feet or rustle of clothing, no ticking of a clock to pass the time. He could hear the soft fall of shoes in the hallway but there was nothing in the room. It was as if Isaac had simply vanished. He strained to hear something, anything, his back began to tense and his heart sped up. The urge to pull the mask off began to grow. Suddenly Isaac's fingers were in his hair combing it carefully.

"Shhhh. Easy. That took less than a minute. I don't need you to think. I don't need you to try to anticipate what will happen

next. I'm sure that is what you've been trained to do. To anticipate the moves of the bad guys. To try to guess what will please
your Dom, but don't. There are no enemies here and I will tell
you what you need to do to please me. Just breathe. Slow and
deep. Focus on where I touch you. I'll do what I like when I like,
and you will please me without needing to guess or prepare."

Jack took a couple of deep breaths and tried to focus on
Isaac's fingers. That first night when they met, Isaac had said he
was touch starved. He hated to admit it but he was probably
right. He continued to breathe and Isaac continued to pet him.
He wasn't sure how long. Things narrowed down to Isaac's
fingers and his own breath.

"Much better. Now, I want you to tell me if you can smell the
tea. There's a little left in the pot. Shake or nod your head."

Jack shook his head. That was not a question he was expecting. What he could smell was whatever the Windsor Club used
to clean their rooms. It wasn't strong but it had a slight floral
scent.

"You know where the teapot is in the room and where it is in
relation to you. Think about where it is then, take a deep
breath."

Jack did as told and this time he smelled it as if it had been
shoved right under his nose. Mild jasmine with the sharp smell
of green tea. This time Jack nodded.

"The human mind is amazing when it comes to filtering our
senses. We'd probably go insane if we couldn't ignore things
when we need to. A clock might tick in our ear all day but we
only notice it at 4:30 on a Friday. Keep breathing in that tea."

Isaac's hand left his head and he frowned. It felt like some
part of him was reaching out trying to bring those fingers back,
but he wasn't moving. There was sound though, beyond Isaac's
voice. There was a shifting of fabric that sounded intensely loud,
like the ticking of a clock on Friday. Even with it happening
behind him, it was as if he could see it. The slick sound of Isaac

removing his belt. The lower sound of him pulling his legs from his pants. The faint click of his nails on his shirt buttons. He was forgetting to smell the tea. Instead he was smelling Isaac. His soap, shampoo, shaving cream, and sex.

There was that hot, sharp, smell of arousal. He heard Isaac's steps, even on the thick carpet, and knew he was standing in front of him. His breath quickened but remained deep. The scent of his own arousal was nearly as strong and his head began to swim in it. Then there was sound, a sound easily recognized by any guy, the sound of a hand slowly sliding across hard flesh. Despite the orders, he began to think ahead. He wondered if Isaac was going to cum on him again, rub it into his skin so he could smell nothing but that. Maybe he'd be allowed to suck Isaac. That had him parting his lips. Maybe Isaac would bend him over, kneel down behind him, and fuck him. He hadn't been fucked in longer than he cared to think about and he did miss it.

"Only the slightest touch, not a drop of pain, and you're ready to cum, aren't you?"

Shame overwhelmed him. No better than a teenager who couldn't control himself. "Sorry, sir."

"Why are you apologizing? Did I say it was a bad thing?"

"No, sir."

"No. No I did not. I like seeing you hard and on the edge. I like knowing that I guided you to that place and that I'll be the one to send you over. Never be ashamed for what your body does."

"Yes, sir." Jack didn't feel that much better. He felt shame at being told not to be ashamed. A small separate analytical part of his mind pointed out that that was messed up.

Isaac's fingertips were suddenly at his lips. He sucked them in, tasting Isaac's lust.

"Very nice, do you like that taste?"

He nodded, unable to answer with Isaac's fingers filling his mouth.

"Taste and smell are very closely linked. Smell a pear while eating an apple. Your brain will scramble up the tastes." He slowly drew his fingers from Jack's mouth. Still trying to breathe deep, Jack leaned forward chasing after them. What he found was the tip of Isaac's cock. He sucked it in, trying to twist his tongue around it but it was wider than what was comfortable or easy to work with. Isaac slipped it out and then back between his lips with shallow thrusts, not even hitting the back of his mouth.

"I knew a pretty boy who couldn't stand the taste of cum. I rubbed cherry chapstick under his nose until he learned to like the flavor. I don't think I'll have to do that with you."

Jack shook his head even as he gripped his hands together hard. He wanted to reach up, to wrap his hands around the rest of Isaac's cock, feel it pulsing and twitching. Isaac seemed to read his mind but it was probably the tensing of his muscles that gave him away.

"Go ahead and touch."

He gladly did as told. Isaac was thick and heavy and he felt like the flesh could burn his skin. He stroked slowly while bobbing his head trying to suck in more.

"Oh, very nice," Isaac moaned softly. "Very good."

Jack sucked harder and breathed deep letting the taste and smell fill him, driving out any lingering scent of tea or soap. Isaac's fingers slipped into his hair. He didn't grasp or pull, just settled his hands which seemed heavier than before, the weight of them sinking through his entire body, anchoring him in place as tightly as any rope or strap. He sped up his hands, the even rhythm of his breathing long gone, now it was shallow half choked desperation as he stretched his mouth wide. And suddenly Isaac was gone, yanked away. Jack leaned forward and reached out but found only air. He could hear though, Isaac's ragged breathing mixed with his own.

"Touch yourself," Isaac growled at him. "Grab your cock as if it were mine." Jack dropped his hands and began to stroke himself. It was like an electric shock and his whole body jumped. Within seconds Isaac's cock was back at his lips. Isaac thrust in the same rhythm that Jack stroked his. Like a strange form of stereo, the sensation began to feedback mingling with the sound, twisting with the taste and smell until Isaac shouted and thrust into his mouth hard and deep. Jack coughed and sputtered, trying to swallow as much as he could. He also tried not to cum. Even as he continued to stroke himself he held back, not cumming until he was told.

"Go ahead," Isaac whispered. "Cum for me. Let go."

It took a few hard strokes and he could not hold back the scream. Fire through every nerve and light behind his still covered eyes. He collapsed forward, his forehead pressed to the carpet, tasting Isaac and smelling himself.

ISAAC DIDN'T CLEAN JACK, OR REMOVE THE BLINDFOLD. HE DID help him to his feet, then to the bed. If he was being cruel, and in the future he certainly would be, he would tease Jack's over sensitized body, perhaps even drawing a second dry orgasm from him, one as painful as pleasurable. But not tonight. Tonight, he watched as Jack drifted, half dozing, overwhelmed by pleasure and release, cum drying on his face and across his belly. It was tempting to kiss him, to wait until his eyes fluttered open and taste himself on Jack's lips.

Not yet. Soon.

He had made a decision that night, the second Jack had apologized for his own arousal. He would take Jack home. He knew he'd already misstepped by not giving Jack a contact number and allowing him to jump the gun, but he was an ideal fit for his needs on so many levels. As long as Jack was willing, he would take him home. The Windsor Club might be clean and posh, with only the finest of equipment available, but take away the gilding and bone china tea sets, it was still a sex club with back rooms for hire. Jack deserved better than that. Isaac had no doubt he would positively bloom if given something better than that.

CHAPTER 6

"I want to bring him home," Isaac said as Murrcat was trying to discreetly steal pepperoni off his pizza. He'd taken a couple of days to mull the idea around his head making sure it wasn't just a midsex, endorphin high idea.

Amalie nodded sliding her own slice of pizza out of the box. "What does he think about that?"

"Haven't broached the subject yet."

Amalie nodded some more, obviously holding back a smile. "Ah."

"Ah? That's all you have to say?"

"I know you, and more importantly I am intimately familiar with your relationship skills and no matter how much you want this, without a solid kick in the pants you will waffle about until hell freezes over, so the question is, should I give you that kick in the pants?"

Isaac wanted to argue but his pizza order, unchanged since college, was testament to how easily he fell into comfortable routine. "I like him."

"You've liked plenty before but haven't tried to bring them home."

"True." He *accidentally* dropped a piece of pepperoni which Murrcat pounced on. "I think, with a bit more feeling around," Amalie smirked. "That we will find our tastes compatible."

"There's no certainty there."

"No. But things are going pretty well so far and I'd like to keep going."

"Okay, but that can be done off site."

Isaac frowned, the certainty he'd been feeling starting to waver. Having a regular sub had always been an ideal but he also trusted Amalie's take on his relationship and interpersonal skills more than his own some days. "If you think I shouldn't—"

"I think if you bring someone home and it goes well it will be good for all of us. I'm just making sure you're thinking with your head and going over things from all angles."

"This is what happens when your wife dates a lawyer."

"Yep. Now, what is it about this guy that makes him special? What bit are you *really* grabbing onto?"

Isaac chewed on his pizza slice thinking. He had lots of feelings concerning Jack but he was a doctor and scientist, he should be able to detach and consider things rationally. "On a purely practical level I couldn't do better. We have complicated schedules but for many of the same reasons. He understands what working for the county means."

"A car can be practical. Doesn't mean you want to drive it."

"True. I think... I think he has the potential to be truly remarkable," Isaac answered slowly. "I think he's been buried under assumptions, his own and other peoples'. I know that feeling quite well. I think if he can be shown that there isn't anything he *shouldn't* want, or *should* be, only what he wants and what he is, that he can be unbelievably amazing. I'm torn between wanting to spank him raw or wrap him in blankets and feed him soup, and I think he needs an equal measure of both."

"And you think you can give that to him?"

Isaac's knee jerk reaction was to answer yes, of course. "I

think I can *now*," he answered carefully. "I think I've learned enough to give him what he needs and I want to be the one to give him that."

"And once you give him that?"

Isaac didn't have an answer. "You're worried already."

She tapped him on his forehead. "You don't detach up here as well as you believe you should." She tapped him on his chest next. "And you're not as good at protecting this as you like to think you are."

"Are you saying I fall in love too easily?"

"No. Quite the opposite. But when you do, you don't hold any of yourself back. I don't want you to get hurt, and if you and him aren't on the same page or looking for the same thing..."

"I don't like getting hurt." An image of Jack flashed through his mind, head bowed, apologizing for his arousal. "But... I think he might be worth the risk."

"Good answer. Make a date, talk to him."

He leaned over the coffee table and gave her a kiss. "You are the best."

She kissed him back. "And don't you forget it."

THE MARIACHI MUSIC COMING FROM BEHIND CAREFULLY PLACED plastic marigolds wasn't so loud as to make conversation impossible and the corner booth was discrete. Jack knew he was unlikely to be noticed by anyone taking a casual look around the restaurant. That apparently included the wait staff. He was trying to wave down a waitress to get some water when Isaac walked into the restaurant, his eyes quickly landing on Jack.

He had been surprised to get a text message from Isaac inviting him to dinner. The message hadn't been particularly date like in its phrasing, more like an invitation to a business meeting or working dinner. He'd still waffled back and forth for an hour over the exact wording of his reply. Isaac spoke quickly to the waitress he had been trying to wave down before sliding into the booth across from him.

"This place has the hottest salsa ever. I ordered us a bowl of the medium which will still send any germ in your system screaming. And I'm saying that as a medical professional."

"Don't you work on dead people?"

Isaac grinned. "Yes, I do, so I know what kills you and what doesn't."

"Not entirely comforted by that."

Isaac laughed. It came easy, just as Jack's words had. They had never spoken like this before, informally and in public. So far, the first thirty seconds had been easy. Now he had to get through the rest of dinner without thinking too much about other stuff or sounding like an idiot.

The waitress brought over their menus along with paper thin corn chips and a small bowl of dark red salsa. He blinked a few times as the smell of the salsa hit his nose. "That's medium?"

"Use sparingly."

He picked up his menu instead. It had all the Mexican restaurant standards, tacos, tamales, chicken, pork, beef. Someone had written GF or V next to some of the items. The untranslated section had lengua and menudo. He still wasn't sure what kind of dinner he was having, but spicy beef stomach soup was probably something to skip.

"The basic tacos are really nice here." There was eagerness in Isaac's voice which made Jack wonder if this was in fact a date. He was hesitant to ask, not sure of which answer he wanted to hear.

"Sounds good."

The waitress came over and Jack ordered a few beef tacos with rice and Isaac ordered the chicken. As soon as the waitress left there was silence between the two of them. He wasn't sure what he was supposed to say or how to act, or even think. He dunked a chip into the salsa and shoved it into his mouth as cover. He instantly wished he hadn't. He tried to chew without any more salsa hitting any part of his mouth but it was an impossible task.

"I did say use sparingly." Isaac dipped only a small corner of a chip into the salsa and ate it. Jack tried to keep his composure but his face burned and his eyes started to run. He broke and chugged a glass of water before eating a few more plain chips, trying to mop up the lingering burn.

"Wow," he finally managed to choke out.

Isaac smiled at him. "Next time I'll order us the mild."

"Good idea." Jack eyed the salsa, trying to decide if it was worth more of the burn to avoid the uncomfortable silence.

"In case you were wondering I thought we should talk in a less formal environment. Get to know each other a bit."

"So, this is a date?"

"It can be if you like. If not, it can just be us chatting about ourselves and each other while eating tacos. I don't actually know that much about who you are and I'm sure you have some questions about me."

Jack did but also didn't. He'd never taken time to get to know his Doms because for the most part he'd only ever known them for a few hours, a day at most. He wasn't sure what he wanted to know about Isaac. Even meeting him in a hole in the wall Mexican restaurant instead of the Windsor was taking him far outside his comfort zone. He shoved another chip in his mouth trying to cover the silence. "How about I start, if you like? Where are you from?"

"Boston." That was a nice and easy answer.

"Really? East Coast boy."

"Born and raised."

"No accent. I wouldn't have guessed."

"My father's doing." Who wouldn't abide anything but *proper* English. "Well, my father and a little too much TV."

"I'm from Oxnard. Bit south of Ventura and I assure you, every tasteless joke that can possibly be made about a city called Oxnard has already been made by its own residents." Jack bit his lip but couldn't hold back a smile. "So, no accent because everyone talks like they're going to be in the movies one day."

"Three beers and I drop my Rs, and I've been told that on the few occasions when I've been seriously drunk I start sounding like Mayor Quimby from *The Simpsons*."

Isaac grinned. "That sounds special."

"I have no recollection of those events so it's all hearsay evidence." Though his sister was always threatening to get him trashed and film it.

"Any hobbies? Aside from Mayor Quimby impressions."

"Not really. It's mostly the job. I work out in my off time but that's more to stay healthy." Jack was aware of how incredibly dull his life sounded and probably was. "I like to ski." He added in hopes of livening things up.

"So do I."

"I'm not very good," Jack added quickly in case Isaac got ideas about them skiing or Jack being the outdoor sporty type. "I mostly stick to the intermediate and beginner slopes, shake my fist at snowboarders like a grumpy old man."

Isaac nodded in agreement. "I usually do one run on a hard slope a year to painfully remind myself that I'm not very good either, then go back to the beginner slopes."

"I probably spend more time in the lodge then on the slopes."

"But you need to justify the fire and hot chocolate by freezing your balls off first," Isaac said, grinning.

"That's about right."

The tacos arrived along with another pitcher of water. Now that Jack had relaxed, he found that he was in fact quite hungry. The first one went down in a few bites with no extra conversation. He was aware of Isaac watching him eat but not with any great scrutiny. He slowed down with his second taco to appreciate the fact that it was pretty good. The meat wasn't over cooked and everything tasted fresh.

Isaac carefully spread a couple of drops of salsa onto his own taco. "I know doctors who refuse to eat out anywhere. They've seen too much weird stuff and don't trust anything but their own cooking, with produce from farms they've personally inspected. They can get really up in their own heads about it."

"Not you I take it?"

He lifted his own taco. "I've yet to cut open anyone who ate here prior to death. I also spent college regularly eating from a place called Pizza 4 Less and my residency involved a lot of questionable food truck food. I figure if I can survive that..."

"I'll take any halfway decent smelling food truck food over some of the stuff we got in the army. I know it was all sterilized and designed to stay fresh for fifty years but man some of that was bad."

Isaac smiled. "See, there we go, I didn't know you'd been in the army."

Jack shrugged. "Not long." There were reasons he didn't go into details about his time in the army. "Four-year enlistment, two on IRR. It wasn't as good a fit as I'd thought."

"And SWAT fits better?"

It was a variation on the questions Jack asked when he was willing to be self-reflective. "Most days."

"Whatever works. And it could be worse. I got all the way through med school and residency before I realized I wasn't cut out to work on real live patients every day. I'm from three generations of doctors. My parents change the subject very quickly when people ask about my specialty."

Jack knew all about parental career disappointment. "My parents tell people I'm a cop but they'd prefer if I was a detective. SWAT doesn't have the greatest rep these days."

Isaac nodded without further comment. Jack understood.

There was a constant urge to go around the country, to certain other SWAT teams and scream 'you're making the rest of us look bad and not making the job any easier'. Most of the cops he knew regularly had the same urge. They fell into silence again and Jack ate another taco.

"Do you want to know anything else about me? Little niggling questions?" Isaac asked again. "Totally open book here."

"Um..." Jack did have a few questions that he didn't know exactly how to phrase. "Your wife?"

Isaac nodded. "Her name's Amalie. She's a genetic biologist. She's currently trying to convince certain types of alga that an oil spill is actually a yummy treat."

"I find anything is edible with ketchup." Jack joked while processing the fact that the wife of the guy he's having sex with is probably some level of genius and has a doctorate in something. All of Jack's qualifications were through the army and of little use or interest.

"I think at one point she was splicing in tomato genes for some reason. I'm always slightly worried that one day she's going to come home with the creature from the black lagoon. We have a cat named Murrcat."

"Meircat?"

"No, Murrcat. I'm sure when he was a kitten we named him Percival or something like that but somewhere along the line we just started calling him Murrcat."

"My sister's cat was called Squeeker. It was giant and terrorized the dog." Isaac smiled at him. It was broad with laughter behind it and Jack noticed it. Really noticed it. There was no formality or rank in front of it. It was just a smile. A nice one. Jack grabbed a chip. He'd been so focused on Isaac's control and personality, the fact that he could get him off with nothing more than a few words and a light touch, he hadn't put much thought into what he looked like. He looked close. With the smile, Isaac looked young. Younger than he probably actually was. His brown eyes were open and friendly. He didn't fall into the category of square jawed handsome or delicately beautiful. He supposed Isaac's features were pleasant, when he was like this, under warm restaurant lights with salsa on his lips. And yet in the Windsor there was something sharp about them. Kind, but with a promise of other things.

Jack grabbed a chip. And uncomfortable arousal settled over him.

"Anything else you'd like to know about me?"

He spun the tip of the chip around in the salsa but didn't eat it. Isaac waited. "You're always asking me questions," Jack finally said. "I mean when we're—" he tipped his head toward the door trying to convey his whole other life. "You keep asking me for permission if you can do stuff."

"Would you rather I didn't?" There was seriousness in Isaac's voice and Jack looked up.

"Most... I mean usually there's some at the beginning but—" Jack put the now far too hot chip on the edge of his plate.

"You are letting me inside your head." Isaac's voice lost the casual humor of earlier. "The inside of anyone's head is a delicate thing and I'm still learning the shape of yours. I ask because I'd rather not run into walls and hurt you in the process. I can stop if you wish. I can simply give you orders and expect them to be obeyed but I'd rather not. Not until I have a better idea of where your walls are and how strong they are."

Jack shook his head. It made sense. If anything, he should be thankful for Isaac's consideration. What he was not thankful for was the massive erection he had simply from the shift in Isaac's voice, soft but firm.

"It would help if you gave me a list." Isaac continued.

"A list?"

"What you know you like. What you know you don't. What you think you might like and are curious to try."

Jack thought about writing out that list. Putting on paper all the things he spent years trying and failing to scrub from his mind. Things he was afraid to even type into google. It would make them real.

"You don't have to—"

"No. I'll think about it. I'll try."

"Thank you. While we're on the subject of thinking about things I invited you here tonight to hopefully broach a subject."

Jack's heart sped up trying to think of what it could possibly be. Isaac wouldn't want to cut things off, not after requesting a list. Did he want to go public? Tell people? Jack couldn't do that. If it got back to his team... They had a certain image of him, and as their leader had expectations about who he was. Yes, they were in public now but this was different.

"I'd like you to come home with me. Not tonight, you need time to think. But I like you and I enjoy our time together and I think we can develop. I'd like to offer you something more personal than the back room of a sex club. You don't have to say yes, there's no time limit, and if you like, we can continue on as we are if that's what you're comfortable with. But if you are willing I'd like to take you home with me. I'd like you to stay the night, and maybe not have to schedule weekends only in the future."

Now Jack's heart was truly racing. That had never even occurred to him. The idea of going to Isaac's home, the place where he lived, spending the whole night. He assumed that they would continue to meet at the club or maybe hotels. Without thinking he shoved the too hot chip into his mouth and promptly choked on it. Isaac chuckled, even as he passed him a glass of water. He chugged the water before shoving mild beans into his mouth trying to sooth the burn.

When he finally was able to blink the tears out of his eyes, Isaac was smiling at him. "Not quite the reaction I was expecting."

Jack took another swallow of water. "I'll think about it."

"That's all I ask."

"How'd it go?" Amalie asked.

"He's from Boston, was in the army, and has a sister whose name I didn't get but who had a cat named Squeeker."

Amalie flicked a rubber band at him, which was pounced on by Murrcat as soon as it hit the floor.

"That's not what I meant and you know it."

He flopped onto the battered love seat that took up half of Amalie's home office. "The medium salsa was spicier than usual tonight." She flicked another rubber band at him. Murrcat ignored that one in favor of a fresh lap. "We talked. I think I surprised him more than anything else. I didn't get the impression that he was against the idea, just a bit startled by it."

"Thought you were going to confine him to sex clubs and motel rooms."

"You make it sound so trashy. I don't recall you objecting to motel rooms."

"When we were twenty and both still living with our parents."

"Remember that manager who thought you were a hooker and tried to get you to sign up for the frequent guest program?" Isaac had another rubber band flicked at his head.

"I hope you use more charm with Jack."

"I do. And he said he'd think about it."

The locker room bench was too hard and too narrow to ever be comfortable, probably designed to keep people from sitting down and not wanting to get back up. Most of his team had headed to their homes hours earlier. Jack had headed to the gym. No matter what kind of decision he made, he was going to be in great shape by the time he made it.

He hadn't been able to stop thinking the entire ride home the night before, thinking about lists, about Isaac. He ended up in his building's pool, swimming hard until nearly midnight.

I want to bring you home.

It made him sound like a puppy that needed to be rescued. He knew he should be thinking about what Isaac had offered. Weighing pros and cons, formulating a plan, but his mind kept running in useless circles.

He jumped slightly at a hand on his shoulder.

"Hey man, you look like you're about to fall asleep sitting up."

He looked up at Dan who was in civilian clothes and probably about to start his shift. Like Jack he was always first in and last out.

"I'm fine, just up in my own head." That was an understatement.

"Yeah? Anything interesting?" Jack shook his head. "Really? And how's that 'it's complicated' thing going?"

Jack didn't answer. He wanted to. He'd been running the same thoughts around until it was a mush of him talking to himself. Dan sat on the bench next to him, but not too close, unlacing his shoes.

"I'm going to take your silence to mean that the complicated thing is still complicated."

He sighed while Dan chuckled.

"So, married or kinky?"

"I don't want to talk about it," Jack lied.

"Or both."

He stood up to open his own locker, Dan getting too close to the truth.

"Both it is." Dan followed him. "You know that can be a workable combo as long as everyone's on board."

"I don't want to talk about it," Jack repeated with not quite enough force.

Dan leaned against the lockers while Jack pulled fresh clothes out of his own.

"I think you absolutely do want to talk about it. Look, if it's the kink but you're not into it then don't, seriously don't, that's not one of those 'yeah maybe I can get used to it things'. If it's a no, it's a no."

Jack leaned his head against the edge of his locker, resisting the urge to start banging his head against it.

"If it's the married thing, as long as everyone's on board..."

"Why are you on SWAT?" Jack asked with growing frustration.

Dan spread his long, well-muscled arms wide. "Look at me? I barely fit in a squad car and being a detective is more of a pain in the ass than I want to deal with."

"I mean why aren't you... I don't know, relationship advice, something?"

"Because lonely bastards like yourself would never actually go to a Relationship Advice Something. I'll tell you this though, whatever it is, it's probably not as complicated as you're making it in your head. You can probably clear any of it up with a five-minute conversation."

Isaac hadn't led him directly to a room this time, instead they sat in a deep booth, much like their dinner, except this time the seats were upholstered in rich leather and the air smelled of fancy cologne and expensive wine. He slid a piece of paper to Isaac. He felt like a spy in a cold war novel, except there was no enemy here. Just secrets.

"It's not much. I realized I don't... I don't think I know as much about myself as I should. Not when it comes to this." It had been hard writing the list. He'd stopped and started a dozen times and it had taken almost the entire two weeks between their dinner and now. He'd gone over every encounter, and every fantasy. He tried to distance himself from the memories, look at them objectively, but that made certain aspects worse. Isaac unfolded the paper and silently read it over. "Thank you for this. I'm sure it wasn't easy. I can't promise I won't misstep with you but this should help lower the odds."

"So, what now?" Jack asked.

Isaac looked back down at the paper. "That's up to you. We can talk about what's on this list."

Jack shook his head. He'd tangled up his brain writing that list and didn't want to think about it for a while.

"We can get a room. Have a little fun if you're in the mood for that." Jack thought about it but oddly enough he wasn't. He didn't feel like he had the emotional energy for it.

"Or, we can order dinner?"

"Actually, I am kinda hungry. I think I might have skipped lunch."

Isaac smiled. "Dinner it is. And we should do dessert. The pastry chef here is excellent."

THE LIST JACK HAD SLID ACROSS THEIR TABLE STAYED FOLDED neatly in Isaac's pocket until he got home. It was two pages, hand written. He'd only glanced over it at the club, somewhat surprised that Jack had done it. He lay it on the small breakfast table in the kitchen, which due to an error in light bulb purchasing, had the brightest light in the house. The list had eraser marks in several places, leaving the paper thin and slightly smudged. He had friends with access to high tech laser imaging computer microscopes that could probably read what had been rubbed out, but if Jack decided he didn't want Isaac to know something, Isaac would accept it, at least until it became a problem.

The likes and dislikes were short lists. The likes were broad, too broad for Isaac's peace of mind, and the dislikes were detailed in a way that spoke of bad experiences. The maybe list was extensive. It looked like Jack had found some kink list online and had simply gone down it, ticking off the ones that spoke to him. And considering that after the first few lines, the list became alphabetical he was almost positive that is what had happened. He laughed out loud at the mental image, then went to find a notepad so he could start making notes of his own.

CHAPTER 7

The front yard of Isaac's home was overgrown but in an artistic way. Patches of flowers that were probably vibrant colors when illuminated by something other than a yellow street lamp, lined the walkway. The front door and porch, with little side windows, were the same as every other house on the quiet street. There were lots of neighborhoods like this one. Rows of tiny houses built by factories or the military in the 40's with each new owner or decade adding on another room or second story, like passing around a Lego house and box of bricks from child to child. There was light coming through the small windows but curtains were closed across the large one.

You can do this. Jack repeated to himself over and over as he sat in his truck outside. He knew what was going to happen, or at least had a good idea. He'd done it before; he'd done it with Isaac. The only thing that was different was the location. That was all, just trading one bed for another. Hardly worth thinking about.

You are so crap at lying to yourself.

He closed his eyes. After each encounter with Isaac, he'd felt more sated and at ease than any previous experiences. Those impossible to scratch itches were soothed. His mind quieted and his body felt right.

And you want that again so get the fuck out of the truck.

He climbed out of his truck. He'd dressed carefully but not formally. Jeans and a clean button down shirt. At Isaac's suggestion, he'd brought a small overnight bag pieced together out of his go bag. He knocked on the door and counted the time. Six seconds and the door swung open. Isaac was standing there dressed in black and purple with bare feet. Jack liked it. He always liked the way Isaac dressed, really the way everyone at the Windsor dressed. No too tight black leather and steel rings. Instead it was silk, wool, and fine linen. Isaac smiled at him.

"Come in. I'm glad you came." He held the door open and Jack stepped in, his eyes sweeping the room. It was habit, making sure a room was clear as he entered. There was no one else. There must have been walls knocked out at some point. The entrance flowed into a large living room with a staircase at one end and then back into a dining room. It was cluttered but in an academic fashion. Full bookshelves lined the walls with more books stacked onto coffee tables.

"Would you like anything to drink? Some water?"

His mouth did feel dry. "Water would be nice. Thank you."

Isaac smiled. "Take a seat if you like. I'll be right back." He headed to the dining room and through the door beyond which presumably housed the kitchen.

Jack looked around and picked up a magazine from a coffee table, feeling the need to do something with his hands. *The American Journal of Forensic Medicine and Pathology*. He flipped it open. *A Retrospective Study of Blade Wound Characteristics in Suicide and Homicide.*

The kitchen door swung open. Jack quickly put the journal down. Isaac glanced at it as he handed him a glass of ice water. "Not the most chipper reading but necessary. Got to keep on top of what people figure out how to do to each other and themselves."

"I only have to catch them. And even then, that's mostly just trying to keep them from running out the back door."

"Still an important job."

Jack sipped his water.

"Why don't you sit down? You look nervous."

He sat holding his water in front of him like some sort of shield.

"You know we don't have to do anything tonight," Isaac said.

"No. I want to," Jack answered quickly while still gripping his glass harder than necessary.

"I could give you a tour first if you like."

"That's okay."

Isaac stood and held out his hand. "Come on. I'll at least show you the ground floor."

As Jack stood there was a rattling at the door, he spun toward it taking a defensive stance, adrenalin hitting his system. Two dark haired women came through it, their lips locked together and tearing at each other's clothes. Isaac cleared his throat and the women parted.

"What are you doing here?" The shorter of the two women asked.

"It's the 23rd," Isaac answered sharply.

"It's the 22nd," the woman said in return. Jack was pretty sure it was the 22nd as well.

"No, it's the 23rd."

The woman pinched the bridge of her nose then turned to Jack smiling. "Hi, you must be Jack, I'm Amalie, it's nice to finally meet you. This is Lydia." She gestured to the other woman then turned back to Isaac. "It's Friday the 22nd."

Isaac pulled out his phone as did Amalie. Lydia held out her hand to Jack. "You look familiar," she said even as she shook his hand. "SWAT?"

"Um... Yeah." Lydia looked familiar as well. "Vega? County Prosecutor?"

"Yep." She tilted her head toward Isaac and Amalie who were having a quiet, if intense conversation and studying each other's phones. "MD and Ph.D. and neither of them can keep track of what day it is. They can't cook either. Dozen recipes between the two of them and half are for different types of margaritas."

"I can cook," Jack said, feeling the need to say something. The sudden rush of adrenaline was bouncing around his body with nowhere to go. "Or, well, I can make a decent breakfast."

Lydia grinned. "Great. Hey you two!" She raised her voice. "SWAT Boy is making breakfast." Before Jack or anyone else could respond she slid her arm around Amalie's waist and ushered her upstairs.

Isaac watched them go before turning to Jack. "Turns out it's the 22nd."

"Yeah."

Isaac took a deep breath then let it slowly out. "That is so not how I wanted that introduction to go."

"That was Lydia Vega." Jack was still processing that. Vega was on the top rung of the County's prosecutors with a good record and reputation.

"Yeah. They've been together for years. They went to high school together."

"Oh." Jack looked around wondering if someone else was going to pop out of somewhere. A cat slipped out from under the sofa, rubbed its head on Jack's ankle then walked off without a backward glance at the now marked stranger.

Isaac laughed. Jack tried to hold in his own laughter but failed. They stood there laughing for a good minute, the weird tension in the room lifting.

"And that was Murrcat," Isaac got out as the giggles began to fade. "Do you want to stay?"

Jack nodded, a few giggles still coming out. He'd made it this far and was *not* backing out now.

"Good."

ISAAC HAD NEVER BEEN SO THANKFUL FOR MURRCAT'S SENSE OF timing and total indifference to humans. He was jealous that Murrcat had gotten to mark Jack first but that was the risk when you lived with a feline.

He led Jack through the house to the downstairs guest bedroom. It had been intended as a play room but with lack of use it turned into the Random Stuff room. Isaac needed a weekend and then some to clear it out. While not as elegant as anything in the Windsor club, he kept the light soft and made the twin bed up in shades of deep blue and green. The equipment he planned to use was neatly arranged on top of a vintage set of drawers.

Jack was looking nervous again as he surveyed the room. Isaac was feeling nervous as well but he kept his face cool. This would be different. A sex club was one thing but this was his home, this spoke of length and commitment, of making Jack feel wanted and valued. This would be make or break. Tonight, he had to be at his best.

Here we go.

"Jack." Jack turned toward him. "Go to the door and lock it. It's a standard push button lock. It won't keep you in but it will keep others out."

Jack hesitated. Not long, just the length of a few heartbeats but those seconds stretched beyond rational understandings of time. Jack gave a sharp nod, snapping time back to its proper shape. He took a few long steps to the door. The small click of the cheap lock filled the room. He turned back to Isaac, clasping his hands behind him. The military training showed through in how he squared his shoulders and kept his eyes ahead.

"Get undressed, put your shoes and clothes in the corner. You won't be needing them in this room. You can leave your phone with them."

"Yes, sir." This time there was no hesitation. He was quick but his movements were precise. There was no fumbling. He took his time to fold his clothes neatly and tuck his laces into his shoes. Isaac appreciated the precision as well as the opportunity to simply watch him move.

"Stand in the middle of the room, legs spread, arms out to your sides, straight, parallel with the floor, palms up. I want to look you over."

Again, there was no hesitation. It wasn't a particularly comfortable position but it wasn't intended to be. Holding his palms up would keep his shoulders rolled back while stretching the brachioradialis and bicipital aponeurosis. Depending on how often he stretched his arms he could begin to feel it quite quickly.

He did a close inspection of Jack's body though there was no need. It was pristine and beautiful in a way Isaac knew he would never achieve for himself. This was about Jack accepting that his body would be inspected on a regular basis. If the state of his cock was anything to go by he didn't mind. It was curved up, swollen thick, and a deep red. His balls were already drawn up and his nipples were at hard tight points. His breathing was regular though, his chest rising and falling on a perfect three count. He cupped Jack's balls and gave them a slight squeeze. Jack's breath faltered.

"You're not to hold anything back from me tonight. I want to hear every sigh, moan, and scream. I need to be able to judge my actions against your reactions."

"Yes, sir."

"Good." He pressed the pad of his thumb against Jack's right nipple and smiled at the small gasp of breath. He switched to his thumbnail and watched Jack shudder. "Your body is beautiful. You take such care with it, I can tell." Isaac removed his thumb and blew softly over the same nipple. Jack made a small noise between a whimper and a hum. His arms were beginning to twitch ever so slightly. "And so responsive." He licked that nipple next and blew on it again. "I want you to know I'm going to mark you tonight. Nothing that will last, but you will be able to feel it in the morning. I am also going to bind you. I have no doubt that you are capable of holding a position if I order it but I don't want that to be your focus. Your only focus should be what is happening to you." He traced his fingers up Jack's body and danced them across his lips. "I will also have you tonight." He lowered his voice and poured his words into Jack's ear. "More softly and carefully than you have ever known. I have been saving that. I have no doubt I could have fucked you that first night. Bent you over and taken you like the others but I knew even then, you are far too special for that."

Jack's breath lost its even rhythm.

"But I will save that for later. Lower your arms."

Jack, to his credit, didn't drop his arms but lowered them slowly and precisely.

"Now, kneel for me." Jack went to his knees. Isaac could tell he was going for that smooth, straight backed, dancer like grace that some subs managed but he didn't quite have the experience to pull it off. He leaned forward to keep his balance and his knees made a soft thud. Isaac ran his fingers through Jack's hair. "Very good. Now close your eyes and breathe." Like that first night, Isaac simply stroked his head until Jack's breathing became settled in that easy three in and three out rhythm. Isaac took the time to steady himself as well. It might have been the light but Jack's body appeared stronger and more sculpted than the last time. He wanted to rub himself against it like Murrcat. "Good boy. You are doing very well."

"Thank you, sir." Jack's voice was hardly more than a whisper.

He gave Jack one more stroke before taking a length of soft rope from the top of the dresser along with a pair of EMT safety scissors. "I'm going to bind your arms now behind your back. Nothing fancy but it will look nice and you won't have to worry about what to do with your hands." Jack looked up at him, then at the rope and scissors he was holding. Isaac watched him, carefully looking for any signs of fear or uncertainty but there were none and Jack said nothing. "Put your arms behind your back and grab your forearms."

Despite Jack's lack of objection, he would keep the bindings comfortable tonight, securing instead of stretching. He uncoiled the rope and found the midpoint. Rope bondage was easier to do with an extra person in the room to hold the ends, but for something simple he could manage on his own. It had been far too long since he'd done complicated rope work. He wrapped Jack's arms to each other with a simple interwoven pattern then wrapped the extra around his waist before weaving in the ends. He took a step back to look over his work. It was painfully simplistic. The white rope didn't look great against Jack's pale skin but Jack's cock was dripping and it looked like it wouldn't take more than a stiff breeze and a kind word to make him cum.

"Very pretty, but I think I can do better. I'll get some darker rope, black or dark blue, something that will stand out. I'll weave it around and around your body like a corset. If I do that often enough your body will get used to it and I'll be able to make it tighter each time." Jack whimpered, his eyes shut and his cock twitching. He stroked Jack's head. "But that's for the future. Let's focus on the now."

Isaac grabbed a simple leather cock ring and ball spreader. He crouched down and managed to get it around Jack's cock and balls before he even knew what was happening. "There, that should help prevent any little oopses." Jack's whole posture relaxed. "Now stand up and spread your legs for me, nice and wide."

He stood but slowly, trying to keep his balance with his arms held in place. Isaac paced around him, examining the rope work from a fresh angle. He traced his finger across Jack's waist where rope met skin. "Very nice indeed."

He went back to the dresser and picked up a riding crop. It wasn't cheap braided leather for amateurs, it was proper with a wide head of cream colored leather. He held it up for Jack to see. "Simple, traditional, yet effective." He checked Jack's expression for fear but his face was still, and difficult to read. "May I use it?"

"Yes, sir." His voice was rough in a way that could be lust or fear. Most likely a combination of both. Isaac didn't like that second bit.

He stroked the leather head across Jack's chest. He shivered. "If the pain is too much, or not doing what it should, you are to tell me to stop. All you have to say is stop. Do you understand me?"

Jack nodded.

"I need you to say it."

"I understand."

"Understand what?"

Jack swallowed hard. "If it's too much I tell you to stop."

"Good boy."

He stroked Jack's body with the head of the crop. Like a paint brush he ran it across his torso, down his legs, across his ass, and up his back. Jack continued to shiver and his cock looked like it was trying to break out of its bindings. He pressed the leather to Jack's lips. Jack kissed it.

"Good boy," Isaac whispered then flicked the crop against Jack's nipple. Not hard, not enough to hurt, barely enough to sting, but the surprise of it sent a twitch through Jack's body. He lay a second, precise little flick on Jack's other nipple. There was a jump in his breathing like a tiny skip on an old record, not truly breaking the rhythm. The next two flicks were on the insides of Jack's thighs, close enough to Jack's balls that he could feel the crop go by and perhaps cause a hint of worry. Each of the four spots where Isaac had left a mark were already returning to their natural color. Isaac hit Jack's left nipple again then the inside of his right thigh. Not hard, not hard at all, but even the most delicate touch can build into pain. Jack closed his eyes and let his head roll back. Isaac continued. He tried to avoid any pattern as he took the crop to the same four spots over and over.

He kept one eye on Jack's face. His lips were slightly parted. And while his body twitched and his breath became ragged, his face stayed relaxed, almost serene. Isaac smiled. The boys he often found himself with were solid masochists who needed a firm whip and strong arm, which Isaac could provide. But that meant it had been a while since he'd done this sort of subtle detailed work. It felt good. Jack's nipples would sting for at least a day every time his shirt moved against them. And there would be that little reminder between his thighs every time he took a step.

Jack gave little mewling cries when the crop hit a nipple and whimpered when it hit his thighs. Isaac was tempted to see if he could get Jack to sing for him with just the flick of his crop.

Jack's cock was purple and straining with beads of pre-cum bubbling to the top and running down its length, and his nipples had gone from pink to a dark red. Isaac stopped and pressed the crop up against Jack's balls. He had no intention of striking them but Jack still held his breath. "Don't worry. I won't hurt you. I need you to be aware. Look at me please."

He tilted his head but he struggled with it. His eyes were unfocused. Isaac tossed the crop onto the bed before stroking Jack's cheek. "Very good." He brushed Jack's nipple and his eyes closed again. "Keep looking at me." His eyes snapped open.

Without breaking eye contact Isaac reached down and undid

the bit of leather that was holding Jack's cock. Jack whined, his whole body shaking but his eyes never left Isaac's face. Isaac began to stroke him, slowly and lightly.

"I'm very impressed. You knew what was happening, you knew the pain was going to build, you didn't flinch or shy away. You didn't try to close your legs. You left your body open to my will. That is something few can do." He stepped in close so his body was pressed against Jack's. "Now I want you to cum for me. Right here like this. I want to feel your breath as you let go." Isaac sped up his strokes not caring about the mess about to be spread across his clothes. It didn't take long. Only seconds. Jack cried out, his body convulsing, cum coating Isaac's hand. He started to pitch forward and Isaac helped guide him down to his knees. He lay his head on Isaac's shoulder and shook while Isaac stroked his back and whispered soft words of encouragement into his ear.

⌘

THERE WAS A LOW HUM IN JACK'S EARS, OR MAYBE IT WAS IN HIS head. It was warm and pleasant. It soothed away all the other chatter. There was warmth curling around his body as well. Hands stroking him. They were rough in places, he knew that, but he only felt softness. His arms were being moved, then they were free, falling limp at his sides. That hurt enough for him to notice but the soft hands were stroking his arms all the way down to his fingers.

"Can you make a fist with your hands?"

Jack didn't want to. He didn't like making fists, throwing punches, but he did it anyway.

"Good, now spread your hands wide."

That was better.

"Now stand up then lay down on the bed. You can rest."

Rest sounded nice. He stood, there was pain in his knees. He lay down quickly, closed his eyes, and rested.

☙❧

THERE WAS A BURN ACROSS HIS CHEST AND BETWEEN HIS THIGHS. He wanted to itch but was afraid to touch. Before even opening his eyes, he flopped onto his back and spread his legs.

"That's a nice look for you. Legs spread, nipples hard, body covered in cum."

Isaac was sitting on the bed staring at him. He was still dressed but his shirt and pants were now stained. He didn't seem to care.

"How do you feel? Honestly."

Jack did a systems check. The warm hum was fading. It always did. It made him worry that this was more like a drug than he wanted to admit. "I'm a bit thirsty. A bit of a headache."

Isaac held out a glass of water which had been sitting on the bedside table. Jack sipped it carefully, resisting the urge to chug it down. Isaac watched him with a small smile on his face as he finished the glass.

"Always a bit of a crash, those endorphins and adrenalin fading away."

Jack nodded in agreement.

"It's more than just neurochemistry though, I believe that. And it doesn't rot your brain and bones like drugs."

There were days when he *did* crave it like an addict might, but he had wanted it before he ever tried it. The desire before he had a name or even an idea, had twisted around the back of his mind and down into his body. He'd fought it for a long time. He still fought it when he looked in the mirror and saw his square jaw and broad shoulders. He tried to beat down those feelings when his men looked at him to guide or order them. When he first went to the clubs, trying to be invisible, watching from dark corners, skinny boys in tight jeans would come up to him, cock their hips and bare their throats. He even tried it a few times, putting them on their knees but it never truly worked, never felt right. Those pretty boys worked it out quick, far quicker than he did. Some stayed and talked with him to try to explain things. Most just left.

Isaac ran his fingers through Jack's hair, dragging his nails along his scalp. Jack pressed himself into it, his eyes beginning to close again. Isaac leaned in close.

"Do you remember what I said I was going to do with you tonight, after I'd bound you and hurt you?"

"Yes, sir."

"What did I say?"

"That you would have me tonight."

"Do you still want that?"

He didn't have to think about the answer. "Yes."

"Good. I want you to lay on your front, close your eyes, and breathe. "I'm going to get you ready for me and I'm going to take my time." Isaac licked his ear with the tip of his tongue sending shivers through him. "I'm going to take such good care of you."

"Thank you, sir." Jack stuttered out. He'd had others say that, but there had always been harshness in their voices and a whip or something similar in their hands. Isaac's voice only had honesty and his hands were empty.

"Lay down."

He lay down and rolled over, spreading his legs as he did. He felt Isaac get off the bed then heard the sound of drawers opening and closing. There were small thumps as objects landed on the bed, then Isaac sat back down. Jack wasn't sure exactly what he expected, but Isaac brushing a soft kiss against the base of his skull wasn't it. There was a slight shift of air as Isaac whispered something, then placed a second kiss not even an inch lower. The kisses were hardly more than the brush of a feather in strength but the sensation filled his body more fully than the bite of any whip. Isaac shifted an inch lower again. Jack got the idea that Isaac was kissing and possibly reciting the names of each of his vertebra.

He was hard and as much as he tried to fight it, he pressed his hips down into the bed. Isaac paused and Jack braced himself for punishment. It didn't come. Isaac stroked his head then continued with his anatomy refresher. By the time Isaac reached the small of his back, Jack felt like his body was melting, except for his cock which had reached the point of pain. And when Isaac placed a final kiss at his tail bone he raised his ass up in invitation.

Isaac pulled away and there were a series of noises he couldn't identify. One sounded like a latex snap but he hadn't heard a condom packet. He was pretty sure the squishy sound was lube. He felt slick latex covered fingers slowly spread his cheeks. The lube was warm, as opposed to the ice cold he usually got. A tiny part of him was offended by the gloves. He'd cleaned well before coming over but he hadn't mentioned that to Isaac and Isaac hadn't asked. That same small part of him wanted to say something but that series of kisses had left him beyond speech.

Isaac ran a finger around his hole and he moaned. He raised his hips, trying to press himself onto that single slim digit, needing it like little else before. "Easy. Don't worry. I'll fill you up before I'm done. I won't leave you wanting." He finally pressed his finger in and Jack nearly screamed. There was hardly even a hint of stretch but he was so close it may as well have been Isaac's cock. Isaac worked that single finger in and out of him at a maddeningly slow pace. He tried to press himself up, to get Isaac's finger in deeper but Isaac always managed to move with him never breaking the rhythm. Sweat rolled down his body, it was absurd to be so close from so little.

"I'm going to put a second finger into you now. You feel so good around me already. It's killing me waiting. I know when I get my cock in you it is going to be amazing but I'm not going to rush this." Jack whined, unable to beg. "You can cum if you need to at any point. I'm sure you're already close. I'm also sure you can catch back up quick."

Jack nodded into his pillow but stopped his thrusting. If Isaac could wait, so could he. There was a slight stretch as Isaac pushed another finger in. He kept the slow and easy pace, sometimes twisting his fingers one way or another. Sometimes dropping a scorching feather kiss along Jack's spine. He lost track of time and most rational thought.

Then Isaac's fingers left him. He tried to squeeze down around nothing. For so little he felt so empty.

"Easy there."

He heard another squirt of lube then felt something press against his hole. It was solid this time.

"Just a little toy. Something to stretch and stimulate. I won't push it all the way in. This is only meant to feel good. Is that okay?"

Jack nodded.

"I need to hear you say something."

He managed to get out a yes but his head was spinning as if slightly drunk.

Isaac pressed in the toy slowly. He could picture it by feel. He'd had them used before. A wand made of a series of balls each slightly larger. Isaac pressed in four then stopped. The fourth one had been the first real stretch. Jack fought the urge to lift his hips, to fuck himself on the larger ones, instead, with no small amount of pride he held himself steady.

"Breathe," Isaac said.

Jack wasn't aware he'd been holding his breath. He let it out and Isaac drew out the toy completely before working it back in. Like with his fingers, he kept the pace slow and steady. It made Jack want to scream. He flopped his head to the side and opened his eyes. The room didn't come properly into focus for several seconds. When it did, all he could see was a blank wall. He closed his eyes again all his awareness focused on what Isaac was doing to his ass.

He counted the balls in and out of his body.

One, two, three, four. Four, three, two, one. One, two, three, four.

Then Isaac kept going, pushing a fifth halfway in, leaving him stretched around the circumference.

"Your ass looks amazing stretched like that. I can't wait to see it around my cock."

Jack moaned, beyond using words, as the fifth ball was pushed in followed by a sixth which burned and pressed against his insides in a way that made him jump and cry out. Isaac stopped.

"Was that a good or a bad yelp."

Jack hoped he said good. His lips felt heavy and thick like the rest of him. Isaac drew the balls out and Jack began to count again.

One, two, three, four, five, six. Six, five, four, three, two, one.

Jack lost track of time again, until Isaac fully pulled the last two out and didn't go back in.

"Roll over. Open your eyes."

He flopped onto his back. It wasn't graceful and it wasn't quick. His legs fell open. Isaac slowly swam into focus. He was smiling. "You look like I've already fucked you six ways to Sunday." Jack smiled back. "Do you think you're ready?"

Jack nodded then mumbled out yes.

Isaac finished undressing, able to do it quickly without looking rushed. His cock looked larger than Jack remembered. Long and particularly thick. He spread his legs wider. "You should spend more time like this, on your back, on my bed, legs spread for me." Jack didn't respond but if he had, it wouldn't have been to disagree. He felt wanton and wild. He could not remember ever wanting to be fucked this desperately. Not even the first time.

Isaac rolled on a condom and knelt between Jack's legs. He bent his knees and raised his hips as best as he could. Usually he was on all fours or bent over something when he did this. He wanted to close his eyes and let his body melt but he kept his eyes on Isaac's face, needing to remember the moment.

Isaac lined his cock up at his entrance and more slowly than he'd done anything else that night pushed himself in. Jack didn't come. He grit his teeth and dug his nails into his palms. He felt his cock jump and strain but he didn't come. Not yet. Not until Isaac was fucking him proper. Instead Isaac stopped, closing his own eyes and let out a moan.

"Oh god. Worth it. You feel so good. So right." He pulled himself out even slower than he went in. Jack couldn't handle it.

"Please," he managed to drag the word from his own lips. "Please."

"Please what?"

Jack shook his head, trying to convey that he simply couldn't speak.

"Should I stop?"

Jack shook his head harder and thrust his hips up.

"Ah, I see."

Isaac thrust back in. Still slowly but with more force. Jack squeezed down around him and that was the cue to really speed things up. He lifted Jack's legs so they were hooked over his shoulders, thrusting hard and fast. Shouts and moans filled the room at random in counterpoint to the rhythmic slap of their bodies. Then Isaac stopped, recentered himself, and thrust up hard. And with a scream Jack finally came. It seemed to last forever.

ISAAC'S WHOLE BODY CONVULSED IN A WAY THAT WAS GOING TO leave him sore in the morning. He had held himself back too long and only came a few moments after Jack, unable to sustain any longer. Jack had looked and felt amazing as he'd cum. So open he almost seemed fragile yet his body squeezed down tight around him, his muscles rippling under his skin.

He slowly drew himself from Jack's limp form his own legs threatening to give out from under him. He managed to find his legs long enough to get the condom into a waste basket before collapsing back down onto the bed next to Jack. Jack hadn't moved. His arms were splayed out and his legs spread wide. His breath was the soft breath of sleep. He found Jack's pulse thumping along strong and steady. He ran his fingers through Jack's hair. He mumbled and turned into the touch.

"Just sleep," he whispered into Jack's ear.

Then Isaac decided to follow his own advice and join him.

CHAPTER 8

J ack's eyes snapped open. He'd hoped that after returning
to civilian life, the jarring zero to sixty wakeups demanded
by the army would fade. It hadn't. It might still take a few
seconds for his mind to catch up but his body was awake
and ready to go.

That few seconds of mental catch up reminded him that he
was in Isaac's house, in his extra bedroom, naked, sore, Isaac (he
hoped) was curled against his back. There was a small digital
clock on the bedside table. It read 7:39. Jack blinked at it a few
times, wondering if it was correct. It had been years since he'd
slept more than eight hours at a shot. Usually he lived off six.
Even after an intense session he'd snap awake before the eight-
hour mark.

He debated if he should move. He didn't want to wake up
Isaac. It had been a long time since anyone had slept next to him
and it was nice. On the other hand, he really needed to pee. As
slowly as possible, he stretched out one arm to draw back the
soft blanket that covered them. Isaac mumbled and rolled onto
his back away from Jack. Jack took the opportunity to speed up
his exit while still keeping it as silent as possible. He grabbed the

bag he'd brought, and still naked, slipped out the door and down the hall to the bathroom Isaac had pointed out the night before.

Once there and having peed he found himself at a loss. Should he go back to bed? Shower? Get dressed? Make breakfast? He settled for cleaning up in the sink and pulling on his jeans and t-shirt, he didn't want to run into Isaac's wife and her lover while completely naked and covered in dried cum. He snuck back into the bedroom. Isaac was still asleep, flopped onto his back and snoring softly. He looked small in the large bed but he supposed everyone looked smaller in sleep, the power of will and personality stripped away.

He hovered in the doorway unsure what to do in the still house. His stomach rolled and made the decision to make breakfast, or at the very least find out if there was coffee.

THE KITCHEN WAS CLEAN BUT WITH AN UNDERUSED LOOK. ON THE counter was an old-school Mr. Coffee coffee maker with a slight brown ring on the bottom of the glass pot. There was also a high-end espresso machine with a thin layer of dust on it. Jack headed to the espresso machine and was surprised to find it hooked up. It wasn't uncommon for people to buy nice espresso machines, thinking 'the kid at Starbucks can make a latte, how hard can it be'. After the third steam burn they go back to their drip coffee or get one of those awful cartridge machines. He took out the filter holder. There were a few bone-dry grounds and slight calcification but no rust. He relaxed. This was familiar territory. He poked around and found some white vinegar and baking soda. He got to work.

Twenty minutes later the water was coming through the machine clean and hot. He liked the fact that he had a backup skill, even if it was a minimum wage one. Then he went looking for coffee. He probably should have done that first. There was a can of grounds only a step away from the instant sitting next to the drip machine. Gritting his teeth, he looked in the freezer. Sandwiched between some frozen dinners and a bottle of tequila was a bag of good coffee. He wished they would print Do Not Freeze in big letters across the front of coffee bags. It did all kinds of damage to the flavor. It was also pre-ground. He'd have to see about getting some whole beans.

Getting way ahead of yourself there.

Jack grabbed the bag of coffee. The muscle memory of tapping in the grounds was still there, careful not to spill any. The sound of espresso sliding into the little pot, the hiss of the steam and the bubbling of milk took him far back in his memory and away from the night before. He'd enjoyed the previous night. He hadn't felt that good in a long time and he knew it, but he didn't want to analyze it, not yet. It was easier to make coffee in the kitchen of someone who was still half a stranger, than to pace around waiting for that stranger to wake up.

"Oh, my god, that smells good."

Jack jumped, nearly spilling the latte across his fingers. "Sorry. I woke up and wasn't sure-."

Isaac slid across the kitchen and took the coffee from his hands. He took a sip and made a noise similar to what Jack had been making the night before. "You made this?"

"Yeah." He waved to the machine. "That was the only good coffee I could find, you really shouldn't keep coffee in the freezer. I did a clean with vinegar to get out the residue but—"

Isaac put his fingertips to Jack's lips stopping the babble. He took another sip. "Every time I tried to use that thing I burned myself."

"It takes practice." Jack mumbled from behind Isaac's fingers.

Isaac lowered his hand. "Summer job?"

"Summer and after school. Coffea Contenuto: Cafe and Organic Bakery"

"That sounds..." Isaac didn't finish his thought.

"Pretentious?" Jack smiled. His time at Coffea Contenuto was some of the best of his life. "We used to roast our beans on site."

Isaac stepped in close, pushing their bodies together, and slightly raising up on his toes, kissed his lips.

You really shouldn't pre-grind coffee.

Was Jack's first thought catching the flavor from Isaac's lips. This was followed by the realization that Isaac was kissing him on the lips. A proper kiss. Before panic or analysis could set in, Isaac pulled away with a shout.

Amalie came in and scurried around the kitchen table, managing to take sips of coffee as she did.

"My coffee!"

"You looked like you were busy with something else. Wouldn't want it to get cold. God this is good."

Isaac made grabby hands toward his coffee while Amalie held it over her head. He braced himself for the imminent mess and scalding before Lydia swept in, perfectly assembled in power suit, makeup, and heels that made her the second tallest person in the room. She plucked the cup from Amalie's hands and took a couple of large swallows.

"Hey SWAT boy, good coffee." And with no other comment she put a kiss on the end of Amalie's nose and walked out the front door, taking the cup with her. Both Isaac and Amalie turned to him looking like kicked puppies.

"So, should I make a couple more cups of coffee?"

THE FLUIDITY OF MOVEMENT JACK SHOWED AS HE MADE THE coffee spoke of long hours of practice and left Isaac wondering if there was a genre of barista porn out there. Probably. The three of them managed to put together a breakfast of scrambled eggs and toast, talking casually as they did. He kept one eye on Jack, the whole time looking for signs of discomfort or general panic. Either he was very relaxed the morning after a scene or he was an excellent actor. It could have been a combination of both.

After breakfast Isaac lured him to a long shower, bringing each other off with soapy hands. It was nearly noon when he sent Jack home with a lingering kiss and a pat on the ass.

Amalie had her feet kicked up in the lounge, with her nose in a science journal. She was of the firm belief that weekends were for lounging around in jammies, unless it was absolutely necessary to get properly dressed. Isaac sat beside her.

"I could have sworn it was the 23rd."

Without looking up from the journal Amalie reached out and patted him on the head. "I love you anyway."

Isaac reached for the mug sitting on the coffee table, only to have his hand slapped away.

"I think you should keep him."

"You're just saying that because he makes really good coffee."

"Yep. But you seem relaxed this morning."

"I'm always relaxed. I'm super mellow."

She put down her journal and finally looked at him her lips pinched. "You know what I mean."

He did. He'd panicked when he woke up without Jack next to him, scared that he had run off into the night, that he had done something that sent Jack into a panic of his own. That had been the only real blip in the evening. A particular part of himself had woken up sated but also hoping for more.

"You like him." Amalie stated the obvious but it was good to have it said out loud.

"I do. How about you?"

"So far..." She gave a slight nod with a shrug. "We should sit down and have a proper talk if he sticks around, but SWAT Boy does make good coffee."

"He does. Where does Lydia stand?" While Lydia had solid reasons for not being out with them, she had a large enough part in their lives that she got a say in certain things. Especially ones that related to her privacy or could intersect with her career.

"She was a little surprised. Muttered a bit about neither of us being able to read a calendar. Assuming you keep him, she'll have to be part of the *big* talk but she didn't seem angry."

"I want to keep him, but I think the ball is in his court now."

CHAPTER 9

Alpha team came storming into the changing room while Jack was pulling on his uniform. There were grumbles and slammed lockers. He stopped whistling as Dan slammed open his own locker and began peeling off his gear.

"What's up?"

Dan rolled his eyes. "They got us all dressed up, baked us in the sun, and our date was a no show."

"I had one of those last month. Got a tip on a stash house turned out to be an empty meth lab."

"We got a tip as well, big deal going down, nothing."

Jack had been thinking about the last bad tip he'd had and another the month before that. "Gonzales had two last month," he said quietly, leaning close but trying to sound casual.

"Yeah, I heard." Dan took a deep breath. "I don't want to say anything too loud but something hinky is going on. It's too many duds too close together. Someone is getting fed bad info or—" Neither of them said the word leak out loud. "I don't want to say it's above our pay grade but..."

"We're both team leaders and it's wasting time and

resources." Jack sighed, his lingering good mood from the weekend diminishing.

"Something to think about I guess." Dan looked Jack over. "So, Mister Whistle While You Work, how'd your weekend go?"

"Fine," Jack answered quickly.

Dan grinned at him. "Yeah, you look fine. I'm guessing Kinky Married Complicated got settled."

Jack wanted to answer, to talk about how amazing he had felt and how relaxed he'd been. Even breakfast the morning after had not been as awkward as he'd feared. He opened his mouth and snapped it shut again before carefully saying. "It's fine."

⬧

EVERY TIME THERE WAS A REPORT OR STUDY THAT CAME OUT declaring the overuse of SWAT beyond its original brief, Jack was forced to agree, even if it was only in private. Their last three jobs had involved serving search warrants by putting a battering ram through a front door. He was pretty sure it used to be a detective would knock on a door and say 'hello, we have a search warrant'. At least that's what happened in the movies.

He checked over his gear again as they pulled up to a rickety house surrounded by abandoned buildings and empty plots. This one was unlikely to be a dud and might actually need SWAT involvement. He could already feel the flood of neuro-chemicals building up in his system. His heart was beating faster, his muscles were tensing, a glint of sun bouncing off the edge of a buckle kept drawing his attention. He fought to keep focus. He was the leader. He'd be first through the door. The team needed him to be able to rationally assess the situation as quickly as possible, while his lizard brain was getting ready to sink its teeth into the throat of some other lizard.

He took deep breaths but tried to be discreet about it. This was where things could go wrong. The lizard was willing to lash out at anything that moved; real threat or scared kid trying to do his homework, it didn't matter. Of course, when there was nothing, just empty buildings, that was a whole different mess of a comedown.

The back doors of the van opened. They had, in theory, good intel this time. Human trafficking, a case months in the making. It was a joint operation with the feds and they'd been heavily briefed, which made for a nice change. High possibility of weapons, high chance of hostages, high chance of the bad guys skipping town in the next 24 hours, high chance of the Big Guy being there.

His team followed him out of the van and down the thin alley between buildings, their job was to stop anyone who tried to run out the back while the feds went in the front. Gonzales's team was split in two, to catch anyone trying to climb out the windows. 'We have the place surrounded' was no idle threat this time.

He heard the heavy thump of chopper blades overhead and a simple call 'go' over the radio. He heard the crash of the front door being forced open. He shoved down his lizard brain, jumped on the adrenalin wave, and got to work.

❦

JACK WAS STARING AT ISAAC'S NUMBER ON THE LITTLE SLIP OF paper when his phone rang. The number on the screen matched up with the doctor's scribble. He'd been debating calling Isaac. That was the problem with never being with anyone more than once, he wasn't sure of the protocol. It had been three days.

"Hello?"

"Hi, it's me." Isaac sounded like he was in a good mood. "Did I catch you at an okay time?"

"Yeah, I'm at home. Was about to make dinner," Jack lied. He'd been thinking about ordering pizza but he wasn't that hungry. He was coming down from the day. It had been a good bust in the sense that the bad guys were arrested, but it hadn't been clean. There had been weapons discharged. One of the FBI guys caught a bullet in the leg. One of the low level bad guys caught a bullet in the head. His team ended up in a hand to hand scuffle. The debrief had been extensive and left him nearly as wound up as the operation itself. Wound up and unsure how to unwind.

"Dinner sounds good. I wanted to check on how you're doing. Haven't heard from you in a couple of days and wanted to make sure you didn't come down too hard."

Jack didn't feel like he'd come down at all. Not really. Not like other times where the crash was hard, leaving him sick, and the itch starting again almost instantly. Or the comedowns from the days like the one he'd just had that left him frayed, unfocused, and needing time on his knees. "I'm fine. Good. I was thinking about calling you but I wasn't sure..." he trailed off.

"You can call me any time you need to, or any time you just feel like it. I want to know how you're doing."

Warmth spread across his body and he smiled, even though no one was there to see it. "I'm feeling fine." He didn't mention work.

"Work okay?"

"Caught some bad guys today so that's good."

Isaac gave a happy little hum that warmed Jack in a different way. "Good. I'm tempted to say something tacky like 'what are you wearing'."

Jack chuckled. "Just jeans and a t-shirt. Nothing exciting."

"Anything can be exciting if worn by the right person."

Isaac's voice hadn't changed, there was still light laughter in it but it made Jack hard. That had been the only downside to the last few days, his dick acting like a teenager's again. He cleared his throat as he shifted on his couch.

"Did you just get hard?"

Jack's face burned and he was glad Isaac wasn't there to see it. "A little," he lied again.

"Are you going to take care of it?"

"Umm... I..." He wanted to. He would have happily whacked off three times a day for the last three days. He hadn't though. It was another bit of procedure he wasn't sure about, but he'd heard other subs talk about.

"You can if you like." Isaac's voice became serious. "I don't need to exert any control over your day to day life. Unless you want me to?"

"Uhhh—" Jack was annoyed at how completely inarticulate he'd gotten as his mind raced in sex based directions.

"How about you take care of yourself as much as you like until the next time we're together and we'll talk about it then. In fact, why don't you keep track of how many times you take care of yourself between now and then."

Shit, Jack thought, knowing full well he was going to do it. "Okay." He swallowed hard a few times. "When can we meet again?"

No, that didn't sound desperate and needy.

"I know I have the weekend after next completely free. Lydia and Amalie are going to some spa to get dipped in mud or something equally unsanitary. And I've double checked the date. You could come over Friday night, stay all weekend if you like. We can just hang out. But if you need to meet sooner—"

"No. I can hang on for that long."

"I don't want you *hanging on*." Isaac's voice was gentle. "I want you comfortable in this."

"I'll be fine."

There was a moment of silence over the line. "Okay, but call me any time you like. You've got my number."

"I will. Promise."

"Good." Isaac hung up the phone. Jack took a couple of deep breaths and unzipped his jeans. He instantly felt much better.

ISAAC HUNG UP THE PHONE SMILING TO HIMSELF. HE'D BEEN worried when Jack hadn't called until it hit him that he might not know he could call. You don't call anonymous one-night stands. That Jack hadn't masturbated since their time together made Isaac tingle. It spoke strongly to wanting more long-term or day to day control even if he didn't realize it.

"Hey, hun?" he shouted from his office to Amalie's.

"What?" she shouted back.

"I invited Jack to come over while you're getting dipped in mud."

He heard her get up and appear at his door only a few seconds later. "Full weekend sleepover?"

"That's the plan."

"That's getting serious."

He knew that. A simple overnight was one thing. Whole days with each other, possibly whole days of submission, that was a trickier test of compatibility and commitment.

"We'll see how it goes. I know he's still got a whole tangle of issues but—"

"Hey, you never know if you can get past the issues if you don't try." She smiled at him.

"And I think he'll look very hot tied up." Isaac said, half deflecting a discussion about feelings until he knew if there were reasons to have them. "Maybe try a corset pattern to start with."

"I can picture that." Amalie had a fair amount of skill at kinbaku herself, but for her it was a purely artistic exercise, that she often referred to as her kinky macrame.

"Speaking of, think I can budget in some new rope?" He really wanted to see Jack wrapped in blue.

"Seeing that I'm about to pay way too much to spend a weekend wrapped in kelp, you can get new rope. With his complexion maybe try to get something in a dark blue or dark green."

"Want to come shopping with me?"

Amalie put on her pretending to think face then grinned.

Isaac clapped his hands together. "Yay, toy shopping!"

CUM WAS DRYING ON HIS BODY AS HE LAY ON HIS BACK, LEGS spread wide. Normally he was cleaner when it came to whacking off. Faster as well. But this one seemed important. He'd taken his time, stripped naked and teased himself. He'd run one hand along his body and slowly stroked his cock with the other. The whole time he'd thought of Isaac, the things that had been done to him, the soft but strong voice in his ear whispering praise.

And there were the things promised and the possibilities of what might happen. Vague dreams, comments overheard, flashes of images quickly scrolled past in the depths of the internet. Things that scared him but sent his hand moving faster.

When he came it had been with his free hand gripping hard in his hair, pulling his own head back, his spine arched, and his body on fire with the thought of what might happen the next time they were together.

CHAPTER 10

" Can I help you two find anything?" asked the heavily pierced young sales woman as they entered Bell's Leather and Equipment.

"We're fine, thanks," Isaac answered politely as he and Amalie headed to the back rooms. The front of the shop was crotchless panties and furry handcuffs for amateurs and lookie loos. The back room had a collection of rope that would put a mountaineering supplier to shame, as well as toys and equipment for the more experienced consumer.

"May I assist you this morning?" asked an elegantly suited, and tightly corseted young man from his desk by the door.

"New rope, and maybe some other odds and ends. I'll look around, see what looks good."

"Of course, sir. We have a new collection of stainless steel insertables, as well as a fresh set of vibrators and plugs that can be controlled and programmed via Wi-Fi or Bluetooth."

"Wi-Fi operated sex toys. I love living in the future."

Amalie tapped him on the shoulder. "I'm going to go pick rope." She had an engineer's eye for the stuff and he trusted her judgment. "You should look at cuffs. Nothing makes a new boy feel special like his own gear."

"Very true." He looked around, except for the ropes along the back wall they'd rearranged since the last time he was there.

"If you'll allow me, sir, I can show you to the leather goods."

"You boys in the back room are always so polite." Amalie commented with a small chuckle.

"We try, madam." He turned to Isaac. "If you follow me, sir."

As they walked through the showroom, Isaac tapped down the desire to request one of everything. He and Amalie were comfortable but he did not need a 900 dollar, fully adjustable punishment bench. His toy collection was already extensive if under used.

He did let himself stop and linger over the cuffs and collars. Amalie was right, he wanted Jack to feel important and comfortable. Second hand cuffs with cracked leather was not going to accomplish that. There was a wide range of thicknesses and padding. Some were so thin as to be nothing more than decorative. Others were industrial, originally designed to hold dangerous criminals in place.

"Decisions, decisions," Isaac mumbled mostly to himself.

"If I may ask what kind of boy you have, perhaps I can help you narrow down your choices."

"Large and strong but in a natural way. Shy but willing. A little delicate." That last bit Isaac said more to himself.

"I see. Perhaps these then." The sales assistant brought over a set of cuffs and a collar in natural leather. "Seven piece set. Wrists, thighs, ankles, and collar. A thick leather with a neoprene padding designed to minimize marking and prevent damage to the leather from sweat. Good for long-term use within reason. There is an option to lock them into place. Multiple D rings of course, and while not rated for suspension they can handle a few hundred pounds of pulling."

Isaac picked up an ankle cuff. It was wide and a good weight.

Not too heavy but you'd know it was there. Nicely padded as well. He wouldn't have to worry about sanding down the leather first or it cutting into Jack's skin.

He knew sets like this fell under the category of If You Have to Ask the Price You Probably Can't Afford It, but Jack was his best opportunity for someone long term in a long time. And considering his history of one night stands he'd probably never had his own equipment.

"I like them." Isaac pictured them on Jack. "Any chance I can get them in a slightly darker color?"

❧

"FIND SOMETHING YOU LIKE?" AMALIE ASKED AS HE JOINED HER BY the ropes.

"I think I got some good stuff. How about you?"

She gestured to several lengths of colored rope and cord. "I figure braided cotton. He's not going to want marks."

"Sadly, no. But I can work with it." He lifted the dark blue rope and ran it across his fingers. He usually used a jute rope because it bit into itself for a secure hold but also bit slightly into the skin, leaving complicated patterns across a subs body if done right. He gave her a quick kiss. "Have I mentioned lately that you are awesome?"

"Yes, but I could always stand to hear it more."

"You are awesome."

She grinned. "I know."

"Are you getting stuff for yourself?"

"Of course, only place I can get that French massage oil I like." She steadfastly refused to buy anything sex related online. "Plus, a couple of other things."

He glanced around the well-stocked room. "Yeah, I think I'll pick up a couple other things as well."

THE CRANBERRY JUICE WAS SHARP AND COLD BUT IN NO WAY WHAT
Jack wanted. Jack wanted a drink, but he'd learned long ago that
on the odd occasions when he really wanted a drink, were the
times he shouldn't be having one. Plus, this was going to be a
loose lips sink ships situation.

It wasn't typical for him, Dan, and Gonzales to be in the
same place at the same time, since one of their teams was nearly
always on the job. As it was Gonzales was on call, meaning they
were at a diner not nearly as far from the station as Jack would
have liked.

Dan sipped his water. "So, we have eleven duds in the last six
months."

"And this month isn't done yet," Gonzales added.

"All tips, or so we've been told. And all connected to drugs,
mostly production, some distribution."

Jack rubbed at his temples. He felt tired and scattered.
"We've got a dripping faucet."

Dan began to draw in his ketchup with a french fry. "Or
someone dumb enough to take bad intel from the same person
over and over."

"I'm more inclined to believe in the faucet with a drip,"
Gonzales said.

Jack rolled his shoulders trying to stretch out his stress
knotted muscles. "This is so far above our paygrade."

"Who are we going to trust though?" Gonzales asked. "I don't
know about you guys but I've got zero useful connections."

"We leak the leak?" Dan suggested. "Some sort of internal
memo. Play dumb about it?"

"I don't know." Jack's army time had taught him exactly how
fast blame could be passed around and how fast shit could roll
downhill until the person at the bottom was buried in it. "And

it's not like we have anything concrete to point to. A few more empty houses than usual. Someone can write that off easy."

"And it's not like we've caught someone sneaking out the back of a place."

Gonzales's phone suddenly played the first four bars of the Dragnet theme. "Speak of the devil." He checked his phone. "I'm up. But if it's another empty I fucking swear—"

"Yeah, us too." Dan waved him out of the bar.

Jack finished his cranberry juice and leaned back into the padded seats of the booth.

"Got any other thoughts?" Dan asked.

Jack shook his head. "Just crap from movies and spy novels. Nothing useful." But that didn't change the frustration that was growing in him. He knew this was going to go bad at some point, he could feel it. "You?"

"Sure, but nothing actionable. Spy movie shit."

The two of them fell into silence. Jack glanced up at the daily specials board. Someone in the kitchen had ambitions above fried eggs and grilled cheese. The dessert was a green tea ice cream with dark chocolate shell.

He was pretty sure he would never be able to *think* about green tea again without remembering being on his knees, his eyes closed, smelling tea and sex.

"So, now that we've completely failed to do anything useful about our work problems, how's your love life?" Dan asked, a tinge of frustration in his voice.

"My love life is fine."

Dan grinned. "Fine means you are admitting to having one." Jack went to stand up. "Nah, sit down. Fine is good. You're good when you're *fine*. Way more relaxed. You don't have that tense brain jumping around thing going."

"Should I be worried that you pay that much attention to my mental state?" Jack asked trying desperately to deflect from the fact that Brain Jumping Around Thing was one of the main things that drove him to people like Isaac.

"We have to back each other up on occasion. I try to pay attention to the overall moods of anyone who is going to be near me with a firearm."

"I'm fine," Jack repeated.

"Yes, you are. Keep doing whatever it is you're doing with Kinky Married Complicated, it's grounding you. That's good."

CHAPTER 11

The smell of the cheap soap stocked in the station showers clung to Jack's skin. It was better than the smell of dried sweat. He was still clenching and unclenching his hands in irritation when Isaac opened his front door.

"What's wrong?" Isaac asked, even before hello, gesturing him in.

"Nothing." Jack answered instantly. The look he got from Isaac was cold. "Nothing important. I don't..." Jack waved a hand trying to convey that he didn't want to talk. Not after the day he'd had. He closed his eyes and felt Isaac's hand gently taking his chin.

"Look at me please." Jack opened his eyes but it wasn't easy. "Take a few deep breaths. As long as it's not something related to us or your health you don't have to talk, but I don't want you to feel that you *can't* talk to me. Understand?"

Jack nodded. "Later." He was scattered and angry. "Just, I need this first." He took a long breath. "I *need* this first." This time there was pleading.

"Okay."

Isaac let go of his chin and drew the curtains covering the front windows. "Get undressed. Leave your shoes and clothes by the door. You can put them back on before you leave, Sunday night. You can bring your phone into the bedroom but only with a work alert."

Jack was hard in a second and the irritation of the morning's fuckups began to slip away. He stripped, taking deep breaths as he did, before carefully tucking his clothes to the side and standing at ease for inspection.

"Hands behind your head."

He interlaced his fingers behind his head and felt the muscles in his back start to relax. He took a couple more deep breaths.

"Close your eyes."

He closed them and continued with long slow breaths, trying to keep his mind clear. He knew Isaac wouldn't want him over thinking, trying to anticipate. Jack didn't *want* to think.

"I'm going to inspect you first. It's been a couple of weeks. Who knows what you've been up to."

Then Isaac was tilting his head down. "You got a haircut."

It took half a second for Jack to remember that he had. He had a standing appointment for a trim every three months for so long he didn't even think about it. "Yes, sir."

Isaac brushed the skin at his hairline. "You need to start wearing more sun screen. I don't want to see you burned."

"Yes, sir." Jack repeated. He knew he'd gotten some sun jogging the day before, but hadn't put much thought into it.

Isaac hummed low and continued. Jack held his position as Isaac traced the muscles on his back then spread the globes of his ass. It felt detached and clinical. Jack wished he'd had time for a proper shower, a long hot one to help him relax and calm down before he even got to the door, but he hadn't had the time. Instead it had been a rush job in the station showers, scrubbing off the sweat with cheap soap and a rough cloth.

"These?" Isaac brushed the collection of small bruises on his upper left arm.

"Skinny meth head tried to flip me." It hadn't worked and it had been a clusterfuck of an operation. One of his guys got a knife in the thigh and was probably going to quit.

"When?"

"Last Thursday."

"This?" Isaac tapped the week-old bruise on Jack's hip.

"Training fall."

"When?"

"A week ago."

"And this?" Isaac tapped a second bruise on Jack's side.

"Same fall."

Isaac hummed again and Jack was tempted to open his eyes to see Isaac's expression, try to guess what he was thinking of the bruises.

He cupped Jack's balls in what was again a clinical manner, but it didn't stop Jack from gasping or rolling his hips forward hoping for more. Isaac let go and Jack waited, and kept waiting. He tried to stretch out his hearing. He could hear the tick of a clock, someone down the street mowing their lawn late. He took a deep breath through his nose and knew Isaac was still standing in front of him smelling of strong soap and coffee.

He wasn't sure how long he was waiting, probably not as long as it felt, when Isaac grasped his chin again. Jack started at the touch but managed to keep mostly still and his eyes closed.

"Is there anything else I should know about? Injury? Illness?"

"No. Just those bruises. I'm healthy."

He felt Isaac step closer to him. "Open your eyes." Jack obeyed and found himself looking directly into Isaac's eyes. It was startling seeing nothing but someone else's eyes. Black points circled by a soft warm brown, yet there was an intensity behind them that caused something to catch in Jack's chest. Isaac stepped back and dropped a throw pillow from the couch at Jack's feet. "Kneel." Isaac turned away and headed to the kitchen, not even waiting to see if Jack followed the order.

Jack did, keeping his hands behind his head since he hadn't been told to drop them. Isaac returned and held out what looked like a glass of water. "Drink this, sip, don't chug."

He took a sip of the cold liquid, jerking back at the salty sweet taste. He recognized it as basic hydration fluid. He took another sip and found it didn't taste that bad, which meant he probably needed it. He'd had a training officer tell him that the better it tasted the worse off you are.

"They wrap you up in ten layers of black, shove you out in the sun or a tactical van, and don't provide nearly enough fluid." Jack nodded at the truth and finished drinking the fluid right down to the slightly gritty dregs of powder that never quite dissolved. Isaac took the glass from him. "Feeling better?"

Jack had to admit he did. The little headache he'd been ignoring was gone and his whole body felt looser. "Yes, sir."

"Good. I'll give you more later. I have plans to sweat most of that glass out of you." Isaac had a naughty smirk which warmed Jack's body in a different way.

"Follow me." Isaac took long strides to the bedroom which Jack was easily able to match.

He looked around the bedroom as he stepped through the door, a small part of his mind always expecting a gun in his face or a meth lab about to blow. The room was thankfully free of firearms or chemistry sets of questionable quality. The thing that caught his eye was four cuffs laid out on the bed.

"I want to be able to restrain you this weekend. The cuffs will leave almost no marks, unlike rope."

The cuffs were wide and well padded. No locks, just buckles and D rings. Also, no sign of a collar that often came with cuffs. Isaac had remembered that. "Thank you, sir."

"Put them on."

He didn't sit down to put on the ankle cuffs. He knew his ass was on the flat side but that it looked pretty good when he touched his toes, or so he'd been told. The wrist cuffs were trickier, especially because he didn't want to use his teeth on the quality leather. When he was done, Isaac came over to inspect him again. He ran his fingers along the edge of the cuffs then frowned before loosening each one of them a notch. "You're going to be in these for a while."

Isaac slowly circled him again, running fingertips along his body in seemingly random patterns before wrapping a firm hand around Jack's cock without warning. He fought to keep himself still, not press himself into that warm hand.

"I told you you could take care of yourself, but I also told you to keep track of how many times." Isaac gave him one long slow stroke. "How many?"

"Fifteen." He muttered, feeling ashamed. He hadn't masturbated that often since he was a teenager. Isaac gave a low chuckled giving him another slow stroke before letting go.

"Go kneel on the bed." Jack complied easily. Isaac pulled up a chair and sat down staring at Jack. He tried not to shift. It was strange. He could stand still while his body was intimately examined, but Isaac's eyes were heavy on him and left him squirming, both lust and embarrassment warring in his head. He took deep breaths trying to simply be in the moment, not worry, not anticipate. He wasn't sure how much time had passed, not being able to see the digital clock on the dresser behind him.

Isaac leaned forward. "Touch yourself." Jack didn't move, it was the last thing he'd expected Isaac to say. "I want to see how you take care of yourself at home when no one is looking."

He took his cock in his hand, his body burning. For all the ways he'd been taken, the things he'd done or had done to him, no one had ever asked to see this. He looked down and began to stroke himself slowly. "You don't need to feel any shame. You are doing this because I want to see it, because it brings me pleasure to know what you look like uninhibited in the quiet of your own life. I want to see how your muscles tense and release, how hard you cum with just your hand on your own cock and my voice in your head."

He stroked himself faster, Isaac's words causing lust to overwhelm any shame. He gritted his teeth, trying to draw it out, trying to last longer than two minutes.

"Relax." Isaac's voice was soft and smooth. "Just let it happen. You're going to be doing it for a while."

He wasn't sure what that meant but he had little brain power left to ponder. With a strangled shout he came, squeezing his eyes tight but still able to hear his cum hit the floor.

He stilled his hand and tried to catch his breath. "Keep going."

He looked up at Isaac who had a small smile and a glint in his eyes. "Keep going," he repeated, his voice firmer this time.

Jack took his cock again but this time winced as he stroked the over-sensitized flesh. He tried to keep his grip loose and speed slow.

Isaac tisked. "You can go faster than that."

He sped up as much as he could take. It wasn't much. His cock had gone flaccid and his body had begun to relax expecting a rest. Now he was tensing again and wishing he had some lubrication other than his own sticky cum. Isaac managed to read his mind and stood up, pulling a small tube from his pocket.

"Don't stop." Isaac squeezed a dollop of lube onto the tip of his cock. It eased the raw feeling that was developing and his cock began to swell again but with an ache. Isaac took his chin and lifted his head so he was once again looking into Isaac's eyes. Isaac leaned in and kissed him, slow and deep. Despite the discomfort his cock rose and he stroked himself faster, Isaac sucking on his tongue and biting his lips. Then he stepped away and sat back down. Jack felt his muscles begin to ache and his balls tighten. He wanted to cum, but that release eluded him.

He wanted to stop but had been told to keep going and he would.

"I can tell you're close. I can tell you're thinking. Stop thinking. Feel it for the pleasure it is. It will happen." And it did. With a painful squeeze and a shudder, he felt the orgasm hit him, not like before though. With nothing but a few drops to spill out he felt rattled. His head spun and his focus was narrowing. His hand stilled.

Isaac stood again and leaned in close, whispering in his ear. "One more." Jack whimpered. "I know you can give me one more." Jack's cock had gone limp in seconds and felt small and tender in his hand. Isaac threaded his fingers into his hair and pulled tight. Not enough to truly hurt but enough to keep Jack aware. He began to stroke himself again, slowly and carefully. Isaac bit the top of his ear and he focused down onto that one tiny spot. The next bite came on his earlobe, hard and sharp but it drew a moan from him, his cock half-forgotten even as he stroked it.

"So good," Isaac whispered in his ear. "Such a good boy." Isaac took a long lick of his neck before nipping again at his ear. "So beautiful." Jack had to close his eyes. They felt swollen and the room was swimming. "Obedient. Good." Jack stroked himself faster, his cock straining back to life, the pain of it a distant second to Isaac's whispers or the nip of his teeth. A tear squeezed from his eye. Isaac slowly licked it from his face and that was enough. The final worries of the day fled his mind. He was his body and hardly even that. Hot points of pleasure and pain twisted together and burned through him.

He knew Isaac was whispering into his ear again, he could feel the bursts of air even if he couldn't seem to make out the words. Finally, a few broke through the haze. "Such a good boy. Come for me."

Jack's body doubled over with lightening pain and pleasure

as he came, his body squeezed dry, a scream in his throat, and soft whispers in his ear.

☙❧

ISAAC RAKED HIS NAILS GENTLY ALONG JACK'S SCALP AS HE RESTED. He wasn't asleep, his unfocused eyes fluttered open and closed. He was drifting, and he would for quite a while if Isaac let him. Isaac had been right during their first encounter. A soft litany of praise had taken Jack over the edge into a third, rough orgasm. He hadn't intended to start things the second Jack came through the door. He figured they could talk, make some plans, see if there was something on the cards other than just sex. Not that he had a problem with sex, but he didn't want this to come across as simply another casual encounter. But every inch of Jack's body had been pleading for this and Isaac was not going to turn him down.

"Good boy," Isaac whispered. "Such a good boy." And he was. He wondered if Jack had been told that often enough, and if it would work outside the bedroom. How much Jack craved or simply needed basic positive feedback. His life choices showed by their definition, a need to serve. Not always. He wouldn't be a unit commander if he was incapable of leading, but in its own way that was a kind of service.

One night stands found in clubs often lacked subtlety or a gentler hand. He stroked his fingers down Jack's face and across his lips. Jack's eyes fluttered open and he darted out his tongue to lick at Isaac's fingertips.

"I'm going to ask you to do that again at some point." Isaac kept his voice low. "Watching you like that, forcing your body to swing between pleasure and pain. You did very well."

"Thank you, sir." Jack whispered, then continued to lick at Isaac's fingertips.

"I'm going to tie you up later tonight. I'm going to do it so you don't have to be good. There will be no need to follow orders or even think. Your submission alone is a beautiful thing." Isaac felt the small intake of breath across his fingers. "Can you kneel for me?"

Jack pulled himself up. His muscles still had a slight wobble to them but he made it to his knees, hands behind his back. Isaac slid his fingers once again into Jack's hair pulling his head back then kissed his lips. He was still fully dressed but the heat of Jack's body soaked through his clothes. He pressed his tongue deep into Jack's mouth then nipped at his lips. Jack kept his hands behind his back but pressed himself forward as much as he could.

"Hands above your head. Lay back," Isaac ordered, his lips still pressed to Jack's.

Jack tried to lay back slowly but it was more of a collapse. Isaac straddled his chest. It wasn't easy, his chest nearly wider than Isaac could comfortably spread his knees. He unzipped his pants and let his cock free for the first time that evening. Isaac liked to wait, to stretch out his own release. He stroked himself and Jack raised his head to watch.

"I'm going to cum on your face." Jack flopped his head back. "I'm going to rub it into your skin and leave it there until morning. I told you I wouldn't mark you in any way that will last, but I'm going to make sure you know the smell of my cum like nothing else." Jack licked his lips. "Mouth closed. I'll give you a taste later tonight. But you are going to wear every drop of this one."

Jack groaned and shifted. Isaac stroked himself faster. He knew he wouldn't last long and had no intention to. This was about marking Jack, making him feel claimed and owned. A few strokes later he came in thick spurts against Jack's cheek.

He smeared it across Jack's face and down his throat, rubbing it into his pulse points like perfume.

Jᴀᴄᴋ'ꜱ ᴅɪᴄᴋ ꜰᴇʟᴛ ʀᴀᴡ ᴀɴᴅ ʜɪꜱ ʙᴀʟʟꜱ ᴀᴄʜᴇᴅ ʙᴜᴛ ᴛʜᴇʀᴇ ᴡᴀꜱ ꜱᴛɪʟʟ the urge to cum again, to stroke himself in time to Isaac's own movements. When Isaac's cum hit his face, he felt some connection between his body and mind snap into place. And when Isaac spread it across his throat he felt collared, but not like it had in the past. No gasp for breath, no need to sprint to the door. Something in his head became quiet. Content even.

"There we go. You look so perfect wearing my cum."

"Thank you, sir." Jack felt the honesty in his own words.

"Don't move. I'll be back in a minute." Isaac climbed off him and left the room. Jack drifted, half asleep, half awake, so aware of his body but not feeling anything but warm comfort.

He hadn't moved when the door opened again. "Sit up."

He didn't particularly want to, but he sat up and took the glass that was handed to him. It was more hydration fluid but it didn't taste particularly bad. Isaac reached down and cupped his balls while he sipped at the salty sweet water. "How do these feel?"

"They ache a little."

"And this?" He ran his fingers along Jack's cock which had softened again.

"A little raw. Not bad."

"Good. I want you to cum at least a couple more times tonight."

"Yes sir." He ached, but there was also a warmth that filled him at the knowledge that he would be able to do as told.

"Do you remember where the bathroom is?" Jack nodded. "Good. Go relieve yourself, brush your teeth, there's toothpaste and a brush in there. Don't wash your face but wash your hands well. Don't get your cuffs wet. Then come back here."

Jack handed Isaac the glass and went to the bathroom. The toothpaste was a brand he had never encountered. A new tube, it was bland to the point of being completely flavorless. The soap was scentless as well. The strongest smell was still Isaac's cum, which had dried to white streaks across his face and neck.

When he returned the lights in the room were brighter. Jack's eyes fell first to the bed. Neatly laid out on it, were coils of dark blue rope. There was also a flogger, the same cream color as the riding crop Isaac had used the previous time.

"Have you ever been used for kinbaku?" Isaac asked casually from where he was leaning against the side of the bed.

"No, well, nothing really complicated. Just sort of basic harness stuff." He'd seen some complicated bindings done that took hours, several people, a dozen ropes, and by the end were beautiful, if really quite sexless.

"That's too bad, you have an excellent figure for it. Do you remember our last time in this room, what I told you I wanted to do?"

Jack ran through his memory, his mind still foggy. "A corset?"

Isaac smiled at him. "Yes. A corset. Nice and tight." He picked up a long coil of rope and a couple of safety clips. "It won't prevent you from breathing, not even close, but it will change how you breathe. More from the chest, less from the diaphragm. Takes getting used to but women managed it for centuries. Men as well. It was quite the fashion for a time." He pressed the rope against Jack's chest. It was soft. "I think that's your color. Look by your left foot. There's a d-ring flush in the wood."

Jack looked down. It was hard to see at first glance as it had a matt finish and was almost the same shade as the wood.

Isaac handed him the safety clips. "When we bought this house, it needed lots of renovations. This room we modified exactly for this use. You, however, are the first person who gets to use it."

Jack wasn't sure what to make of that. Did that mean he was the first one Isaac ever brought home? Maybe they'd moved recently. It didn't feel like it.

"There's another clip about three feet to your right. Strap yourself in."

He pushed away the flutter of thoughts and reached for his ankles. It was tricky and he felt the stretch in his calves and thighs. He tried to make a mental note to stretch more, but when he stood up his legs were spread and firmly attached to the floor.

Isaac lightly scraped his fingernails along his torso.

"Hands behind your head so I can work."

Jack placed his hands behind his head. "Depending on the person this can be very intense, or you'll simply be humoring my desire to see you wrapped in blue. If it gets to be too much, you can say stop and I'll cut you out."

"Yes, sir."

Isaac split the coil in half and started low on Jack's torso, almost at his hips. The last time Jack had been put into a complicated rope harness, it had been with well used hemp that bit into his skin. This felt more like soft cotton. Isaac wrapped it around twice then twisted it in some way and pulled. The ropes tightened noticeably and Jack began to think of what that would feel like around his waist and chest. He gasped.

"Easy." Isaac reached down and fondled his balls. "Just close your eyes and relax."

The rope was wrapped around and around again, each time twisted and pulled tight. In between each layer Isaac teased his body, stroking his balls or cock. Twisting or pinching his nipples.

As Isaac pulled the ropes tighter, Jack understood what he'd said about changing the way he breathed. It was getting harder to take a deep breath. He tried pressing out his stomach. Isaac slapped him on the ass hard and he gasped. As he did, the ropes were pulled tight. "Horses try that trick when you're cinching on a saddle. You deal with it the same way."

"Sorry, sir," Jack mumbled flushing with shame. He'd been

told what was going to happen and it was his position to accept it. Isaac chuckled and pulled the ropes tighter.

As the rope was wrapped up his chest, the tweaks and caresses were interspersed with the occasional slap on the ass. Jack's breath was coming faster and harder. Isaac stopped.

"Jack, hold your breath for a three count then let it out slowly. You need to breathe slowly and higher in your body. Don't try to force what you can't do."

Jack took another slow breath his chest expanding and his shoulders pulling back.

"Perfect."

He took a dozen more slow breaths before Isaac continued his work. Around and around, twists, knots, and gentle strokes.

"Put your arms down and hold this tight." Jack grabbed the two ends of rope Isaac was holding out. "Time for something extra."

He took a pair of screw on nipple clamps from his pocket and a length of string. He attached the clamps to Jack's nipples, which had already been teased to hard points. A shudder went through him and his breath hitched again causing him to wobble. Isaac gave them a tug, making sure they were secure. Then he took the length of string and began to weave with it, through the loops on the clamps, down into the ropes, and back out again. "Take a deep breath."

Jack breathed deep. His chest expanded, the ropes stayed in place, and the clamps pulled. Another moan and a shudder. He could still breathe, nothing was hindering his breathing, his arms weren't even bound but he had a choice now, he had to focus on control. A fast gasp of breath would lead to a sharp tug which would turn into another gasp. He felt like he might cum.

Isaac took the ends of rope and tied them off below Jack's nipples. He took a step back. "Gorgeous." There was a rough edge to Isaac's voice. "Your body was made for this I swear. The things I want to do to you. The things I want you to do. Things I *know* you can do." Isaac took a large hand mirror from the bed and held it up so Jack could see himself from at least the waist up.

His cock was hard and straining. The ropes cinched his waist noticeably with twists in a V pattern adding to the trim look. The clamps on his nipples looked mechanical and crude by comparison, but that only highlighted the careful weaving of the string.

Isaac picked up the flogger next and held it out. "Hold this behind your back."

He took the flogger. If he was flogged like this it would be impossible to control his breathing, to manage the clamps. "I'm not going to flog you now. That will happen tomorrow after breakfast, but you are going to hold that flogger until then. If you do something that requires both hands, drape it around your neck. You will know that flogger before I take it to your body."

"Yes, sir." Jack placed his hands behind his back, forcing his chest out as he did.

The flogger wasn't particularly heavy but it was solid. He ran his fingers down the braided leather of the handle.

Tomorrow, after breakfast.

Waiting was always the worst part of anything. He didn't consider himself an impatient man, but he was a fan of getting things done when the opportunity presented itself.

He felt the ends of leather brush the back of his leg. He began to think about what they might feel like when wielded by Isaac. Would he flick them hard leaving them to sting and bite, or would he start softly and build up the burn.

He couldn't control the shiver that went through him.

"Do you appreciate how much raw sex you are putting out right now?" Isaac's voice was low with a growl. Jack wasn't sure how to answer that. "I have an urge to wreck you in some way. Bend you over and fuck you raw. Leave you desperate and begging." Isaac ran his tongue along Jack's neck sending another shiver through him. "But I won't, I wouldn't. I never take what is not fully offered." He nipped Jack's ear. A tiny clip of teeth, but to Jack it felt like fire. He squeezed the handle of the flogger wishing his hands were clipped together. He wanted to touch himself. Even with his skin still raw and balls sore, he was hard. He wanted to cum. Not just cum but to fully drop and drift away.

He rocked forward, nearly losing his balance.

"Can you speak?" Isaac whispered in his ear.

Jack nodded then. "Yes, sir."

"Good. I want to fuck you but I am going to give you the option as to how."

Jack shook his head. He didn't want to make a decision, even one as simple as that.

"You don't want me to fuck you."

Jack shook his head again. "No, I mean yes. Fuck me please, sir."

"Would you rather I decided how?"

Jack nodded.

Isaac ran a thumb over his lips and he sucked it in. He slipped his other hand between Jack's butt cheeks and teased at his hole. Jack pressed his hips back. He felt empty.

"Would you like me to fuck your ass?"

Jack nodded again, vigorously. Isaac bent over. There were two little snicks and Jack's ankles were freed from the floor.

"Kneel on the bed, face down, keep your arms behind your back."

The few steps to the bed were strange, the ropes changing how he walked. It felt like there was more movement in his hips and shoulders. Getting into position wasn't easy either, scooting on his knees before half falling over, his face pressed into the sheets. He could still breathe but it was tricky. His nipples ached but he didn't care about that. All he wanted was for Isaac to fuck him. The desire overwhelmed his mind and filled his body. He couldn't remember the last time he felt such need.

"Close your eyes."

Jack closed them gratefully. He heard clothes hit the floor. There was the sound of steps around the room. Drawers being opened and closed. The bed behind him sank and he spread his knees. His cheeks were spread, but it wasn't Isaac's cock or even fingers that entered him. There was the cold wet of lube then what felt like some sort of wand or thin dildo. It was hard and unyielding. "I'm not going to stretch you much but I'm going to work the lube in deep." Jack rocked his hips back. It wasn't enough, not even close. Isaac pulled out the wand, added more lube and pressed it back in.

"Please." Jack gasped out, nearly in tears. It was hard to get a full breath, his nipples burned and his arms ached. "Please."

"Can you be a good boy and hold still for me?"

"Yes." His lips were feeling thick. It was hard to form words.

"What exactly do I want you to do?"

Too many words.

"Be a good boy and hold still for you."

"Perfect." The wand was removed. There was a crinkle of a condom wrapper then Isaac was pushing into him, so slowly. Time slowed and stretched. He wanted to push back. To bury Isaac in him.

Be a good boy, he told himself and don't move. His thighs began to shake from the strain and his ass burned as it was stretched, but there was no pain, not the way he normally knew it. It was perfect and desired. His body filled and controlled. Tears squeezed from the corners of his eyes. Another thing he could not control.

"Good boy," Isaac said softly. "Such a good boy."

Then Isaac began to move. Steady and controlled he pushed Jack ever closer to that wild edge.

Jack didn't know what he was saying anymore. Sounds were

being ripped from his throat that made no sense to his own mind. He might have been begging but he wasn't sure for what. Then Isaac's hand, cool and slick was around his cock. "Time to be a good boy and cum one more time."

Jack screamed.

⚜

ISAAC MANAGED TO HOLD HIMSELF TOGETHER AS JACK CAME, screaming and clenching down tight, he wasn't far behind, his release shattering any sense of control or composure. He had no doubt that there would be ten small bruises on Jack's hips by morning and he would take the time to kiss each one.

He pulled out and Jack collapsed flat, his hands still gripping the flogger behind his back. Isaac was impressed.

"You can roll over," he said as he stripped off the condom. Jack didn't move. Isaac checked his pulse. Strong and steady and his breath was even, so simply out. He took pride in the fact that he'd managed to fuck someone completely out, but it did make for some logistical issues. It was one of the problems with favoring physically large subs; moving them when they're out or so deep they can't really move themselves. Luckily, Isaac had experience moving dead weight, literally. It was a matter of leverage.

He pried one of Jack's hands off the flogger and managed to roll him on his back. He wouldn't be able to completely remove the ropes until Jack could sit up, but he could loosen them. Technically he could cut them, but quality rope was expensive and it wasn't an emergency.

He removed the nipple clamps next. The quick shock of pain was enough to snap Jack awake, though his eyes were unfocused. Isaac lay down beside him tangling their legs together and pulling Jack's face to his chest. Skin to skin contact should help anchor him as he eased himself up.

After several minutes, Jack moaned softly then went limp again. Isaac didn't move, just kept close and waited for Jack to wake up.

He did a head to toe systems report on himself while he waited. Everything appeared to be in one piece. He ached but in the best possible way and felt nicely grounded. Jack had looked absolutely beautiful in the ropes, and he hoped at some point in the future he would be allowed to do something more complicated. He didn't like doing anything too intricate without at least one other person present for safety sake.

And Jack had reacted so well to it. Jack's cock had been dripping by the third loop. It really was about the praise and surrendering of control for him. He'd half expected Jack to call a stop to it when he started cinching his waist down tight but he'd done as told, changing his breathing as directed.

"Good boy," Isaac began to whisper.

And he'd been so desperate to be fucked, to be taken. Isaac had seen the wild, almost manic look in his eyes, craving that final step, the last shreds of the stress of the day long gone.

"Such a good boy."

He already had plans for the morning if Jack wanted to continue. He would set the pace for Jack's submission in the shower. He would feed Jack breakfast as he knelt next to him. And there would be the flogging. He was looking forward to that. Jack wasn't a pain slut, but he'd taken both the spanking and Isaac's work with the riding crop so well, he was sure the flogger would make him fly.

CHAPTER 12

I t was Jack's stirring that brought Isaac fully awake. He'd been drifting in and out of sleep to the sound of Jack's soft breaths. "Can you sit up?" he asked softly.

Jack rolled slightly, his eyes only fluttering open for a moment, but with Isaac's help he managed to sit.

"I'm going to unwrap you now. You're going to want to take a deep breath but keep it slow and even until we are done. This can shift your blood pressure and give you major head spin."

Jack nodded and Isaac got to work. He tried to keep the rope neatly looped but Jack was still wavering, some muscles limp and others twitching, so he went for speed and let the rope hit the floor by the side of the bed in a big tangle.

"You can lay back down."

Jack crashed back down shivering slightly. Isaac pulled the blankets over him and held him close. Skin to skin, body heat to body heat. Jack was asleep within seconds.

ISAAC COULD TELL JACK WAS WAKING UP AGAIN BY THE WAY HE breathed. Deeper breaths at a faster rate. Isaac stroked his head. "Are you okay with me getting up for a moment? I want to get you some orange juice, I'll be right back."

It was several seconds before Jack nodded. Isaac hurried to the kitchen. He poured a tall glass of orange juice for Jack then took a long swallow out of the carton for himself. He grabbed some saltines and a bowl of grapes he'd set aside earlier.

Jack was sitting up in bed, coiling the rope, the flogger draped around his neck. His movements were jerky, his fingers uncoordinated, and he was still shivering.

"You don't have to do that."

Jack stopped but didn't speak. "I know that was intense for you. Also, beautiful. Give yourself a few moments to get back together. Here, drink this."

He took the juice and began to chug it.

"Easy. Little sips. You don't want to make yourself sick." He stopped but it seemed to be a struggle. Isaac could see where the sweat had dried on his body. When the juice was done, Isaac handed him some crackers and grapes. Even after those were finished he could tell Jack would need at least another couple of hours of gentle cuddle time.

"You can lay back down again." Jack did but there was an unsure stiffness in his movements and he was still nonverbal. He wondered how much aftercare he usually got from one night stands and how deep into subspace he went with them. Not enough, was probably the answer to both those questions. He guided Jack onto his side so they could lie face to face and Isaac could easily stroke his body. He kept the touches nonsexual and hopefully comforting.

Jack didn't fall asleep again but he did relax enough for Isaac to kiss him softly. He didn't put any heat into it, simply affection. Truthfully, another round of sex would make it hard to walk come morning. He placed kisses on Jack's cheeks and over his eyes.

Slowly Jack continued to relax until he gave a small hum, the first noise he'd made since waking up, and gave a small kiss back. Isaac smiled.

"Can you say anything?"

Jack licked his lips a few times. "Yes." His voice was rough.

"Good. I want to make sure I hadn't completely broken you."

Jack shook his head. "No."

"Are you warm enough?"

"Yes."

Isaac didn't comment on the one word answers. "Would you like another cracker?"

"Yes, please."

He grabbed a cracker from the plate on the bedside table and gave it to Jack. "Normally I have rules about crumbs in bed but I'll make an exception this time."

"I'll change the bedding."

Isaac smiled, they were up to four words. That was a good sign. "In the morning."

Jack ate the cracker then a few grapes that Isaac held to his lips. Hand feeding him the rest of his meals was most definitely on the agenda.

After that he went back to holding Jack close.

"Are you aware enough to tell me what happened today that got you upset?"

Jack tensed then sighed. Isaac didn't want to kill the mood, but he also wanted to make sure it wasn't something that would affect the rest of the weekend.

"We got stood up. Got all dressed up, kicked in a door, place was totally empty."

"That sounds frustrating."

Jack shook his head. "It keeps happening." His voice was

heavy and serious. "Last few months, my team, Dan's, Gonzales's. We get told that we're raiding a drug house on a tip and instead we get empty buildings, half cooked meth, and the coffee still warm on the table."

Isaac's stomach sank. "Somebody is tipping someone off."

"Or giving bad intel, or playing both sides, over a dozen in the last six months between the three teams. One of these days we're going to go in, and instead of an empty house, someone is going to decide to shoot back or booby trap the place, and someone is going to get killed and—" Isaac combed his fingers through Jack's hair trying to calm him. He let out another sigh. "No one wants to say the big L word but—"

"A leak is a big deal."

"I know it's not me, Dan, or Gonzales. We're all in the same boat and we're never given info until five minutes before things go down, sometimes not even that much. It's no one on our teams, for the same reason. Other than that... I want to say I trust the brass but—"

"There's someone you shouldn't be trusting but you're not sure who."

"I'm not good at trusting people in general. Not really."

Isaac kept stroking his head. Those words hurt to hear, but it was an easy enough assumption to make about Jack's personality. The question was who had betrayed Jack's trust and when? "Neither am I to be honest. But I do trust a few. Would you like me to talk to Lydia? She has sources of her own. I can leave your name out."

"She'd know it came from me. Unless you're sleeping with anyone else from SWAT."

Isaac saw Jack freeze as the words came out of his mouth. They hadn't talked about anyone else. They should have. Jack knew about Amalie and had since day one, and he was sure that Jack wasn't sleeping with anyone else, but they hadn't talked about taking other partners or not. Isaac kicked himself. He knew Jack was insecure and they should have had that talk much earlier.

"I'm not sleeping with anyone else and I have no plans to."

"Thank you." Jack's voice was rough and Isaac knew he'd said the right thing.

THE BLARING OF HIS PHONE SHOT THROUGH JACK'S SLEEP JARRING him awake. He sat straight up, his heart racing, every muscle tensed and ready for action. A second later, before even stopping to remember where he was, he stumbled out of bed and grabbed his phone which he'd left on the dresser.

"Hello?"

"Burnside," his S.O. barked. "Feds have something big going down. Big enough they asked for county backup. All teams are up."

"Yes, sir." His boss hung up without further comment. The rest of his team would be getting robo calls but the team leaders got personal ones. He looked around, the sleep burning off and his mind waking up. Isaac was sitting up in bed looking at him.

"I'm sorry," were the first words out of Jack's mouth. "I—"

Isaac waved a hand cutting him off. "Nothing to apologize for. This is exactly why you and I may just be an effective match."

"I'm still sorry." He glanced around before remembering his clothes were by the front door. "I have to go."

"You are covered in sweat and cum. You need a shower first."

He looked down at himself. Not only was he covered in sweat and cum, but he absolutely reeked of sex. He was also still holding the flogger.

Isaac jumped into the shower with him, helping him scrub with maximum efficiency.

"Text me when you're done."

"I will." Jack left off the 'sir'. As much as he didn't want to, he needed to remind himself that in just a few minutes, a group of well-trained men would be looking at him to lead them into a potentially dangerous situation. He'd rather be in bed with Isaac, getting petted and praised, but how much praise did he deserve if he didn't do his job to the best of his ability?

Isaac's house was closer to the station than Jack's apartment and at three in the morning the roads were clear. Despite that Dan and most of his team were already in the locker room when he arrived.

Dan yawned so wide his jaw audibly cracked. "Oh, fuck me," he muttered rubbing his eyes. "What can possibly be big enough that the Feds want *all* of us at this fucking hour of the morning. I mean how hard is it to wait until at least six."

"It's either drugs, weapons, or terrorists."

"Or a combination of all three."

Dan ended up being right. A ship was coming into port on the morning tide, supposedly full of weapons, with links to terrorists, and a side order of drugs and human trafficking. Jack hated dealing with human traffickers. It made him lose what little faith in humanity he had left.

Multiple agency SWAT teams were going to climb up the side once it docked, drop down from helicopters, and rush the gangplanks. They were being issued extra strength body armor, flash grenades, and the big guns. It was going to look like a Tony Scott movie. Hopefully with a smaller body count. But as he stood on the dock, hiding behind a shipping container, while an honest to god black helicopter fwhumped overhead, all he could think was *this is going to suck.*

ISAAC FUMBLED WITH HIS PHONE, CONFUSED BECAUSE HE COULD hear ringing but there was nothing on the screen. Only a clock telling him it was just past six in the morning. It took a few seconds of wondering if his phone was broken before he realized it was the land line ringing. The only people who called his land line were his parents and work. Neither of them ringing at that hour on a Saturday was a good thing.

He reached over Amalie's side of the bed to grab the phone. He hadn't felt up to staying in the downstairs room when it still smelled of Jack and sex.

"Hello?" he mumbled.

"Sorry Isaac," his boss said. "Looks like the feds went and killed a bunch of bad people, but they want all the investigation and reports done in double time."

"And since when are we taking orders from the feds?" Isaac complained even as he knew that there was a good chance Jack had been involved in whatever had happened.

His boss sighed. "Since they bought us our own Inductively Coupled Plasma Mass Spectrometry set up. Now get your butt out of bed, suck some coffee, and help me kiss some federal ass."

"Yeah. I'll be there in thirty."

If you're lucky.

IT WAS CLOSE TO NOON BY THE TIME JACK STUMBLED INTO HIS OWN apartment. He hadn't bothered showering at the station. When the adrenalin of the operation had worn off, he found himself beginning to feel the places on his body where Isaac had worked him the most. His cock felt raw. His nipples ached and he felt well fucked.

He began to drop back into that warm fog just thinking about what Isaac had done to him and still could.

What he could see of his own back by twisting around looked clear, free of rope marks from the corset. There was nothing noticeable on his wrists or ankles. There were however, ten tiny bruises. Five on each hip. Not deeply colored but Jack could feel them. Not just the tiny points of small ache, but the memory of the fingers that put them there.

He stepped under the shower, not using any soap, wanting to smell like nothing, just the way Isaac had had him not even a day earlier. He did get hard again. It was only Saturday. In theory, he was still off for the rest of the weekend.

Careful not to touch himself he made it back to his bed and picked up his phone.

Finally made it home. In theory, off until Monday morning.

There was no immediate reply. He closed his eyes and began to drift. He was nearly asleep when his phone buzzed.

Got called in to help clean up the mess the feds made last night. Going to be stuck here until late. :(I'm so sorry. Not how either of us wanted the weekend to go. Hope you are doing well. Getting some rest. Maybe Sunday morning breakfast?

Jack's heart sank, but Isaac pointed out that first encounter that they both ran the risk of late night callouts and triple over-time. He had been thinking of the weekend as a test. If they could spend more than a night together. If he could spend multiple days in submission or just in each other's company. He guessed this was a sort of test as well. Could they accept the disappointments and inconveniences that came with their jobs? He still didn't like that they'd left the weekend hanging. It left him feeling frayed and on edge.

Sorry about the mess. Wasn't my team. Everyone we found just put their hands up. Breakfast sounds nice if you're not too tired.

This time Isaac texted back quickly.

:-) I'll text you in the morning. We can Brunch. (I'm told that's a verb now). You should get some sleep. Take care of yourself. ;-)

I will.

Jack wasn't sure if he would *take care* of himself. It didn't feel right, touching himself and fantasizing about all the things Isaac might have done with him while Isaac was stuck at work. Instead he closed his eyes and just tried to sleep.

CHAPTER 13

The sun coming through the window of the restaurant and bouncing off the glass of orange juice was too bright. The chatter of families and older women still in their early morning church dresses was too loud. He felt hungover, but in truth he was just tired and frustrated. Mostly frustrated.

The blue button down shirt Jack was wearing was tight across his chest. In his sleep deprived state Isaac found himself mostly focused on a couple of buttons that looked like they might pop if Jack took the time to flex.

Jack was speaking.

"Sorry, I missed that."

"What time did you get off work?" Jack repeated, a deep frown on his face.

"Umm. Twoish? There was a lot of paperwork."

"Did you sleep in your office?" There was a disturbing squeak in Jack's voice.

"Not the first time."

"You should probably go home."

Isaac knew he was right. "You could not imagine the things I want to do to you right now."

Jack flushed red and glanced around, but all the other diners were focused on their own eggs and pancakes.

"Or maybe you can. This is the problem with being over thirty, your body starts re-prioritizing sleep over sex without asking your brain first." Jack smiled, which is what Isaac was hoping for. "What does next weekend look like for you?"

Jack frowned again. "Training Saturday, on call Sunday. And the narcotics division has gotten into the habit of serving warrants on Sundays. I don't know why, it's annoying."

"Maybe they figure everyone will be hungover from Saturday, little less quick on the draw."

"Maybe. Still annoying."

Isaac sipped his orange juice, knowing from hard experience that coffee would do him little good in his state. "I know there was a time in med school when I could have done a shift twice as long and been fresh as a fucking daisy. I'm sorry."

"It's okay. I mean we sort of knew there were good odds this would happen." Jack poked at his half-finished breakfast.

"Yeah, I was hoping it wouldn't be first thing. How are you doing? I know that was a rough yank up?"

Jack shrugged. "I'm okay, I've had worse."

Isaac wanted to argue that having had worse wasn't the same as okay. "What can I do to make it better than okay?"

Jack gave a shy smile. "I really am okay. Was a little rough at the start but I'll be fine."

Isaac still wanted to argue, but he was so tired and with their relationship as new as it was he found it hard to find leverage. "Okay, but until we see each other again I want you to call me if you feel even a little bit off. Or even if you just want to talk."

Jack nodded. "I can manage that."

JACK HAD LIED. NOT A BIG ONE BUT HE COULDN'T SAY HE WAS 100%. There were edges of his mind that were still ragged and ripped instead of neatly rolled up. It was a feeling he was accustomed to. He could never afford to make a bond, he couldn't risk lingering after a scene. He had practice taking care of himself. Grounding himself back to where he *should* be, even if it wasn't where he wanted to be. He knew Isaac would have taken care of him. He had in the past and with any luck would in the future, but it would have felt selfish to ask for that while Isaac was half asleep in his eggs.

Instead, he ran at a pace more than a jog but less than a sprint, out to the edge of his neighborhood and back. A steady meditative pace that would burn out any residual restless energy. He'd spend the rest of the day doing mundane chores and errands, have a salad for dinner, and by Monday, in theory, he'd be as good as he ever was.

Not ideal but good enough to get through.

IT WAS PROPERLY DARK WHEN THE FRONT DOOR CLICKED OPEN. Isaac was spread out on the couch half asleep, his mind drifting from one random thought to another. Amalie dropped her overnight bag by the door.

"Hey there, have a good weekend?" Isaac asked first, lifting his legs so she could sit on the couch.

She sat down and Isaac put his legs across her lap. "Had just about every bit of me massaged, wrapped in kelp, and massaged again."

"Sounds like fun. How's Lydia?"

"I think I got her to relax for twenty, maybe even twenty-five minutes."

"Go you." Isaac held up his hand. Amalie grinned and gave him a high five.

"And how was your weekend?

"Friday night was great. I mean, fuck me he looks spectacular in rope. I need to get him up to Kevin's place for some real rigging."

"I'd love to see it when you talk him around to it. What happened after Friday night?" Her voice took on a serious edge.

"Saturday morning, three A.M. his phone rang. Six A.M. my phone rang and I didn't get back to sleep until about two A.M. Sunday morning and that was in my office. Jack and I managed brunch and I almost passed out in my eggs. I'm sure I used to survive on less sleep."

She gave his legs a sympathetic rub. "I'm sorry. That sucks."

Isaac shrugged. "I guess it's kinda good in a way. Part of our problems with finding someone long term has been finding someone understanding when the phone rings at three in the morning. At least we got that test out of the way early."

"Still leaves both of you wound up and short a sexy week-end." Isaac shrugged again. "Have you set a make-up date?"

"No. He's got training and on call next weekend and I haven't checked my schedule yet."

"I'll spend the next weekend at Lydia's, give you some space—"

"No." He took Amalie's hand. "I don't want to kick you out just so I —"

"No," she cut him off "You two still need to know if you are compatible beyond a quickie in a club. Put yourselves in a bubble for a couple of days, and see how it works before having someone else hanging around. I'm as invested in this working as you are."

Isaac tried to shrug off a little creeping guilt. Not for wanting Jack but for not being able to find someone long term sooner, leaving their relationship noticeably out of balance with Amalie taking on more emotional support than was fair. "Will Lydia be okay with that?"

Amalie smirked. "She has jury selection next week. By Saturday she'll need a good long fuck as much as I bet Jack does."

"I love it when you talk dirty, yet practical."

"Yeah, I know."

CHAPTER 14

You don't hear the clock until *4:30 on a Friday.*

It was actually 11 A.M. on a Saturday but he'd been up all night, again. Getting called out for duds was one thing. Getting called out in the middle of the night 'to get the jump on the bad guys', then being forced to hang around while evidence was collected, 'in case the bad guys come back' was another level of time and resource waste. The residuals of the adrenalin rush with nowhere to go was as unpleasant as anything else.

He had told his guys to go home and get some rest but he knew plenty went off looking for something to drink, fuck, or fight. Not that Jack wasn't interested in doing at least one of those things. It would be another week before he saw Isaac again. He'd texted and called a few times just to make sure Jack was okay, doing better than just holding on. Jack would have been fine with a couple of hours at the Windsor Club, but he knew Isaac wanted more and he wanted to be able to give it to him.

He stared at his locker and tried to make plans for the rest of his weekend. Most of his thoughts were turned to sleep, or at least bed.

A warm hand rested slowly on his shoulder. It felt nice and he closed his eyes.

"Jack!"

Jack's eyes snapped open. Dan was standing beside him, hand still on his shoulder.

"Can you sleep sitting straight up with your eyes open because I called your name three times?"

He shook his head. "Sorry, was just staring into space I guess."

"Must be the most interesting space in human history. Go home and get some sleep."

"Yeah." He stood and stretched his back. "That's a good idea."

"And drive *very* carefully."

"I brought curry!" Lydia's voice echoed through the house and up to Isaac's office.

"Down in a sec!" he heard Amalie shout back.

There was a theory that each week they would have a 'family' dinner. They would cook, and eat at the table like adults and not talk about work. The reality was it happened more on a two to three week schedule, it involved some variety of take out, and most of the talk was about work.

Isaac headed downstairs to get a word in with Lydia before Amalie finished up.

"Hey, I hear your weekend with SWAT boy got interrupted." Lydia was laying out plastic containers of rice and curry on the dining room table.

"It was going to happen sooner or later," he replied with a shrug. "How was getting wrapped in kelp?"

"Surprisingly relaxing." She put a bottle of wine on the table and Isaac went for the glasses.

"While we're talking about Jack—"

"Not my type, but continue."

"SWAT's got a leak." Lydia froze. "Or at least someone above SWAT has a leak."

"Evidence?"

"Circumstantial. Last six months they've knocked down a dozen doors, all drug related, all on tips, all empty, and according to Jack, half the time the coffee is still hot on the table and the meth is still bubbling on the stove."

Lydia opened the bottle of wine. "Any possible names?"

"Not that he mentioned. He's pretty sure it's not any of the team leads since they've all been in the same boat. He thinks it's someone above and he's worried about walking into an ambush instead of an empty building."

"Would he be willing to talk to me direct?"

"Not sure. Maybe. He seems to play his cards pretty close to his chest."

"Okay." They heard Amalie come down the steps. "I'll sniff around. See what I can find."

THE VIBRATOR IN JACK'S PHONE WAS LOUDER THAN THE RING AND it was sending an itch down his leg and up his back.

"Are you going to answer any of those?" Dan asked from his side of the restaurant booth.

"Nope."

"You on the outs with Kinky Married Complicated already?"

"No, it's just my brother."

Dan grinned. "So, things are good with KMC?" Jack just sighed. "I'm asking because you've seemed a little wound up the last couple of weeks."

"I'm fine. I've been fine."

Dan managed to take a bite of a burger in an impressively judgmental way. Jack's phone buzzed again. He'd checked the first message hoping it was Isaac.

"Seriously, are you going to check those."

"My brother lost a passive aggressive pissing match with my mother over his own wedding arrangements, and is now halfway down a bottle of merlot and I'm the only one who he can complain to who won't take mom's side. Actually, my mother is completely right but I don't care enough to say anything." Who schedules an outdoor wedding in Boston in July?

Dan paused with his burger half way to his mouth. "Okay, in the I'm not sure how many years since the academy, that is the most I've heard about your family. That's the first I've heard about you even having a family. Just sort of had you pegged as an orphan.

Jack sipped his coffee. He had reasons not to talk about his family. "They're all back east." There was another buzz and Jack took his phone from his pocket to mute it completely. There were 23 messages from his brother, and one from a number with no name attached that Jack swiped open.

How are you doing?

Jack smiled.

"Now *that's* not your brother. At least I hope not."

I'm fine. Grabbing a late lunch. About to start shift. He typed in reply, ignoring Dan.

Hope it's an easy one. See you in the morning.

He heard Dan chuckle. "That is definitely not your brother."

CHAPTER 15

The lights on Isaac's street were still sodium yellow, not yet changed to the blue LEDs of the central city. Jack knocked quietly. He was early, multiple hours early. He'd texted before driving over and was told it would be okay. The door opened after only a second. Isaac must have been waiting despite the late hour.

"Come on in," he said, his face tight with worry. He was fully dressed in slacks and a button-down shirt. He must have changed after getting the message.

"I'm sorry." The plan had been for Jack to come over early, they would have breakfast, then start over. But Jack needed to be grounded, now. If Isaac hadn't answered his phone, he would have been very tempted to go back to the Windsor Club or even just some bar. He liked to think he was beyond that but he wasn't sure.

"What happened?" Isaac led him to the couch and sat him down.

Jack shook his head.

"No," Isaac responded. "That's not stress on your face, that's rattled, bad. What happened?"

"A cook house went up. We were a block away, felt the whole van shake. We were supposed to go in. Seriously, my guys were a block away from getting killed. If we'd hit a green light instead of a red. If we'd driven a little faster, if the briefing had been a little shorter." He felt his hands begin to shake. "One extra block and..."

Isaac cupped his cheek. He leaned into the touch. He felt raw. His nerves and emotions were frayed. The wind had blown the smoke in the opposite direction but he'd still stood under the hottest shower he could for as long as he could, and scrubbed every inch of his body he could reach over and over.

"Hey, I see that one extra block every day. A step earlier crossing the street. A moment later leaving the house. The fish instead of the chicken. Everyone has a thousand moments like that every day that they never know about. You can't dwell on that 'what if'. It didn't happen. You are here. You are safe. Your team is safe. Do you understand?"

Jack nodded. He knew all that. He was safe, his team was safe, but the van had shaken so hard he thought they'd crashed into something.

"Can you rest tonight if I put you into bed or do you need to be brought down first?"

"Down," Jack whispered. He'd gotten through the night with his chin up and holding firm to command in the chaos, but now his hands were shaking.

"Okay. You know where the bedroom is. Go there and get undressed. I want to inspect you."

"Yes, sir." And with those two words Jack began to calm.

THERE WERE FOUR LEATHER CUFFS AND A FLOGGER ACROSS THE foot of the bed. It was the one Jack was supposed to hold until it could be used on him. He stripped quickly and took it in hand.

The leather was cool to the touch but the solid construction was comforting. He clasped his hands behind his back and spread his legs.

"Did you get near the fire?" Isaac asked.

"No, sir."

"Your skin is very red." He leaned in close and took a long sniff of skin then ran his fingers over Jack's torso. "Don't do that again. Comfortably warm showers and no more scrubbing than necessary to get off the dirt. You are not to injure yourself, even in a passive manner." Isaac's voice was firm in a way that bore no argument.

Arousal and shame rocked through Jack followed by a calm. "Yes, sir."

"May I put the cuffs on you?"

"Please, sir." He remembered the feel of the leather, how they kept him in control so he didn't have to be.

Isaac strapped them on efficiently. The weight was minimal but it felt like they were dragging him to his knees, which was where he wanted to be. When Isaac was finished, he cupped Jack's balls.

"How many times did you masturbate while we were apart?"

"None, sir."

"That is not good." He began slowly stroking Jack's cock. "Two to three times a week to maintain health. You don't have to orgasm if you don't feel you've earned one, but you should give things a good drain. Go kneel on the bed."

Jack clenched his hands around the flogger and got on the bed. Isaac lubed up his right hand. "I'm going to drain you now. Nice and slow. We're going to save a proper orgasm for tomorrow. For tonight you are going to only focus on my hands on your body and accept that I will make your body do what I want it to do. Your will or desires have nothing to do with it. I will be taking care of it. And after that you will sleep. Do you understand?"

"Yes, sir." Jack understood. He was going to be taken care of. There was guilt and shame for wanting and needing this, but so much relief it overwhelmed nearly everything else.

Isaac began to stroke him. He went slow and gentle, covering his whole cock. It was a teasing touch but he still found himself sighing softly with pleasure. Isaac wove his other hand into Jack's hair and yanked. Jack gasped at the sudden sharp pain then Isaac let go. He gave another half dozen slow strokes and yanked again, the pain crashing into the low and slow build of pleasure. He repeated that pattern over and over. A few strokes of his cock then a yank of the hair. Both were sending different types of arousal through him, like the wake of a boat crashing into the rising tide. It fast became overwhelming. He made no attempt to control the sounds he was making or the uneven thrusts of his body.

It wasn't just the pleasure that was building but an overall desire for more. To be touched, filled, bound, fucked. To serve and be praised. To kneel and be petted. To surrender.

"Oh, god."

Then there was nothing. Isaac's hands were gone from his cock and his hair. He felt his cock twitch and his balls squeeze. He looked down. Cum was flowing thick from his cock but there had been no orgasm, no fire of release, just shattering exhaustion. He gave a sob and Isaac's hands were on him again stroking his back and rubbing circles on his chest. Isaac kissed his jaw just below his ear and it sent one last squirm of pleasure through him.

"So beautiful," Isaac whispered in his ear. "Strong and beautiful. You please me greatly, accepting that you would not be receiving pleasure tonight. I know you are tired. I can see the exhaustion in you. You are going to continue to obey. Lay down now, close your eyes, and sleep. Just sleep and rest. Replenish your body for all the amazing things it's going to do in the morning."

Jack nodded. Sleep seemed like an excellent idea.

IT TOOK AN HOUR OF WATCHING JACK SLEEP BEFORE ISAAC FELT comfortable slipping from the bed and back upstairs to change. He hadn't been sure what the situation would be, so he had gotten fully dressed. It had been a good idea. Jack needed to be brought down fast, which meant Isaac had to kick into a dominant headspace more quickly than he liked. It was hard to do that in plaid pajamas. Luckily Jack had reacted well. Isaac usually saved ruined orgasms as a punishment meant to frustrate, but he took a gamble that putting Jack on that sexual edge would put him and keep him in a submissive state better than a quick hand job. And after the fright he'd had, he didn't want to put Jack into bondage or use any kind of impact play.

He tried to be quiet as he slipped into his bedroom but Amalie cracked an eye open.

"Jack here?" she mumbled.

"Yeah, got him to sleep."

"What happened?"

"He and his team got caught a block from a meth house when it blew."

"Shit." She opened both eyes. "Is he okay?"

"Physically yeah, mentally rattled pretty bad. Playing the 'what if' game."

Amalie nodded. "Have I ever mentioned how glad I am you're not in the field work side of law enforcement?"

"A few times."

She took his hand and gave it a squeeze. "I guess this is another test from the universe. Can you handle a relationship with a cop in a high-risk job?"

That was something that had been on his early pros and cons list concerning Jack, though not as far up the con list as a full civilian might have put it. "That is going to be the question. If he keeps coming to me, rather than doing something dumb to cope, I think we'll manage."

"And if something really bad happens?"

If he'd been that one block closer?

"That'll hurt. I know that already."

"Worth the risk?"

Yes Isaac wanted to answer but knew that was jumping ahead. "I think I'm going to find out."

CHAPTER 16

Jack's mind felt quiet. His breath came easy and there was warmth that sank deeper than even his bones. He was waking up but it didn't feel early. There was no painful jerk of his mind into the 6 A.M. daylight. Bits of memory floated to the surface. The heat and smell. The roar of the fire. His mind running in loops of fear and doubt. A thousand 'what ifs'. Then Isaac was there giving orders. Strong and sure, to be obeyed without question. The cuffs on his wrists, his hands on the flogger, Isaac's hands on his cock and in his hair. Driving him mad yet making him feel safe.

He opened his eyes, the room was only lit by the green numbers of the alarm clock but it was enough to make out Isaac's shape. He was on his back and Jack was pressed to his side. He had some morning wood pitching a tent in the blankets. He wanted to reach out and touch it, feel the heat and weight in his hand. He wanted to relearn the taste of it. He took a deep breath and could smell harsh soap still on his own body. Isaac took a deep breath as well and turned his head.

"Good morning," he whispered. "How are you feeling?"

"Better," Jack answered. "Quiet."

"Quiet is good."

"Yes."

Isaac yawned and stretched before looking over Jack to the clock. "It's after eight."

"Really?" He couldn't hide his surprise.

"Are you up for making some coffee for us?" Isaac asked with another yawn.

"I can manage that." He could make coffee half dead in his sleep.

Isaac gave him a kiss. "Go to the bathroom, take care of yourself, make a couple cups of coffee and bring them back."

He rolled out of bed, remembering at the last second to fish out the flogger that had slipped under the blankets.

In the kitchen he found a surprise. Instead of fishing a bag of pre-ground out of the freezer, there was a new coffee grinder and a bag of whole beans waiting. He checked over the bag recognizing the small batch café it came from. Organic, fair trade out of Angola. He opened it breathing deep before popping a bean in his mouth. Medium roast, good oils and flavor. He smiled. Isaac had put some thought into this, and considering the can of Folgers still sitting beside the drip coffee machine, it had to be to keep him happy. Something warm that he didn't want to think about yet, settled into his chest as he began cleaning and checking the espresso machine. People didn't appreciate that a good espresso machine was a unique and sophisticated piece of equipment. He might have no plans to sling coffee again, but that didn't mean he didn't keep his skills up.

He downed the first shot of espresso for himself to check the quality. It felt wonderfully warm on his still raw throat. He was steaming milk when he felt a hard but furry bump against his ankle and looked down. Murrcat head butted him again.

"Good morning." Murrcat made a noise, showing off where he got his name then rubbed himself on Jack's ankles. "There are probably rules about feeding you and I don't know what they are." Murrcat jumped up onto the counter and used a paw to open a cupboard door revealing a shelf of cat food cans. "Yeah, you're going to have to ask your person about that and I'm not your person." Next to the cans was a bag of gourmet liver cat treats. Murrcat purred and batted at the bag. "Okay, just to keep you from following me." He pulled out one treat and threw it to the far side of the kitchen then grabbed the cups of coffee while Murrcat chased his bribe.

By the time he got back to the bedroom, a cup in each hand, Isaac was sitting up and the lights were on. He patted the bed next to him. Jack slid in and handed over one of the cups. Isaac took a sip and moaned long and low.

"Do you make coffee for your other partners?" he asked.

"No." Jack wasn't expecting that question. "I never... I mean I was never in someone's home."

Isaac looked him over, his face unreadable. "More fool them."

That was the last comment Isaac made and they finished their coffee in silence. When they were both done, he took the cups and placed them on the bedside table, then he reached out and brushed his thumb across Jack's cheek.

"Are you feeling settled enough to pick up where we left off? Do you need more time to—"

"No." He craved this, every time his mind had a chance to wander. He needed to know what it was like to be wanted for more than a quick evening of fun. To know what it was like to be completely settled and fully claimed. Even if it never went further than that weekend, he needed to know. "I'm good. I want this.

Isaac smiled and put a soft kiss on his lips. "Good. I want you to go to the bathroom now. Take off your cuffs. Clean yourself fully, make sure your shower is warm but not too hot. When you're done don't dry off, just kneel on the bathmat next to the tub and wait for me. I want to inspect you before I put your cuffs back on and continue with the day.

The burn in Jack's cheeks was now as much lust as embarrassment and his cock was hard. Something about being ordered to perform the most basic of tasks was twisting in him and dropping his mind into the place where what he wanted most was to please. "Yes, sir."

Grabbing the flogger, he hurried from the room.

THE PLAN WAS TO HAVE JACK WASH HIM. HE SEEMED LIKE HE would react well to giving that kind of service, and Isaac was always up for some pampering, but if Jack had never been to someone else's home, maybe it was best not to push him this first full weekend. The realization that Jack had never been taken home made him both sad and glad. Sad because Jack was an absolute gift and one that had been obviously underappreciated. Glad because Jack would have these first kinds of experiences with him and trusted him enough to come to his home when things were bad. It was one thing to be in a club or even a motel where technically there were other people around, a safety net, if a thin one. There was far more risk in a private residence.

Jack had left the door open and he could hear the shower run. The hot water would bring up any marks and bruises he might have missed the previous night. He'd mentally set aside the first part of Saturday to get Jack back into the right headspace, and the second half of Sunday for recovery and general aftercare. He hadn't hesitated to pick up the flogger, so it would certainly be used after breakfast, he'd promised after all. Breakfast on his knees. And more rope at some point. Nothing too complicated but Jack had taken to it incredibly well.

He also wanted to play with Jack's ass some more. He had a

nice collection of dildos and plugs, many of which vibrated. Isaac smiled to himself. Maybe he could bind up Jack during dinner with something in his ass on low. Watch him squirm and drip through the meal.

Isaac teased himself. Forcing orgasms out of Jack during their interrupted session had been extremely satisfying. Maybe binding him with something in his ass on high would be a nice way to spend the evening.

He heard the shower turn off. He gave Jack another minute to get into place before heading to the bathroom, grabbing a handful of clips on his way.

THE SMALL EXTRACTOR FAN DID LITTLE TO PULL THE STEAM FROM the room. Jack's usually pale skin was pink, but he was kneeling with the flogger in his hands. Isaac kept the door open, helping some of the steam escape. The moisture wasn't good for the leather on the flogger or the cuffs. They'd have to be cleaned and oiled later.

"Stand up. Spread your arms and legs."

Jack stood and spread. It was tricky to walk around him in the small bathroom but Isaac managed. "Did I leave bruises on you last time?"

"A few."

"Were they unmanageable?"

"No, sir."

He pressed his pinky finger into Jack's hole finding it clean. His cock was nicely hard.

"Kneel again."

Jack dropped to his knees. Isaac slipped the cuffs back on then clipped his wrists to his ankles bending his back.

"I'm going to take a shower now. Tomorrow you are going to

clean me. Today you are going to watch." Jack's cock jumped. Isaac smirked.

"Yes, sir."

Isaac ruffled his clean, damp hair. "Good boy."

Isaac was usually one for a quick and efficient shower but he took his time, made sure Jack could see everything he was going to want, even took time to play with himself. He watched as Jack's tongue poked out in concentration. It would be so tempting to step out of the tub and rub his cock across that tongue but he'd save that for tomorrow.

Once he'd finished and dried himself he stood in front of Jack. "When I unclip you, I want you to strip and change the bed then put away the clips. They go in the closet in the bedroom. There is a utility closet at the end of the hall. There are clean sheets and a laundry bin in there. You can leave the blankets. Do you understand?"

"Yes, sir." Jack answered immediately, his cock twitching. Isaac wondered how he'd ever survived the army without a permanent erection.

"Good. I'm going to make breakfast. Contrary to Lydia's opinions of my cooking I can scramble eggs and make toast."

Isaac undid the clips and handed them to Jack to put away.

"Yes, sir."

JACK HURRIED BACK TO THE BEDROOM, DRAPING THE FLOGGER around his neck as he got there. It had become second nature already.

He opened the closet door to put away the clips. He froze. The closet was beautifully organized and filled with *things*. There were coils of rope, mostly white, hanging from a bar. There were shelves of plugs and dildos, cuffs, collars, leashes, spreaders, and gags. Crops, paddles, and multiple floggers in a rainbow of colors and sizes. There was a disassembled *something* he couldn't identify. An electrostym setup and a few things he only recognized from the internet. There was a collection of small drawers of the type usually seen in workshops, for holding different types of nails and screws. And for some reason a picnic basket. He opened the little drawers one at a time finding clips, clamps, and chains until he found one that matched the type of clips he was holding.

He found himself staring at the gags. There were multiple varieties. He'd never liked gags because he had to be able to tell people that he needed to go. That he had to get to his phone because work was calling, or sometimes simply to explain that he needed to get out. He needed his voice, usually.

Things were different with Isaac though. Maybe..?

He shook his head and got back to cleaning.

By the time the room could pass inspection it was getting close to ten and Jack could smell toast, eggs, and bacon coming from the kitchen. His stomach rumbled.

In the kitchen, Isaac was dressed in jeans and a dark blue t-shirt. He was placing strips of crisp bacon onto a well loaded plate. There was only one chair at the kitchen table but there was a pillow on the floor next to it.

"Find everything?" There was a smirk on Isaac's face and he knew Isaac was talking about the closet of sex toys more than the closet of cleaning supplies.

"Yes, sir."

"Good." Isaac gestured to the pillow and Jack knelt.

Isaac sat in the only chair and held out a piece of bacon. He felt like a dog being fed a treat, but his stomach really didn't care and he took an eager bite.

"It's not particularly good for you and I can't condone daily consumption, but you were very good in coming to me last night so I thought you deserved a treat."

Jack took another bite this time licking at Isaac's fingers.

"Good boy."

The praise only added to him feeling like a dog but he was rewarded with a second piece of bacon. Murrcat rubbed against his feet then jumped on the table. "No, you've had your breakfast and you have done nothing to earn bacon. Go catch a mouse or something." The cat was pushed to the floor then walked out giving Jack a dirty look.

After that, breakfast was a leisurely affair with Isaac feeding him bits of bacon, toast, and eggs and occasionally presenting his fingers to be sucked on.

From where he was he could see Isaac's cock hard in his jeans and his own cock was craving touch. When the plate was clean, Isaac cleared the table then slowly washed the dishes by hand, leaving Jack to wait and think. Jack had told him what would happen after breakfast the last time and there was a reason his hands were still wrapped around the flogger.

Finally, Isaac came over and took his chin tilting his head back.

"Get up, and go to the living room."

"Yes, sir."

CHAPTER 17

Jack stood in the sunny room. Embarrassment and a thread of shame grew in him as he waited. The curtains were pulled tight over the main windows, but it was late enough in the day that the sun came through the high windows and filled the room. He could hear cars go past, a lawn mower in the distance, the footfalls of someone running with the scratch of dog nails on cement keeping pace. He felt naked and the flogger that he had carried the whole morning felt like lead in his hands. He shifted uncomfortably.

"It's different in the daylight, isn't it?"

"Yes."

"We are afraid of the dark, as a species, but there is a strange safety in it. And a freedom. Almost as if we are not accountable in the same way. It's much harder to do somethings in sunlight than in moonlight."

Isaac held out his hand. Jack placed the flogger into it.

"I'm going to use this on you now, here in the daylight."

Jack felt his skin begin to burn as if Isaac had already begun.

"No one will see you, no one will know. Just like the warm

and safe darkness. And when I'm done with you it will stop mattering, I promise."

Jack slowly placed his hands behind his head and spread his legs.

"You can close your eyes if it makes you feel better."

"No."

"Watch the dust motes in the sunlight." Isaac stepped behind him.

The first blow was soft, landing on his right shoulder blade, quickly followed by another soft strike on the left. A figure eight, slow and lazy. The dust motes whipped around in the air stirred up by Isaac. There was no pain, not really, the soft fall of the leather on his back warmed him in the same way the sun warmed his front. The sound of it on his skin drowned out the distant lawnmower and the Saturday joggers. He heard Isaac shift his stance and saw a flurry of dust motes rush in opposite directions before the first blow fell across his ass. It warmed him, but stung just enough to clearly focus his mind on his body. The strips fell across his back again. He wished he could step out of his body, see what pattern Isaac was using to cover him so fully.

He was hard and losing time. He closed his eyes as his vision began to tunnel. The soft blows had layered into burn, but not the kind that would have him run away. He wanted to lean into it, to feel more. He locked his knees tight, hiding any wobble in his legs. He wanted to show Isaac, to please him, prove that not only could he handle this but that he wanted it. He felt that break in him, so rare but always sought for, the pure submission, the freedom of it. More of mind than body. He could not move now if he wanted to, not because he had been told not to, but that it had been his choice, to give away that control, freely and willingly.

The even, steady sound of the leather on his skin intermingled with random gasps and cries, small pleading words, and as long as Isaac wanted his pain, desire, and submission, he knew in that moment he could last.

⚜

THE SNAP OF THE LEATHER ON JACK'S SKIN WAS LIKE A WORDLESS mantra to a meditation, putting Isaac into a state of absolute focus. He was good with a flogger, he always had been. From the first time he picked one up, it had felt natural in his hand. He knew he would never have the raw strength of some Doms, but he had control. He could leave bruises that would last for weeks or a burn that would vanish in a day. For Jack he wanted a burn that would last until Monday morning.

He smiled as Jack's skin slipped from pale white into deepening shades of pink. And he could tell the moment when Jack slipped into a headspace of pure compliance and desire. The moment when strong muscles relaxed, and the whimpers of pain vanished into moans of pleasure and conflicting cries for more and release. Drips of pre-cum darkened the floor between Jack's feet.

Next time he would bind Jack to a bench or table. Save him the energy of standing and have him already spread and ready for Isaac when he was done. The sun glinted off the D-rings of Jack's cuffs. He wished he could have Jack in a collar, complete the set properly. He could guess why Jack wouldn't want one. He seemed sensitive about his neck and throat. Someone misstepped somewhere. Maybe at some point Jack would understand the meaning that could exist behind it. He'd have to want it though.

As Jack's skin shifted into properly red and Isaac could feel that spot on his chest Amalie had tapped before, begin to grow and change. He stopped and listened to Jack's ragged breathing and hard gasps that were nearly sobs. He raked his nails down his back and Jack screamed, his whole body shaking. He pressed himself against Jack's back, wrapping one arm around his middle and the other hand around his cock, letting the heat of Jack's body sink into him. "My good and beautiful boy." He stroked Jack's cock slowly but with a tight grip. "Cum for me."

Jack screamed again as his cum splashed onto the floor and his legs went out from under him. Isaac couldn't prevent the fall only control the descent.

ॐ

JACK WAS MOST AWARE OF THE WARMTH. HE'D SELDOM BEEN ABLE to drift this long. Not deep, but relaxed, sort of Zen but naked. Not that he cared that he was naked. He only cared that his head was on Isaac's lap and the sun coming through the high windows was warming his body. His eyes drifted along the bookshelves that filled the room. Something tickled in the back of his head, something that was trying to drag him up and out. He let himself focus on a few books. *Pandora* by Anne Rice, followed by *Parasitic Diseases Fifth Edition*, then the *Oxford Handbook of Clinical Medicine*.

He twitched. He tried his best to beat down that twitch into nothing because it didn't matter, it didn't matter in the slightest. How someone else kept their books was no one's business but their own, and that damn twitch was all his father's fault.

He must have tensed.

"What's wrong?" Isaac asked.

"Nothing." The book after the *Oxford Handbook of Clinical Medicine* was laying on its side, too tall to stand up on the shelf.

"Something is wrong."

"Nothing that matters," Jack insisted. It didn't matter, he kept repeating to himself.

"Everything matters to someone. What's wrong?" Isaac asked again, his voice firm.

There were paperbacks stacked on top of the book on its

side. Jack squeezed his eyes tight, the warm bliss of the morning rapidly disappearing. "You arrange your books alphabetically, by title, sort of."

"Those books get organized maybe every three years. I usually make a start then get sidetracked reading something I'd forgotten I had."

Jack would not let himself whimper in pain.

"Really, that's sort of the public library anyway. The books I use regularly I keep in my office and Amalie keeps hers in hers."

Jack took long breaths trying to relax again, to find that nice peaceful place a good flogging and an orgasm had taken him to.

"Would you like to organize my bookshelves?" Jack told himself Isaac wasn't laughing at him, but he was still sure he could hear some humor in the words.

"Yes. I mean I don't *want* to, I *really* don't want to but…"

"The fact that two people with advanced degrees can't keep their books in any sensible order is bugging the crap out of you, and is going to stick in the back of your head until the end of time."

Jack nodded gritting his teeth as he did.

"Go ahead, but no getting dressed." Isaac patted him on his still sore ass.

He hopped up, hating himself for this, but at the same time feeling more relaxed just for having permission to do it. He spun around, mentally taking in the rough number of books, the size and shapes of the shelves. Doing a perfect shelving wouldn't be possible. There were too many odd sized books, they'd need their own section. And the fiction looked like he might have to separate out hard and soft covers to make it all fit but he could do this.

"I can do this."

Damn I hate my dad some days.

"Can I get a note pad and a pencil? And maybe some post-it notes"

Isaac smiled at him. "Sure."

It was a rookie move to take every book off the shelf at once. He whipped around the room pulling all the fiction first (there was less of it), and felt better for having fiction and nonfiction separated. Once that was sorted he slipped into what he called The Shelving Zone. He made rough notes as to which shelves would handle what kind of texts and began sorting.

The piles were rough. He was pretty sure the forensic books fell under the R section of the Library of Congress Catalog with the rest of medicine, but wasn't 100% sure where. All of the books that were probably Amalie's were stacked into QR.

There were also sex books, quite a few of them. Jack only let his eyes quickly skim over the covers feeling the blood rush to his face. He knew where most of those went; HQ75-76.8, HQ79, HQ997. Not that he'd ever handled those shelves, but he'd always let his eyes skim over the titles as he walked by, not even really sure why. He reached for a book but Isaac picked it up first.

"Ever read this one?"

Jack looked at the mostly black cover. *The Ritual of Dominance and Submission*, by David English. He shook his head.

"Ever read any of these?" Isaac tilted his head to the pile with the HQ post-it note next to it and a copy of *Erotic Bondage* on top. Jack shook his head again even though he recognized a few of the titles. "How about if I put a few aside for you to read later. It won't all be relevant, no one size fits all in this, but it might give you some things to think about."

Jack nodded, his blood warming more than just his face. He'd managed to forget that he was naked. He had the sudden urge to hold a book in front of his privates, except the book in his hands was *Leathersex* by Joseph W. Bean. He felt his whole body begin to flush. Maybe this is what Isaac had meant that first night, about the naked and the nude. Even stripped, flogged, and fondled he hadn't felt as naked as he did in that moment.

Isaac kissed him while lightly pinching one of his nipples. "Get back to shelving. I want this done before dinner."

Jack tried not to moan. Somehow his nightmare childhood summer chore had turned into an act of erotic submission.

"Yes, sir."

Isaac smiled and sat back down between the piles for ND1290-1293 and QR75-99.5.

Jack got back to sorting, but this time was truly aware of Isaac's eyes on him. It was getting him hard again. He wondered if he should make some sort of show of it, but he was doing plenty of bending and stretching as he shelved. Each move highlighted the subtle burn of his back and ass. Isaac had told him to finish by dinner. It wouldn't take him that long. Maybe another two hours. Then... He wasn't sure what Isaac might have planned next. He was sure watching him organize books hadn't been on any plan, but Isaac didn't seem annoyed and he was getting his books put into at least some logical order.

ISAAC WATCHED AS JACK STRETCHED TO PLACE A BOOK ON A HIGH shelf. He could honestly say he'd gone through his life without any dirty librarian fantasies, until now. It was giving him a nice insight into Jack's mind. There was a librarian or years of library work somewhere in Jack's past, probably family. He had a solid long term and detailed memory as he appeared to have the Library of Congress system memorized. Some obsessive tendencies judging by the way he had been twitching as he looked over the bookshelves.

He would definitely be slipping a few books into Jack's bag, but only after putting bookmarks in certain sections. Even the best books had parts that would not fit with Jack's personality or the bits he was gleaning of Jack's past.

The sun was creeping across the floor and the shelves were

beginning to fill. He got up and made a couple of sandwiches, poured some juice then went back to the living room.

"Come and eat. I still plan on spending another 24 hours tormenting you. You need to keep your strength up."

Jack turned bright red, head to toe, but he sat and ate. Isaac didn't force any conversation, simply watched as Jack all but inhaled his lunch then got back to work. Isaac ate at a more leisurely pace, enjoying the view. When it looked like Jack was getting closer to finishing he stood up.

"I'm going to grab a few things, keep working."

He went to the bedroom and stood in front of the closet. He tried to picture what Jack might have done when he first opened it. Had he reached out for one thing or another? Run his finger through the strands of the floggers.

Isaac picked up the picnic basket, a gift from an old friend, and began filling it with bits and bobs before heading back to the living room.

Jack was still sorting but there were only a few shelves left empty, all at floor level. Isaac lounged across the sofa.

"Tell me Jack, do you enjoy having your ass played with?" Jack froze and began to turn. "No, no, keep working." He kept his voice casual.

"Yes, sir." Jack half mumbled, his cock swelling and his skin going pink.

"Do you like it stretched and filled? Heavy plugs? Nice thick dildo?"

Jack nodded sliding a few more books onto a low shelf, his ass high in the air still striped red. "Yes, sir." Jack mumbled again.

"Good. I have a couple of toys I want to use on you before dinner. And a few after."

"Yes, sir," Jack said again, his cock fully hard.

He finished filling the last few shelves then turned around several times looking over the entire room.

"All done?"

ADA MARIA SOTO

"Yes."

"Good, talk me through it. University was a while ago, I need a refresher."

Jack began explaining the system. He'd put a sticky note on each shelf denoting which books went on it. The fiction was separate from the nonfiction. He apologized that he had to put the oversized books and journals in a separate area because they wouldn't fit, but basically there was a place for everything and everything was in its place. Isaac was impressed and said as much.

"Honestly, even when we first moved in, the books in this room were never this organized and I certainly never believed that they could be arranged this quickly."

Jack shrugged.

"I need to reward you for this. What would you like?"

Jack shrugged again, his eyes to the floor, still unused to praise.

"Would you like to suck my cock? You've been staring at it all day, don't think I haven't noticed." Jack mumbled. "Say that again?"

"Yes, sir I'd like to suck your cock."

"There is no shame in a request like that. No need to mumble. But first bend over the coffee table so I can put something in your ass." Jack bent over the table, spreading his legs wide.

"Beautiful," he said, but other words had nearly slipped out instead at Jack's eagerness. It was something he'd think about later. Amalie was right. He wasn't as good at detaching and compartmentalizing as he should be. He pulled a large black plug with a twelve-speed remote control vibrating function out of the basket along with an irrigation syringe preloaded with lube.

"I'm going to put a plug in your ass. It's a large one. It's going to stretch and fill you. You'll find it hard to focus but that's what I

160

want. I don't want you to focus, I don't need you to think. You just gave yourself a solid analytical workout. Now you get to be mindless for a time."

"Thank you, sir." Jack said, true relief in his voice.

Isaac ran his hands over the globes of his ass. They put out a nice heat where he had flogged them. "I'm filling you with lube first, lots of it." He pushed in the plastic tip of the large syringe. Jack started at the cold. "Easy. I could have put this in the fridge first." A small tremor went through Jack's body.

"Now the plug. I'm going to go slow and I want you to hold still. Try to relax and tell me if the pain becomes sharp. I want to hurt you a little, not damage you."

Jack nodded. The plug was three large bumps the largest being a good two inches in diameter. Jack tensed as the tip was pressed against his hole but he took a few breaths and relaxed. Isaac pushed in slow to give Jack's body time to adjust and his mind time to become aware of the size. He watched as a drip of pre-cum hit the shiny surface of the coffee table.

Jack moaned low as Isaac pressed the second bump into him. "Too much?" He shook his head. "Can you take a little more?" Jack nodded. Isaac pressed in the last of the plug as slowly as he could manage, watching Jack's ass twitch and stretch then squeeze as the last of it slipped in, the wide base spreading his cheeks.

Jack was breathing hard and there was a trickle of sweat on his back. "How does that feel?"

"Good." Jack's voice was rough again.

"Good." Isaac sat down on the couch and unzipped his pants. "Come and get your reward. I know you want it."

Jack almost tripped over the coffee table as he rushed to kneel between Isaac's spread legs. There were few things Isaac loved more than someone eager to suck cock. He stroked the back of Jack's head as Jack sucked him in. "That's right. Such a good boy. Keep going."

Isaac kept up the soft litany of praise as Jack took him in ever deeper. He wondered if he could teach Jack to deep-throat. That would be a wonderful thing. Even without that, Jack had talent and Isaac knew he was close. That he hadn't cum in the last two days didn't help.

"I'm going to cum soon," he managed to say with what little mental focus he had left. "I expect you to catch every drop." Jack nodded but didn't stop sucking. "Don't swallow. I want you to hold it. You don't get to swallow until I say so."

Jack nodded again. It would be as good as a gag. Isaac tightened his grip on the back of his head and thrust up into Jack's mouth with a growl.

࿇

JACK HAD NEVER BEEN TOLD *NOT* TO SWALLOW BEFORE. HE PUFFED out his cheeks trying to catch every drop like he'd been told. The load felt huge and he struggled to obey. The plug in his ass had him so on edge it was hard not to cum right along with Isaac.

He leaned back on his knees and it felt like the plug was pushed in that much deeper. He moaned and felt some drool escape the corner of his mouth.

"You are very good at that. I hope you've been told that often."

It had been mentioned a few times but it felt different coming from Isaac, more honest or maybe more important.

Isaac tucked himself back in and stood. "Come with me."

Jack followed him back to the bedroom taking small steps and unintentionally wiggling his hips. Isaac ran his hand over the tightly made bed. "Damn you are good. You could bounce a quarter off this thing."

Jack shrugged. Getting yelled at and made to do pushups taught him to make his bed properly and quickly. In truth, he never made his bed at home. A tiny act of rebellion against his own past and parts of his personality.

Isaac took one of the pillows and lay it length wise in the middle of the bed. "Straddle that pillow for me and lean forward."

If Jack thought the simple walk to the bedroom had been hard, every move needed to climb onto the bed made him feel like he was only seconds away from cumming.

Isaac sat on the edge of the bed and stroked his back. "You've gotten a look at the supply closet now." Jack nodded. "See anything interesting in there?" Just about everything had fallen under the category of 'interesting'. Jack nodded again. "Good. I'm going to secure you again. You won't even have to think about not moving."

Isaac moved to the closet. Jack was expecting more rope but instead he heard the clink of metal. "Spread your knees and ankles and put your arms back." Isaac turned around holding a heavy looking metal bar with some welded-on loops. In less than a minute his ankles and wrists were attached to the bar forcing his legs apart and his ass high in the air. The plug in his ass began to vibrate. He jumped as much as he could and nearly swallowed.

"Yeah, that's remote controlled, twelve speed, some preset patterns, and mini USB rechargeable. The future is so cool." Jack whimpered and squeezed his eyes tight. "It's okay. You can cum as soon as you want, just relax into it. And as soon as you cum you can swallow."

The plug vibrated fast and hard. It was like an electric shock and he tried to thrust down into the pillow, cumming hard and finally swallowing. He screamed the second his mouth was clear. The vibrations eased up but they didn't stop. "Your face is amazing when you cum. Open and absolutely free. I want to see it again. And maybe a couple of more times after that. So relax. Don't think."

Jack tried to relax. The vibration and the sensation of still being filled kept him from going fully limp. He'd almost managed to catch his breath again when the vibrations became stronger and began to throb. It wasn't quite like being fucked but the hard to soft pulsing of the plug had his body rocking, his cock looking for any touch, even just the pillow that he couldn't quite reach. Isaac was stroking his back again.

"I know this feels strange but I know you can do it. I know you want to do it. Giving pleasure is important to you and I take so much pleasure in seeing you like this. Mindless and knowing nothing but sensation."

Jack tried to raise his head, he felt like he should say something. Maybe even explain himself though there was nothing to explain. He flopped his head down again. There was only one thing to focus on now. One sensation that was slowly overwhelming all else. The pulsing rhythm stopped and again became a single hard vibration. Again, it was like an electric shock. His ass squeezed tight and a second orgasm crashed over him, this one hard and painful, burning thought from his mind and all other sensation from his body.

The vibration didn't stop or even slow down this time. It became stronger, nearly pulling a scream from his throat and bringing tears to his eyes. There was a voice whispering in his ear as he thrashed.

"So strong," he heard. "So strong. So beautiful."

Fingers were put to his lips and he began to suck them hard. It felt better, he wasn't sure why but it felt right. He wasn't sure how long the third orgasm took to happen. Seconds. Forever. He whimpered. His body shook. His balls ached. There was one last extra hard shock of vibration. This time he did scream then it was gone. His muscles clenched and shook, his breath was ragged but there was stillness in him.

"Good boy," the whispering and stroking continued. "Good boy."

CHAPTER 18

The first time Isaac had seen a pretty sub forced through multiple orgasms, his cock twitching trying to squeeze out nothing, tears running down his face, he knew he'd encountered something beautiful and an absolute fetish. He hadn't found many subs who could handle more than two or three however. He stopped at three with Jack though he knew Jack could have kept going. He could have probably wrung one dry orgasm after another from that strong amazing body until he passed right out.

He wanted Jack awake though, for a given value of awake. He liked Jack like this, deep in subspace. Not just because it made Isaac feel good for being the one to put him there, but because it was what Jack was looking for. He wondered how many times Jack had truly found it.

He stroked Jack's sweat slicked back. "Can you understand me?"

There was a pause before Jack nodded.

"How do you feel? You can nod for good, shake your head for not good."

Jack blinked slowly then nodded his head.

"Good. I want to keep you like this for a while. Mindless. Peaceful. Secure. How does that sound?"

Jack nodded his head again.

"Good. I'm going to take out that plug now. You wore it well. I think I'll make it a point to always keep something in your ass." He twisted out the plug slowly and carefully. Jack still hissed and his stomach muscles clenched. He stroked Jack's lower back. "Easy. Your hole looks so open and inviting. I want to put my cock in you. Cum deep inside you. Plug you up. Leave it in there." Jack nodded. "No. Not yet." Despite the fact that Isaac knew he was healthy and the Windsor club required blood tests, there were some talks that had to be had when all parties were fully coherent. Jack did not fall under the category of fully coherent and probably wouldn't until sometime on Sunday, at least if Isaac did things right.

Next, he unclipped Jack's wrists but not his ankles and helped him stretch out and roll over, laying his head on the cum stained pillow. Then he attached Jack's wrists to the headboard and ran some rope from each end of the spreader bar to the sides of the bed.

"Take deep breaths." Jack took a long breath, his chest expanding, then another. "Other people might look at you and think you are exposed. You are not exposed, you are safe. Others who don't understand might think you have no control. You have complete control. You have presented yourself to me, allowed this, like the most beautiful of gifts and you can take it back whenever you wish." Jack's breath hitched for a second. "So much strength and beauty in this. Others don't see it. I don't think you always see it, but I will show you. I will show you your own strength."

Isaac sat on the bed and stroked Jack's hair until he was on the verge of sleep. He slid his hand down and tweaked Jack's right nipple. His eyes opened.

"I'm going to play with your chest. Get your nipples nice and swollen. Make them as sensitive as the rest of you." He watched as Jack's nipples hardened at his words. "You're going to want to cum again just from my breath on them." Jack's hips rose up, though his cock was still drained and limp. He was so beautifully suggestible in this state. Isaac knew he'd have to be careful. Jack's mind was as malleable as his body and far easier to damage.

He got up and grabbed some things from the closet. His office might be in a chronic state of disaster and he may not keep his books sensibly organized, but he knew exactly where every sex toy he owned was.

He sat cross legged next to Jack and started with the pinwheel. He kept it so light it would be more of a tickle and an itch. Back and forth over one nipple then the next. They had been designed by a doctor to test nerve sensitivity. Isaac was pretty sure there was nothing on earth that hadn't been turned into a potential sex toy by the kinky minded. He hummed slightly as Jack began to twist, seemingly unable to decide between pulling away from the sensation and pressing harder into it.

He set aside the wheel as Jack's breath began to speed up. "Easy, we've just started." He waited until Jack calmed again then picked up one nipple clamp and one strong nipple suction cup. One would pull extra blood into the nipple, the other would cut it off. There was something to be said for asymmetrical stimulation.

He squeezed the bulb on the sucker tight before putting it over Jack's left nipple and letting it go. Jack gasped as the flesh was pulled up into the plastic tube. While Jack was still reacting to that he clamped the other nipple tight.

He flicked at each one more or less at random and watched as Jack's cock, which had been slowly expanding, came fully to life. "Feels strange doesn't it? You're not sure which sensation to focus on. The suck or the bite. One hurts now but the pain is building in the other. It's good pain though. Your cock enjoys it. I'm sure you'd be dripping if you had enough in you. I think that will be the goal. I'll tease your nipples until you drip." Jack raised his hips and thrashed his head. "Do you want me to stop?" Jack shook his head this time instead of thrashing.

"Good." Isaac roughly removed the sucker and the clamp and quickly switched them. The clamp having engorged flesh to grab on to and the sensation of blood rushing into the other nipple was amplified as it was sucked into the tube. Jack cried out, his voice raw. "This is getting your nipples nice and fat. I'll be able to bite them. I can have my cock deep in you and just lean over and bite down." Jack's cock was jumping and Isaac's was hard as well. He could easily fuck Jack now in a dozen different ways, or simply take himself in hand and cum over Jack's body. It would be easy beyond belief, but Isaac would wait for the right moment as opposed to the easy one. This was, after all, all about control.

He pulled off the clamp and the sucker and switched them again, leaving Jack to moan and twist. One more change over, Jack's nipples now a vivid red and swollen. He twisted and flicked them until Jack was crying out. Then he pulled off the sucker, leaned over Jack's right nipple and bit down hard. Jack's hips lifted into the air and a single bead of pre-cum pushed its way from the tip of Jack's cock.

Isaac let go and instead licked at Jack's raw nipples and blew across them gently, leaving Jack shaking and occasionally thrusting his hips up into nothing.

THERE WAS PAIN. IT FELT LIKE BOTH FIRE AND COLD ON HIS CHEST but he didn't want it to stop. It was good and he wanted more. More of the fire and ice, but his ass felt empty and his cock bare. He wanted to feel full again. He always wanted it when he was in this mindless place. He lifted his hips as much as he could, tried to pull up his knees to explain. He wanted to ask but there were no words. Speech abandoned him like it seldom had before.

There was pain again, this time sharp and burning, the pinch of teeth, not metal. His ass squeezed around nothing and his hips lifted into the air which gave him no release.

Then the teeth were gone. Tongue and air now. Soft. Too soft, it was nearly as bad as the burn. He still felt empty. He lifted his hips again and pressed them back down, trying to explain still no words in his head, only flashes of images and sensation. He couldn't even open his eyes, there was too much.

"If I put that plug back in your ass I think you'd gladly fuck yourself on it."

Yes.

Speech still wasn't working. He nodded as best as he could.

"Well okay then."

Jack felt Isaac get off the bed and begin to shift things in the closet. He could open his eyes to watch, he wasn't blindfolded, but he felt like he maybe should be. It was better with his eyes closed. There was so much sensation already.

He hoped to feel the bed sink again, but instead his legs were released from the bed. Still forced apart by the spreader but he could bend his knees. That was better.

"Feet in the air. Hold them."

He awkwardly lifted his legs. The bed shifted as Isaac crawled across it. He still didn't open his eyes and he couldn't put his legs down. Something was attached to the spreader bar and anchored somewhere near his head. He flicked his eyes open just enough to make out rope then closed them again.

No work, no thinking. Didn't even have to hold his legs up. Something pushed at his hole. It wasn't the plug. It was thinner, hard and cold but rubbed inside him in a way that drove out those few developing threads of thought. It was pulled out and pushed back in. Isaac was fucking him with something and he was going slow. Almost lazy, Jack could hear him humming.

"I wonder how much cum you'll put out. I drained you dry before. Your cock is certainly back in the game and your ass craves this, I can tell. I wonder how your balls are doing."

Jack needed more, needed it faster, but he couldn't even press his hips down now. Still Isaac continued, slow, steady, lazy, humming some nameless tune to himself. There was noise coming from Jack's mouth now. Not words. Words were still too much, but begging all the same. He was burning and he wanted more.

Isaac pulled out whatever he had been using. Jack cried out in frustration or desperation, but in seconds he was filled again, this time properly. It was something long and thick. It gave one quick hard buzz and Jack came screaming.

ISAAC PULLED OUT THE SIMPLE VIBRATOR AND UNCLIPPED THE spreader bar as soon as Jack came. His head lulled to the side. He was either spaced out or out cold. He removed the spreader bar and unclipped his hands from the bed.

It was always an interesting dichotomy; what subs said they liked, versus what they went absolutely mad for once they were in subspace. Nipple play hadn't featured particularly strongly on Jack's lists of preferences but it had obviously been doing it for him. There was also no mention of gladly taking extra-large vibrating dildos, but that could just be self-consciousness. Wanting to get fucked is one thing. Begging to get stretched and filled while being pushed to the edge over and over was something harder to say out loud.

He pressed his fingers to Jack's neck finding a strong and steady pulse. His eyes were twitching under his eyelids. He must have fallen instantly asleep. He wondered what Jack was dreaming about. Had the sex followed him into his dream state, or was he staring at a math test and realizing that he hadn't been to class all year and wasn't supposed to be back in school anyway, but the teacher was glaring because he had a number 3 pencil.

That might have been Isaac's reoccurring stress dream but that didn't mean there weren't other people who had it.

He pulled a blanket up over Jack then rushed to the kitchen to grab some water, juice, and grapes. When he got back Jack had flopped an arm over his own face and was snoring softly. There was a cuteness to it that made Isaac smile. Sleep was the great leveler of appearance. He figured Jack would easily sleep until dinner and Isaac decided to join him.

CHAPTER 19

He was thirsty. That was his first awareness. His mouth felt sticky, dry, and his throat rough. He tried to swallow but there was nothing to swallow and his throat was stinging. There was warmth pressed to his side. He cracked his eyes open. They also felt rough and raw. Isaac was there against his side, asleep, his face mashed into a pillow. Beyond him on the night stand was an entire pitcher of water. He felt like it should be in a spotlight with an angelic chorus in the background. He wanted to reach for it but his limbs felt heavy and his head ached. There was a war. How thirsty he was versus how much he didn't want to move.

He tried to swallow again and winced at the pain. There was no way of reaching the water without either waking up Isaac or getting out of bed and walking all the way around it. He wasn't sure if he could walk. The muscles in his legs were twitching. He groaned and Isaac opened his eyes.

"Hello. Are you waking up or going back to sleep?"

Jack opened his mouth to respond, even though he was pretty sure he couldn't make words happen. Nothing came out except for a rough half cough.

"Let's get you some water."

He could have cried in relief as Isaac poured a glass and held it to his lips. He wanted to gulp it down but all he could manage was a series of tiny sips. Isaac stroked his head. "It's okay. Go at the pace you need. We're in no rush. No need to do anything."

He closed his eyes again.

No rush.

He still had a night and a day of this if he wanted. He could say stop. He could call a halt to it all. It was more than he'd ever done. He'd done overnights in a hotel but nothing this long. Twelve hours at the most. And it wasn't just the time. He'd never gone this far before. Oh, he'd sunk down, come close but not like this, not to the point when he truly no longer recognized his own body or mind. He'd never felt that wild, that desperate for more. It was terrifying and he ached. His body ached but already his mind wanted more. Isaac had said it wasn't a drug but at that moment it felt like it. Like he could easily stay like this forever. Bound, fucked, serving, but being fed sips of water and petted like something precious.

He sipped some more water simply focusing on the way it soothed the burn in his throat. Time was still drifting in a way. Isaac gave him sips of water or juice and petted him. When he glanced at the alarm clock on the dresser he was surprised to find it was after seven. His stomach rumbled. Isaac smiled.

"Hungry?"

Jack nodded. "Yes."

"Getting your voice back?"

"Yes."

"How are you feeling?"

"Sore. Quiet."

"Feeling quiet is good. Too Sore?"

"No.

Isaac held him close and ran his fingers through his hair. He pushed into the touch like a cat. Isaac chuckled. "Think you're up for dinner?"

"I think so."

"I want to feed you on your knees again if you'll let me."

"Okay."

"It's just that you are amazingly sexy eating out of my fingers and I'd like to see you do it at least a few more times before Monday."

Jack wasn't sure what to say. He was never good with compliments so he defaulted to a simple 'yes, sir'.

"Let's see if you can stand up." Isaac got out of bed first, giving Jack space to roll over and get his feet on the floor. He stood slowly. His legs wobbled at first but he took a few steps and felt the strength return. He couldn't say he felt normal. His ass ached, clearly reminding him how much he'd had shoved up there. And his balls ached after being drained over and over. But it was all a good ache. It fed something warm deep in the back of his mind.

"Got your legs under you?"

"Yes."

"Why don't you use the bathroom while I start dinner? How does steak sound?"

His stomach rumbled again. "It sounds great."

ISAAC PULLED ON HIS PANTS AND GRABBED A FEW THINGS FROM THE closet before heading to the kitchen. There were only a couple of really nice dinners he could make that could be done quickly and be hand fed to someone. Steak, green beans and sliced heirloom tomatoes was his best.

First thing he did though, was open a can of Fancy Feast. It wouldn't prevent Murrcat from trying to steal food, but he'd be less demanding about it if he'd already been fed. He heard the cat flap bang open and wondered if anyone had ever done research as to how far away a hungry cat could hear the sound of a can opening. It was like the auditory equivalent of a shark smelling blood.

He pulled out the steaks and veg as Jack came in. He paused by the kitchen table eyeing up the things Isaac had left there.

"Can you slice the tomatoes into wedges?" Isaac held up the large purple tomatoes he'd gotten at the farmers' market.

"Sure." Jack gave the things on the table one last look before taking the tomatoes and standing in front of the cutting board.

"How do you like your steak?"

"Um... Medium rare leaning on the rare side."

"Good, me too." Isaac had gotten two thick scotch fillets that would take time to cook, even rare. He handed Jack the beans to get ready while he spiced the steaks. They worked mostly in quiet and it was nice. He'd found that the ability to simply be quiet with someone was nearly as important as the ability to talk to them.

Once the beans were in the steamer and the steaks were settled into the cast iron pan, he turned to Jack. "How are you feeling?"

"Good." Jack frowned. "You keep asking me that."

"Yes. It's important. If you're not feeling good, especially after we've been doing something intense, then I've probably done something wrong. The whole point of aftercare is to make sure the nice up feeling of a scene doesn't turn into a hard and ugly crash."

Jack's eyes flicked to the floor and he didn't respond. Isaac growled in his head, but was careful to keep the emotions off his face. There really should be some sort of professional type registration and certification process for Doms that included testing and regular recertification. And where you could file complaints if you found subs that hadn't been receiving proper aftercare, at least not regularly. Massage therapists had to do it and they weren't sticking their hands up peoples' butts. Usually.

"Did you like it when I hand fed you at breakfast?"

"Yes."

"I'd like to do that again. You are very attractive on your knees, and not because it makes you seem smaller. If anything, it highlights your strength." Isaac pushed on, not giving Jack room to respond. "I also want to tie you up. Nothing overly constrictive. More decorative than anything else."

"Yes, sir." Jack's cock was swelling again, which after the previous twenty-four hours he would have believed was impossible.

"Good. There are rules about sex in the kitchen. They've been broken a few times but we try not to."

"I used to have my Massachusetts Food Safety Certification."

Isaac flipped the steaks over, bringing a fresh round of sizzling from the stove. "So, no real life hot barista fantasies for you."

"I didn't have any workmates who weren't at least a decade older than me, and lesbians."

Isaac grinned. "Tell me this place still exists because next conference in Boston I'm going there."

"It exists. I stopped by to say hi last Christmas and ended up working a nine-hour shift."

Isaac wasn't much of one for role play but some ideas involving coffee, whipped cream, and candy canes were bubbling up. He turned off the steak. "Those need a few minutes to rest. Plenty of time."

He led Jack over to the table where the pillow still sat from breakfast, though now it was occupied. "That's not yours." Murrcat opened one eye, stared at Isaac then closed it again. He gave the pillow a nudge with his foot. "Shoo you brat. Don't think I won't cut off the Fancy Feast supply. You'll be on dry kibble." He gave the pillow another nudge. Murrcat got up with a long slow stretch, making it very clear that it was his idea to move and he was in no way giving in to name calling and threats. "Nothing like a cat to undermine your authority and remind you of your true place in the universe."

Jack was failing to keep a smile off his face.

"Put your hands behind your head." Isaac picked up the short coil of rope he'd brought. Under it was a large stainless steel anal hook. Jack's eyes locked onto that. "Just going to do a simple chest harness to start." It was one of the first bits of rope work Isaac had ever learned how to do. He even did it on himself once to prove a point. The rope highlighted Jack's well developed pecks and left a strong handle between his shoulder blades. He didn't fully tie off the ends of the rope. He grabbed the hook off the table next, taking note of Jack's erect cock and the way his body was relaxing. He wished he had the space and rigging to do some serious rope work with Jack. He obviously got off on it.

"Ever used one of these?" He held up the hook.

"No, sir."

"Know how it works?"

Jack nodded and looked down, his cheeks flushing. "Yes, sir."

"Good. Put your hands on the table."

Jack leaned forward, and with a squirt of lube Isaac slowly inserted the business end of the hook. It wasn't a particularly thick one, with only one ball at the end. But like all steel it was unyielding. Jack gasped and his lower back tensed. Isaac rubbed it until he began to relax. He threaded the leftover bits of rope through the top of the hook securing it in place. Then gripping the harness, led Jack to his knees. He gasped at each small move and his eyes were already becoming unfocused. He finished the look by securing Jack's wrists at the small of his back.

The end effect was of a proudly displayed chest and perfect posture.

"Perfect." He held his fingertips to Jack's lips. Jack licked at them delicately. "Save that thought. I'm going to dish up."

THE HOOK WAS MAKING JACK AWARE OF EVERY MUSCLE TWITCH IN his body. The smallest shift either pulled it in deeper or stimulated him in a way that left him close to cumming. Isaac had said perfect. He didn't feel perfect, not with the way the energy in his body was building up, making him feel itchy. He wanted Isaac to touch him. His nipples in particular, were craving touch. He'd never encountered that before. Not like this.

Isaac sat at the table, turning sideways in the chair, and held a piece of steak to his lips. It was warm and rare with a hint of pepper and he licked the juice that covered Isaac's fingers. He grounded himself on the flavor of each small bite he was fed, and the texture of Isaac's fingers as he licked them clean. At one point he felt a furry face claiming his feet as territory, but the cat was shooed away.

Isaac gave little murmurs and words of praise each time Jack cleaned his fingers. He began running his tongue down Isaac's palm. As the meal was finished Isaac pressed two fingers to his lips and Jack sucked them in hard.

"Shit. Okay, I'm going with the 90's presidential definition of sex." Isaac pulled his fingers from Jack's mouth and undid his own pants. Jack leaned forward, pulling the hook in deep, and took Isaac's cock in his mouth. "Fucking perfect." Jack never understood why this felt as right as it did. The smell, the heat, the taste, the weight on his tongue and the steady hand on the back of his head. "Swallow every drop." Jack bobbed his head, taking in as much as he could each time. He wished he could wrap his hands around the rest. Or better yet suck it all in, but it was a trick he'd never mastered. Not that he'd ever given himself much chance to learn it.

Isaac slid his hips closer to the edge of the chair. Jack slid himself back to accommodate and gasped. The angle was wrong or maybe right. With every bob of his head it felt like he was being deep fucked. He whimpered and tried to ignore it. Tried to focus on his task. Tried to squeeze down enough so the hook wouldn't move, but that made it worse. He wriggled his hips but it was no use. The cock in his mouth was overwhelming two of his senses. His eyes were squeezed shut. He could barely hear over the sound of his own heart thumping, and the shifting of the hook was relentless. He was going to cum. There was a bizarre feedback loop going in his brain and he couldn't stop it. Stop.

Suddenly Isaac's cock was gone from his mouth and Isaac was kneeling in front of him.

"What's wrong?"

Jack couldn't answer. He was about to ask the same thing.

"I felt you say stop. What's wrong?"

"Going to cum. Can't— Couldn't stop. Shouldn't—" Shame burned through him. First simple rule. Don't cum unless told. They both looked down. Cum was still sliding in slow spirts from Jack's cock even though he hadn't orgasmed.

"It's okay."

Jack shook his head, squeezing his eyes shut. It was not okay.

"It's okay." Isaac stroked his back. "You didn't do it on purpose. And you said stop when you thought something was wrong."

No, Jack thought. *Should have been better.* Jack shook his head.

Isaac grabbed his chin and forced his head up. "Look at me and understand me. You have done nothing wrong. Accidents happen. Do you understand?"

Jack nodded but couldn't say he believed it.

"Lean forward and put your head on my shoulder. I'm going to untie you now."

Jack pressed his forehead to Isaac's shoulder. He wanted to

cry. There was the crush of shame, the sting of fresh forgiveness, and an undertow of frustration born from an orgasm that didn't happen.

His arms were released first. He let them flop at his sides. The hook was removed slowly. He hissed and it clanked on the floor. The rest of the ropes were easily loosened and removed, Isaac stroking each freshly revealed piece of skin.

"There we go," he whispered as the last of the rope hit the floor. "Sit back on your knees again for me." Jack rolled back, keenly aware of how empty he felt. Isaac took the napkins from the table and cleaned up the sticky cum that had covered his belly and thighs.

"That couldn't have been very satisfying. I know ruined orgasms can leave someone even more on edge. That's not what we're going for here. Can you stand up?"

Jack stood slowly, his legs shaking from the time spent on his knees. "Come on. Let's go lay down for a bit."

☸

HE WAS PROUD OF JACK. PROUD THAT HE WAS ABLE TO SAY STOP when something was wrong, even if he wasn't fully aware he was doing it. He was also annoyed at himself. He had not intended for things to go this way. Jack had handled far more in terms of stimulation and it hadn't even occurred to him that it was likely to happen in the middle of a blowjob. The hook was meant to tease, certainly, but he hadn't intended to push Jack into a ruined orgasm. He didn't believe in setting subs up to fail and he didn't want Jack to think he had done that.

Then there was Jack's reaction. He had looked so guilt ridden and defeated, like he was about to cry. He was probably expecting some sort of punishment. Yes, not cumming without permission was a pretty standard rule in this kind of situation, but it wasn't like Jack had grabbed his own cock. If there was one thing Isaac had learned as a doctor, it was that sometimes the human body does what it wants and gives your mind little choice in the matter.

"Let's lay down on the bed. I want to hold you. It's still early."

Jack lay down but his body was stiff and his muscles tense. Isaac curled up next to him and started running fingers through his hair. He said nothing and felt Jack growing tenser by the moment.

"I'm sorry," Isaac started. Jack shook his head. "No. It was not my intention for you to be in a situation where you would be overstimulated to the point you were. I wanted to tease you but I should have paid closer attention to what was happening. I apologize for this. It's on me. Understand?"

Jack was still for a long time before he nodded. Isaac was sure that nod was a lie, but it would be hard to call Jack out on it.

"You've never done this before have you? Spent this long so deep."

"No," Jack whispered.

"It does build up, especially the first time. If it's gotten to be too much you can say so. I'll understand. We can spend tomorrow relaxing, go out for breakfast. You can go home if you feel you need to."

Jack shook his head.

"Okay." He hugged Jack close. "I want this to be a positive time for you. I want you to wake up Monday morning feeling more strong and sure about yourself than you ever have before. And I want you to be able to trust me enough that you'd be willing to do this again. I'm sorry I misstepped."

Jack nodded again before pressing his face against Isaac's shoulder.

There was nothing but his hot breath for a long time before he heard Jack speak. It was muffled beyond where he could make out any words.

"If you want to tell me something you're going to have to

raise your head."

Jack became still, then slowly raised his head. "It was like a feedback loop. Like putting a mic in front of speakers. The more I sucked made it feel like there was more in me and I couldn't move in a way that didn't..." Jack petered off.

"So, you like the idea of having cock in both ends." Isaac said trying to shift Jack's thoughts away from what had happened.

Jack flushed and his nod was small. "When I'm... deep, the things I want are more and different and... more. Like there are two mes, almost but not."

Isaac had heard similar things before, especially from men in high power, high responsibility jobs. Some even used different names, not for anonymity but to separate out the part of themselves that didn't fit with how they thought the world saw them. He'd seen it lead to some nasty self-loathing and destructive habits.

"There's only one of you. You just have slightly more complex and layered desires than those dull mundane people walking around out there. It's one more thing that makes you interesting."

"I'm not interesting."

"Yes, you are. You're an ex-army SWAT commander who used to be a hippy shop barista and somewhere along the line you memorized the Library of Congress cataloging system."

"Not the whole system." Jack mumbled. "Just the first couple layers of categories."

"That's still something that makes you stand out. You're more than just a cute smile and a tight bod. You've got some solid brain power going on up there." He tapped the top of Jack's head. Jack shook his head and buried his face back into Isaac's shoulder.

And there we have intellectual inferiority complex. Probably been called a dumb jock a few times too many.

He held back a sigh and stroked his fingers down Jack's still tense back.

He could feel Jack's frustration in the way his muscles twitched under his skin. He was obviously not a man who handled failure well, perceived or real, but he knew few in law enforcement who did. He'd kicked some trash cans and hit the bar early himself, when a bad guy got off. He'd seen Lydia spend a hundred bucks on cheap dishes and glassware, just so she could go out and smash them. Any lingering fears from Friday's meth explosion were probably not helping.

"Have you ever actually been taken from both ends before?"

"Once." Jack mumbled.

"Did you enjoy it?"

"Yes."

"Would you want to do it again?" Isaac knew a couple of Doms he'd be willing to trust but not this early on in the relationship.

Jack shook his head, though Isaac could feel his cock twitch. "Too many people."

There weren't many in the community who knew in detail what Isaac did, but there were a few and they could possibly track Jack to his job. Not that they would. Isaac trusted them but it was a big ask to ask Jack to trust a stranger. And quite frankly Isaac was feeling possessive.

"Okay. I do like the thought, you filled on both ends. Filled completely. The way you handled that giant plug earlier impressed me."

"Thank you, sir." Jack's face was still pressed against Isaac, but it was the first thing he'd said since they got to the room that wasn't half a mumble.

Normally if a sub called stop, Isaac would bring them all the way up and make sure they stayed there until they were more grounded and they had worked through whatever had happened. But in Jack's head he'd failed and he wasn't going to let this go until he could prove himself again.

"That ruined orgasm must have left you frustrated?"

"Yes, sir."

"I have to say I'm feeling on edge myself." Jack immediately started to shift himself down the bed. "Nope." He gave Jack's hair a gentle tug to stop him. "As always, I love your enthusiasm for sucking cock but the idea of seeing you *properly* stuffed on both ends has intrigued me." For the first time since they entered the bedroom Isaac could see Jack's body begin to relax. "So, I'm going to do just that." Isaac rolled out of bed. "Hands and knees. Press the soles of your feet against the headboard then roll yourself back so your ass is pressed to the headboard as well."

Jack got into position.

"Very nice. Do I need to secure you?"

"Please, sir."

That was not the answer Isaac was expecting. Maybe he shouldn't have completely unwrapped him. He seemed peaceful while in binding. He pulled the heavier hardware from the closet. Spreader bars on wrists and ankles and a telescoping bar running between the middle of each. Jack's movements would be limited to rocking back and forth on his knees and shuffling.

"Lean yourself forward." Isaac stuck a large dildo with a strong suction cup into place and liberally covered it in lube. He slowly guided Jack back until he was impaled on it. He stroked Jack's lower back. "Here's what's going to happen. You are going to finish sucking me off while you fuck yourself on that nice piece of rubber cock back there. At no point is it to completely leave your body. Keep it in there nice and deep. If it comes out, I'll put a very short leash around your balls and attach it to the headboard as well."

Jack shivered. "Yes, sir."

"You are going to keep fucking yourself until you cum, and after you do, you are not going to stop. I want to watch you grind out a few more orgasms without your cock ever being touched."

Jack was licking his lips and swallowing hard. "Yes, sir.

Thank you, sir."

THE FIRST TASTE OF ISAAC'S COCK WAS THE LAST THING NEEDED TO properly ground him. He wished he could deep-throat. He wished he could stretch his neck out and let Isaac fuck it.

He would try to learn.

He rolled his body on the dildo as he bobbed his head on Isaac's cock. It felt good. He could almost pretend it was Isaac's, it was a similar size, Isaac somehow duplicated, taking him both ways at once. He tried to put all his focus onto Isaac. He wanted to make sure he was good, as perfect as he could be in the situation. To make up for what had happened before, losing control and leaving Isaac unsatisfied.

Isaac's hand was a firm and comfortable weight on the back of his head, guiding him. He kept his eyes closed focusing on the shape in his mouth. He leaned forward trying to take more but felt the dildo about to slip out. He slammed his hips back and nearly came. He locked onto Isaac's cock again and tried to find that perfect point of balance.

Isaac's hand tightened on Jack's hair and Jack did his best to suck in as much as he could. Isaac thrust twice, hard, hard enough to make Jack cough and gag but he still clamped his lips around Isaac's cock, desperate not to spill a drop. He swallowed as much as he could. It felt like more than any other time before, but still he sucked and licked until every drop of cum was gone from Isaac's dick.

"Good boy." Isaac purred. "Good boy. Now let's see you do it."

Jack hadn't stopped moving but now he picked up speed and strength, never pulling off more than half way and slamming himself back hard. "Next time it's not going to be a rubber cock. Next time you're going to ride me. I'm going to lay back and let you do all the work."

Jack whimpered and instantly pictured Isaac kneeling behind him fingers tight on his hips.

"Or maybe I'll see if you can *really* cum with no stimulation on your cock. A nice strong cock cage, something made of steel. I'll stick that big plug back in and make you cum over and over, your cock never getting any proper relief."

"Yes," Jack gasped out.

"I'll have you bound when I do it. Wouldn't want you to hurt yourself trying to claw through the cage. On your knees, thighs to ankles, waist cinched tight. I'll tie your hands right above the plug so you won't be able to reach it if you wanted to. Not that you'd want to. Not even when I turn that plug up so high it feels like electricity in you."

The picture being painted in Jack's head was so vivid he could feel the ropes already.

"And I'd leave you like that for as long as I wanted."

Jack came with a scream of relief. Like an itch finally scratched, seldom had anything felt so good.

"Keep going," was whispered in his ear.

He kept going but slowed down. A marathon was different from a sprint. He didn't know how many times Isaac would want to see him cum. In the past it was three or four. Jack knew it would be hard. He was oversensitive and it was already beginning to hurt but he would keep going. He rolled his back getting the right spot so he never went completely soft.

"Your nipples haven't been played with enough. Maybe that's what I should send you home with. A nice pair of clamps. Every night you can screw them on a little harder and leave them a little longer while you stroke yourself, until the idea of cumming without them feels strange."

Something in that image landed deep in his core. Teasing his body, even while alone, training it to react as Isaac wanted. He started fucking himself faster, wanting that dick to be deeper and real. Wanting it to be Isaac's dick. He felt Isaac's hand on the back of his head. The next orgasm pushed through him in a way that brought tears to his eyes. The muscles in his arms and thighs shook. Sweat pooled in the small of his back.

"Can you keep going for me?" Jack nodded. "Good boy."

Isaac was stroking his back now. Long slow strokes that encouraged him back.

"One more for me." Isaac's voice was low and commanding. "You can do one more. Your ass is so fuckable. You take it so beautifully. Watching you impale yourself over and over. You are beautiful bound and beautiful in motion like this. I want to tie you up so you cannot move and I want to see you run, see you sweat and your muscles strain. See all that strength so perfectly controlled and brought right to the edge."

He pushed back hard and there was a sharp slap on his ass causing him to jump and break rhythm. He pushed back and there was another slap on his other cheek. "There. Now my hands are on your ass. I could send you home with this. Tell you to attach it to your wall, so every night you can fuck yourself on it. Keep your body ready and desperate for the real thing."

Jack thought he might have nodded. He might have even have said yes, but what he knew he had to do was keep going until he simply drowned in the sensation and came again.

☙❦❧

THERE WERE TEARS COMING DOWN JACK'S FACE WHEN ISAAC finally told him to stop. His whole body was trembling and slick with sweat. Isaac freed his hands and he collapsed. He cupped Jack's face and his palms were kissed with reverence.

He freed Jack's legs and moved aside the heavy bars. Then he lay beside Jack and held him close, held him tight. Jack continued to shake. Isaac whispered over and over that he was a good boy.

CHAPTER 20

It was early for Isaac when he woke, barely past seven. Jack was still asleep and Isaac started trying to re-plan the day. The plan had been to take a shower, feed Jack breakfast, maybe do some rope work, then spend the afternoon relaxing. He knew that needed to change. While he still loved the idea of feeding Jack on his knees, it might reawaken the distress of the perceived failings from the night before. At the same time, Jack had a serious need to prove himself and would probably take eating at the table as criticism.

Fucking society.

He could attempt to get Jack to eat out. There were a handful of really good breakfast places within walking distance. They were always crowded on Sundays but he was sure they could get in if they timed it right. After the early birds but before the brunch crowd.

Jack was still curled up tight against him. He had cried out a lot of pain the night before, before Isaac had been able to slide him fully into bed.

Fucking society. Isaac thought again. The human body and the human mind can hold up to amazing amounts of pressure in the moment. It's the spring back that gets ugly. The stretching that shows where all the cracks are. He brushed a wisp of hair from Jack's face. He'd put money down that Jack's failure issues started with his family. They were usually the first culprits. An A minus on a test isn't good enough. Second place in a race might as well be losing. First time he'd met Amalie was sophomore year at college, when she'd been drinking herself stupid at a party because she'd gotten 95% on a midterm paper and her parents had been a little disappointed. That had been nothing compared to the fit his parents had thrown when he finished med school, and then went to work on dead people.

The military or the job would have easily amplified Jack's issues. Messing up in combat could leave someone dead. Kicking in the wrong door could have the same results. Messing up during a scene means cleaning up and trying again. Or at least it should.

When he was a kid, his neighbor fostered rescue dogs but only large breeds like Mastiffs and Great Danes. It was always strange to see these giant dogs, often bigger than he was, skittish and trying to hide but so grateful for a simple treat or a kind pat.

There was one, an Irish Wolfhound with a missing eye and front paw, who would stand on its hind legs and easily drop tennis balls over the shared fence into the back yard. Isaac used his mother's tennis racket to knock them back over the fence. He'd listen to the scatter of paws on grass, then the thump of the dog running into the fence to drop the ball over. He'd spent most of a summer doing that until one day the fence fell over. The dog pounced instantly, nearly crushing him under a hundred pounds of weight, and half drowning him with licks and drool. Eventually the dog had rolled off him for a belly rub, but it was enough to freak out his mother and the neighbor. The dog was sent somewhere else, which Isaac found grossly unfair, and he had voiced his objections by stamping around and slamming doors.

He gave Jack a squeeze and felt him take a deep breath then open his eyes. Salt from the tears had dried on his cheeks.

"Good morning," Isaac whispered.

Jack frowned. "It's morning?"

"Sunday morning. You slept all night."

Jack's frowned deepened. "Sorry."

"No need to be. Would you like some water?"

"Yes, please. I have a headache."

"Not surprised." There was still a half a glass of water on the night stand which Jack drank eagerly. "I've been thinking about what to do today."

"I'm supposed to wash you."

Isaac didn't like the words 'supposed to'. "I would enjoy that but it's not a requirement. We can just take showers."

"No. I want to." Jack's voice was firm and trying for confident, but Isaac could hear the waver.

He leaned in close and kissed him. He kept the kiss soft and slow. Jack kissed him back just as carefully but something warm, other than lust, started to pool in Isaac. He pulled back.

"Go take your own shower. Take your time. Give yourself a nice deep clean then wait for me by the tub."

A small smile touched Jack's lips. "Yes, sir."

Jack's legs wobbled as his feet touched the floor, but it only took seconds for that military perfect posture to return. Isaac made a show of looking him up and down before he headed to the bathroom.

Isaac lay himself back in bed and spread his legs. He teased his cock, lightly running his fingertips over it while thinking about all the thing's he'd like to do with Jack, or the things he would do with Jack when Jack was more comfortable, and trusted him more. Jack fucking himself on that dildo had been amazing to watch. He'd like to see it again but with little weights on Jack's nipples, maybe stretch his balls, dividing his focus, making it that much harder.

He'd like to train Jack to deep-throat. It was not something everyone could do, and it took practice but Jack seemed like the type who would practice. He could tie him on his back, spread-eagle, his head back over the edge of the bed, slowly show him how to open his throat, relax into it. Take pleasure in developing a new skill.

He'd certainly like to take the flogger to Jack's body again. The red marks were already fading. Use more steel on him, and more silk. Maybe both at the same time. Such contrasts, but they could be used to obtain the same means. Maybe, maybe some time in the future he could take Jack to an old friend of his who was set up to do complicated rope work, including suspensions. And he would fuck Jack, regularly if he was able.

He gave his cock a tight squeeze then let go. He heard the shower shut off but didn't leap up right away. He wanted to give Jack a few minutes to finish readying himself.

Only when his own arousal was beginning to ease up did he walk casually into the bathroom. Jack was kneeling on the bath-mat, head down, and hands behind his back.

He stood behind Jack, running fingers through his hair, then tilted his head back forcing him to look up.

"Warm up the shower. Hot but not unmanageable."

Jack leapt to his feet, adjusting the knobs. Every so often Isaac made a note that they really needed to remodel the guest bathroom. There was something unpleasantly generic about it.

It didn't take long for the room to begin to fill with steam, the pipes still warm from Jack's shower. Isaac stepped in and motioned Jack to follow.

"Well?"

Jack grabbed the bottle of shampoo and got to work. Aside from the pleasure of Jack's strong hands on his body, Isaac was impressed. Almost stroke for stroke what he had done to himself the morning before, Jack was doing now. His hair was washed and rinsed. His body well lathered in soap. His cock and balls

were washed with reverence and Isaac couldn't even begin to
prevent his own arousal at it. The heat amplified the flogger
marks on Jack's body. And Jack was nearly as hard as he was.

We are absolutely doing this again.

Jack cleaned carefully between his toes. When he was done
he put aside the bar of soap and knelt in the bottom of the tub,
hands once again behind his back.

Isaac knew that being a Dom, at least a decent one, was
about control. Not control of others but control of self. There
had to be an ability to step away from any moment and view it
on a rational, even logical level. But even at the best of times,
sometimes raw lust reared up to the point of being nearly blinding. He grabbed Jack's chin and his own cock.

"One more thing to do."

Jack didn't hesitate and took Isaac in with gusto, his own
eyes heavy with lust.

"Fuck, you are perfect."

Jack whimpered and sucked harder, taking him in until he
began to choke, but he continued sucking as much as he could
of Isaac's dick and wrapping his hands around the rest.

Isaac didn't hold anything back or give a word of warning,
simply clenched his fist into Jack's hair and came deep into
Jack's throat, watching as he swallowed and licked up every
drop.

"Good boy."

ISAAC TURNED OFF THE WATER AND POINTED TO THE THICK TOWEL
folded by the sink. Jack leapt from the tub, ignoring the ache in
his knees and jaw, and held the towel out so Isaac could step into
it. Even in the plain suburban bathroom he felt like he was in a
roman epic, attending to an emperor in the bath house. But that
didn't work. Not really. He wanted this too much to be some

slave boy in the background. He had been treated too well. Isaac praised him, called him perfect, told him he was good, even as his own doubts said otherwise.

He understood the desire, even the need, some subs had for a collar. Something to show the room who they tended, prove there was someone who wanted them to serve. Someone who wanted them. Some days he wished he could handle that.

He dried Isaac, careful not to leave his hair unmanageable or moisture in unfortunate places.

"I was thinking about going out for breakfast this morning."

Jack was pretty sure his heart stopped, even as he kept drying Isaac's legs.

"There are a half dozen good breakfast places within walking distance, and it's a nice day out."

Jack wasn't sure how to answer. Going out? People would see them. Yes, they'd been out before but that was different. And that was before everything that had happened, had happened. And if he was a regular somewhere they would recognize Isaac, but they would expect him to be with someone else, like his *wife*. And what if someone from the department did recognize him? It's a small world. He once ran into a guy from high school while he was stationed in Arizona. He ran into Isaac at a place he thought he was guaranteed to meet no one familiar! And then there was his dick. All Isaac had to do was use a particular tone of voice and he was rock hard and half into a submissive head space.

"We don't have to if you're not comfortable." Jack was aware he hadn't answered despite how fast his brain was turning. "I just thought it might be nice." He finished drying Isaac's feet. Isaac reached down and tilted his chin up again. "I would never do anything to embarrass you or make you feel uncomfortable. You can say no if you like."

Jack nodded his head.

"Is that yes to no or yes to going out?"

He didn't answer because he wasn't entirely sure. There was something unreal about the last day. A soft fantasy bubble where he was someone else. Outside, things were real. He was a different person, or so he always wanted to believe. Going out would mean popping the bubble and seeing what existed in the daylight.

"How about if you dry off and change the sheets while I get dressed. You can think about it. No pressure either way."

Jack nodded again and reached for a dry towel. "Use the same towel."

His cock, which had started to go limp, sprang to life again. Isaac smiled at him while he shivered. "Yes, sir."

HE WAS ON COMPLETE AUTOPILOT AS HE CLEANED THE ROOM AND made the bed.

He coiled the rope first, remembering the one failed summer he spent in boy scouts. There had been a lot of knot tying and general stuff with rope. There had also been poison ivy, a broken leg, and a strangely intense fight with the scout master's son over the nature of god. The next summer he'd gotten his job at Coffea Contenuto.

His mind was raging back and forth. The 'it's just breakfast and there are a million lies you can tell if someone recognizes you' warred with the 'people will know' camp. Someway, somehow, complete strangers will look at them and know what they get up to behind closed doors. A very small voice argued how ridiculous that thought was, and why should it matter even if it was true. That voice was not getting a lot of traction.

Isaac returned as he was sliding the pillows back into place. He was completely dressed, right down to a pair of shoes. The full truth of his own nakedness hit Jack. He didn't even have his cuffs on. They were still sitting neatly in the bathroom.

He was suddenly chilled. The room wasn't that warm. He wanted to get dressed. Get dressed and go out. Go out with Isaac. He said he wouldn't do anything to embarrass him or make him uncomfortable and so far, Isaac had done nothing but protect him. Even from himself.

"Come to any decisions?"

"Yeah. Yes." Jack found it hard to find his voice. "I think going out might be nice."

Isaac smiled and Jack felt the warmth of praise even if it was unsaid. There was one issue though that Jack couldn't figure out how to deal with.

"Um..." He looked down at himself. He was hard and waving in the cool air. And even if he was allowed to cum right at that moment, his control had been reduced to a teenaged level. It wouldn't take much for him to end up sitting in a restaurant with major wood.

Isaac's smile widened. "Do you trust me?"

"Yes." Jack didn't even think about his answer. It just came out. Here at least, in that moment, he trusted Isaac more than he trusted himself.

"Good." There was a softening in his posture. "I'm going to go get your clothes. Take care of yourself. You can cum on one of the clean pillows. When you're done, we'll take measures to make sure there are no little accidents while we're out."

Isaac turned and left with no other comment. Jack took himself in hand. The rush of relief was staggering. He started stroking himself fast and hard, images of the previous day flashing across his mind. He was near the edge already but for some reason he wasn't cumming. He squeezed his eyes tight in frustration. He could feel his balls drawn up and the burn low in his belly. He pinched one of his nipples hard. Then he felt lips pressed softly to his shoulder followed by a hard bite of the muscle.

He cried out, his hips bucking, and stroked himself faster and harder than ever.

"I thought I told you to take care of yourself," came a low growl in his ear. "Do you need me to fuck you? Should I bend you over now? Drop my load in your ass and plug you up. Walk you around holding my cum?"

A second hard bite was applied to his shoulder and Jack finally found his release. His legs wobbled and he locked his knees forcing himself to stay standing.

"That was gorgeous. Keep your eyes closed."

Jack nodded. He doubted he could open his eyes. Even with his cock going limp in his hand there was still a painful lust and emptiness in him. He heard the closet open then close.

"Let go of yourself." Jack hissed as a cold wet wipe cleaned his cock, shrinking it that little bit more. Then there was more cold, this time metal, behind his balls and tight around his cock.

"Open your eyes and look at yourself."

Jack looked down. His cock was encased in a solid steel tube, curving it down between his legs, a small lock attaching it to the steel ring behind his balls. His breath caught and his legs wobbled. "Go ahead and take a feel."

He wrapped his hand around the tube, feeling nothing but the warming metal. He couldn't get hard if he wanted to. He couldn't cum no matter the desperation. It was one thing to say he had no control, but now he truly had no control over this most basic part of his body. He had never wanted to be fucked so badly.

He couldn't keep his balance and pitched over, barely catching himself, his face inches from the cum stained pillow.

"Is that an offer?" Isaac's voice was rich with humor but Jack couldn't share the joke.

"Please," he begged. "God, please."

"If I'd known I'd get this reaction I would have caged you up earlier. Maybe I'll leave it on the rest of the day."

Jack whimpered and spread his legs, his mind narrowing down to nothing but desire and Isaac.

He heard a zipper lowered, the crinkle of a condom wrapper, a quick squirt of cold lube then Isaac pressing in. It hurt and Jack wanted more. His cock tried to fill again but was denied. All he could do was take Isaac's cock until Isaac was done with him. He pushed back.

"Fuck," Isaac hissed. "Fuck. Next time this is going on the second you walk in the door and isn't coming off until you leave. I'll wrap you up tight. Only way you'll be able to cum is if I'm fucking your ass hard and only if I let you."

Jack nearly cried again. It sounded good. It sounded right. Out in the sun he might be horrified by the thought, by his approval, but here in the moment it sounded perfect.

CHAPTER 21

So much for missing the brunch crowd.

Isaac would be surprised if he could even get Jack out of the house in this state. He'd used cock cages before for a bit of teasing or discipline. He'd never been into the enforced long term chastity that some Doms used. He liked watching his subs cum too much. He'd known plenty of subs who were into it. Especially younger ones for some reason. But he had never seen anyone drop so hard and fast as Jack when that tube clicked into place.

It was that tiny little 'please' that had nearly snapped something in Isaac. Maybe with another sub he would have said no. Teased and played with him, maybe even forced him out in that state but he wasn't going to deny Jack. Not this first time. He thought he'd discovered Jack's 'thing' with the ropes but this was working on a whole special level.

Jack was panting as Isaac pulled out. His muscles trembled but the begging had stopped. He guided Jack until he was sitting on the bed then kissed him softly and kept kissing him until his breath settled out and the shaking stopped. He grabbed the pack of wet wipes and cleaned Jack's face. There were strings of pre-cum stuck to his thighs but he ignored them. He was sure if he got his hands anywhere near that cage it could quite possibly send Jack right over the edge again, and frankly he was getting hungry.

"Can you look at me?"

Jack raised his head. His eyes were focused, if hesitant. They made Isaac want to kiss him again. Kiss him and push him back on the bed, fucking him unconscious.

"I could use some breakfast, and so could you." he said carefully. "I'm going to get you dressed then we're going to go find something to eat, if you can manage it."

Jack nodded.

"Can I get a verbal response?"

"Yes."

"Good."

For Jack's sake Isaac got him dressed as efficiently as possible with no touching or teasing. When he was completely dressed, Isaac stood him in front of a mirror.

"There you go. Exactly the same as when you walked in here on Friday night. You even smell like the locker room soap." Jack nodded again, but his eyes were focused on his own crotch. Isaac picked the cage he had because, even under tight jeans, it wouldn't show in the slightest. With Jack's more sensible fit, it was truly invisible.

"Let's get going."

He put a hand at the small of Jack's back and steered him out the door. Isaac took a deep breath. This was going to make or break them, he was sure. It was one thing to trust someone in a club, or the privacy of a home but this was reality. He made a decision to take Jack to The Four Way Stop Cafe. It was a mile walk and usually had the fewest people of all the local breakfast spots. Hopefully the walk would take enough time that he could get Jack's head back into a more public space.

"So, how does a SWAT army boy end up spending time slinging coffee at an organic bakery?" Isaac asked after a block.

"What?" Jack blinked and almost tripped over a piece of uneven sidewalk. "Oh. Um... I was fourteen and I wanted a new computer. My father said that he would pay for half if I could get the other half. It was an expensive computer and I'm sure he didn't think I could actually get a job, or keep one long enough, or save well enough or something. I could tell when he said it."

Isaac filed away the old hurt in Jack's voice as a reminder not to like Jack's father if they ever met. "Nothing more dangerous than underestimating a motivated teenager."

Jack smiled. "I spent a week wandering around getting turned down for everything. And I passed by this sign that said part time afternoon barista wanted. I walked in and there was this old lady there. Okay, she was fifty which isn't old, but at fourteen it seems ancient. She had short green hair, tattoos on her arms, and I could see her nipple rings through her t-shirt because she doesn't believe in bras, and I wasn't sure if she was awesome or terrifying but I asked for a job."

"And she gave it to you?"

"She asked if I knew what a barista did and I said no. Then she asked me why I wanted the job and I explained, and I'm still not sure if I amused her, or she liked the idea of sticking it to someone like my father, or lost a bet where she had to hire the next person who walked through the door, but I started the next day. Had burns on my hands for a week and all the other employees were over twenty-five, dyed, pierced, tattooed lesbians but I worked after school and full time during summers and holidays." Jack was smiling and clear eyed at the fond memories.

Isaac smiled as well. It was good to see Jack opening up about his past. "They sound like a fun group of ladies."

"They were like a weird little coven of older sisters and aunts that I never knew I needed. I think they had a contest going for which one of them could teach me the most random thing."

"Example?"

Jack sighed. "I know how to choreograph a maypole dance so that you actually get a complicated woven pattern in the ribbons around the pole."

Isaac couldn't help laughing at the idea of a teenaged Jack dancing around a maypole. "You weren't being metaphorical about the coven bit, were you?"

"No. I can also make a vegan gluten free orange cranberry scone that's... Okay, I'd be lying if I said it was good, but it's edible. If you were really hungry you wouldn't turn your nose up to it."

"That counts as a useful skill in some circles."

"Clare and the Organic Witches of Boston."

Isaac was now curious how a teenager who spent his formative years with tattooed pagan lesbians ended up in the military, then the police. Family probably had something to do with it. It usually did.

"So, did you get your computer?"

"Yeah. And I'd never seen my dad so pissed. Didn't say a word just handed over the check. The fact that my brother and sister were both laughing hysterically didn't help. He showed up at the cafe a week later and Clare scared the fuck out of him. My dad wore three piece suits to work and carried a pocket watch."

"Couldn't handle the nipple piercings?"

"Nope." Jack's smile was broad and his steps long and proud. Isaac was glad he had a reasonably good relationship with his father. Jack's sounded less than perfect.

Isaac steered them toward breakfast while Jack told a few more stories about his adventures at Coffea Contenuto, many of which involved him trying to shield his poor virginal eyes from random lady bits, then getting to tell other boys in gym class that they were full of shit because he'd seen the real stuff they'd only just imagined. There was a conference in Boston the coming year that Isaac had been thinking about attending, but it was now moved up to absolutely attending just so he could meet Clare and the Organic Witches of Boston.

He opened the door to the Four Way Stop Cafe and gestured Jack in. A waitress looked up at them and motioned for them to take any table. Jack froze, glancing around at the people. Isaac was certain the place was a front for something. The food was reasonable but there were never more than four or five people in there and the parking was nonexistent. He couldn't work out how it was still in business but it had been around forever.

Isaac sat them at a booth in the back and the waitress came to take their drink orders. Jack froze again.

"Two coffees and two large glasses of orange juice."

The waitress left, leaving them to look over the menus.

Isaac leaned across the table. "It's okay. It's just breakfast. You've had it several thousand times in your life. This is just one more."

Jack nodded but also squirmed in his seat. Isaac wanted to lean all the way over, whisper naughty things in his ear, make him blush, but he'd promised no embarrassment.

"I'm thinking about having the pancakes and the fruit salad, because they actually put fruit in their fruit salad instead of just two types of nasty melon and three grapes. How about you?"

Jack looked around the cafe again as if someone was about to judge his breakfast choice. "I think I'll have the waffles."

"I've never had the waffles here. Maybe I'll have those as well."

The waitress brought over their coffee and took their orders, Jack managing to speak this time. Isaac sipped his coffee. "Yours is much much better. Two mornings and you've spoiled me."

Jack blew on his coffee and took a sip. "Over roasted to compensate for a mild bean, pre-ground, kept in cold storage.

South American. Columbia probably. It's been a while." He poured milk into the coffee.

"Impressive."

"Never thought I'd be a coffee snob but..."

"Ghosts of careers past."

Jack smiled.

As they waited for breakfast, Isaac managed to keep the conversation on coffee and Coffea Contenuto, the goal being to keep everything normal. To help Jack forget about, or at least not care about, the steel tube between his legs. Every so often he would shift and a pink flush would grace his cheeks, but they managed to keep the conversation rolling.

The waffles arrived heaped with butter, syrup, whipped cream, and fruit.

"I usually don't let myself have this much sugar with breakfast." Jack commented, looking down at his plate.

Isaac smirked. Maybe one little naughty thing. "I'm sure we can find some way to work it off."

Jack flushed, he squirmed in his seat and began to eat. It was with the measured pace of someone who didn't want to look like they were bolting through their food, but also had somewhere else they needed or wanted to be. Also known as how Isaac had dinner with his in-laws.

Isaac kept up, because for all his hunger and his pride at getting Jack outside, he now wanted to get Jack back inside.

And back inside of Jack, the perpetually adolescent part of his brain added with a snicker.

ISAAC'S LIPS WERE ON HIS AS SOON AS THE FRONT DOOR OF THE house closed. They still tasted like strawberries and syrup. "I am very proud of you," he said after he pulled away. "I know that was scary on many levels, but you did it and I'm proud of you."

Jack didn't answer. It wasn't scary, it had been terrifying. There were moments when he had managed to forget what was going on, then he'd shift in a particular way and it would all come flooding back. He was sure everyone who passed on the street, and every person at that restaurant had somehow been able to look at him and just know. Know what he was wearing, know what he'd been doing. Isaac would manage to distract him for a few minutes until he remembered again.

"Are you willing to get undressed for me one more time?"

"Yes, sir." His clothes had become itchy on the way back and felt tighter than he knew they were.

"Strip here, go get your cuffs, and meet me in the bedroom."

Jack fell into Isaac's words. It would be the last time today, possibly for a while, he'd get the chance to do that and he let himself fall.

He stripped quickly, hyper aware of the metal preventing the erection that wanted to break through. In the air his whole body felt sensitive. His nipples were craving touch and his ass felt empty. He grabbed the cuffs and rushed to the bedroom. Isaac was waiting for him. There were ropes on the bed. Along with clips, spreader bars, and multiple plugs and dildos. More than could possibly be used in a few hours but there were certainly options. Isaac took the cuffs away from him and strapped them on tight. Then he picked up two more thick ones from the bed and strapped them around his thighs.

They felt comforting.

"I want you to go to the closet and pick out one other thing for me to use, or you to wear. Your choice but I maintain veto power."

Jack looked in the closet. There was so much and he had to think clearly. It was Sunday. As much as he wanted to feel that flogger again, it wouldn't heal by morning. His hand hovered over a collar, wanting the symbolism of it but he instantly felt his throat begin to close. He grabbed a gag instead. The one with the rubber bar that looked like a bit for a horse.

He held it out to Isaac.

"I thought gags were on the no list?"

They usually were but he could talk around this type with a bit of work, and Isaac would listen. "I trust you."

Isaac took the bit and turned it over in his hands. "Thank you," he said, his voice soft and his face unreadable but there was a weight in the words. Jack was sure something important had just happened but wasn't sure what.

"Open your mouth."

Jack opened his mouth. The rubber bar was pushed between his teeth and the strap cinched tight behind his head. He bit down. The bit of rubber felt much wider than it looked and he wasn't sure where to put his tongue.

"I'm going to tie you up again. Tighter this time. I believe you can take it. I'm going to pinch and weight your nipples while I do. I'm going to fill your ass and make you cum, your cock still in that tube."

Jack moaned around the bit and felt his legs wobble as if it were already happening.

"Kneel in the middle of the bed. It'll make the rope work trickier but I don't want to risk you falling over. Next time I'll get out a frame so I can keep you on your feet."

Jack crawled onto the bed.

"Can you keep your eyes closed? I want you focused on your body."

Jack closed his eyes.

"Good boy."

He fought the urge to anticipate actions that came with closing his eyes and instead focused on his body as Isaac said. There was an itch and emptiness. He heard Isaac move around the room and felt the bed sink behind him. Something cold and rubbery parted his ass cheeks and a small plug was pushed into him easing the need to be filled but also making him aware that he could handle so much more. Isaac moved around the bed. There was a mechanical pinch on his right nipple as a clamp was screwed on tight, and a soft bump against his chest.

"That is a weighted clamp." Isaac flicked it. It felt like someone was trying to stretch out his nipple but it didn't let up. A shudder passed through him. Would these leave his nipples swollen? Would they be longer? Isaac attached the other then flicked them both. They hurt. They pinched and burned in a way Jack usually wouldn't tolerate, but instead the pain was sending a direct message to his cock and his ass. With every flick he squeezed down tight.

"And one more thing before we begin." Isaac moved behind him again. There were a couple of clicks and the cuffs on his thighs were connected to the ones on his ankles. There was now no way he could get up from the kneeling position, and if pushed onto his back it would leave his legs in the air.

"Your cock is already leaking. It's beautiful."

"Thank you, sir," Jack said around the bit.

"It's only the truth. Now for a little more decorations, but it really is gilding the lily."

Jack was already associating the feel of the rope with control and peace. He kept his hands behind his head. The first wrap of rope went around the back of his cock then around the top of each thigh, allowing the corset part to start all the way down at his hips. Each strong pull of the ropes caused the weights on his nipples to swing. When Isaac reached his waist he stopped, pulled out the small plug and pushed in a larger one.

"Your ass really is designed to take all I can give you."

Jack didn't respond. Words were gone. There was only the feeling of the rope. The burn of his nipples. The fullness of his ass. And Isaac's hands on his skin as he worked. It was easier to change his breathing this time. He knew how it was done and the transition was seamless.

As the ropes were wrapped around below his nipples, Isaac brought his arms down and wove his wrist cuffs into the work just below his shoulder blades.

He couldn't move his arms, couldn't stand, couldn't speak clearly, couldn't have an erection, could hardly form a coherent thought, and all he wanted was for Isaac to fuck him again.

He pulled out the second plug and put in a third. This one was large and Jack was pretty sure he recognized it. It was the one Isaac was going to use to push him over the edge, he was sure of it.

He heard Isaac move around the room then there was quiet.

"Open your eyes."

In front of him, propped up on a chair, was a mirror large enough that he could see himself. He couldn't recognize himself though. His eyes were glazed. His cock was dripping, and he looked decorated. The weights on his nipples were blue teardrops of glass. The rope woven around him was blue and dark green, alternating and twisting together. He reminded himself of a maypole.

"This might be a good bit of ego on my part, but you look stunning."

Jack closed his eyes.

"Open your eyes."

Jack opened them.

"I'm going to make you cum now. I want you to watch yourself for as long as you can. I want you to watch how wild you are."

Isaac reached into his pocket and a low vibration filled Jack's body. He closed his eyes then snapped them open again, remembering his orders.

The vibrations increased steadily until it felt more like electricity in him. His cock was jumping even if it couldn't expand. His hips were trying to thrust, only succeeding in rocking his whole body, stretching his nipples. Drool ran from the corners of his mouth and down his chin and pre-cum came from his cock in a steady stream. He tried to focus on breathing instead of the wild stranger he was looking at, with swollen lips and knees spread wide.

It was no use. There was one more step up in the vibrations and the orgasm roared through him like a fire. He watched as cum oozed from the tip of the tube where his swollen cock should have been. It didn't feel real. It felt good, there was release, but also a disconnect. He wanted to touch himself.

The vibrations slowed but not by enough. Isaac pulled off the clips and he screamed in pain as the blood rushed back to his nipples. He tried to thrust his hips again. He heard the clink of the little lock against the metal tube and finally squeezed his eyes shut. He fell onto his side but only heard Isaac laugh. The vibrations became stronger again. Less electricity and simply fire.

There was no distinction anymore between pain and pleasure. There was no other him than who he was in that moment. There were no thoughts. Only his body out of his control.

The second orgasm was like a lightning strike.

Later he would try to remember if there was a third or even a fourth, but there was no solid moment to hang a memory on to.

When he became aware he was on his back, the plug was being pulled from his body. His knees spread wide and his legs still bent. Isaac hovered over him for a second, looking more than human, like something beyond him, and he fought for a breath.

Then Isaac was naked and pushing into him and that felt right. Possibly more right than anything in his life.

CHAPTER 22

T he clips holding Jack's thighs to his ankles came off first, letting him stretch his legs. Then the bit. Then Isaac freed Jack's arms and loosened the ropes. He wouldn't be able to get the ropes off until Jack was aware enough to help. At the end he seemed animalistic, his higher mind gone.

Isaac loved it. It was going to take a while to bring Jack back up from that, and steady himself for the outside world again. He knew he was liable to crash himself if he wasn't careful.

Jack was starting to shiver. He pulled a blanket over the both of them and held him close, tangling their legs together and sharing the heat. He felt Jack fall properly asleep.

It was an hour before Jack jumped into his own wakefulness pulling at the ropes.

"Easy. Easy." Isaac grabbed the safety scissors off the nightstand. He had hoped he wouldn't have to cut the ropes. Good ropes weren't cheap and there was the sweet spot between new and overused, that he hadn't gotten to yet. "I'll get it, deep breath."

As he snipped through each level of rope Jack pulled it off, slowly calming as he went. When the last piece of rope had been flung to the floor he fell back onto the bed.

"Sorry, sorry."

"No." Isaac set the scissors aside. "No. My bad. I should have tried to keep you awake and gotten them all off first."

"I thought they were snakes. I had this dream, and there were snakes and one was crawling up my neck and—"

Isaac pulled him close but didn't hold too tight. He stroked Jack's back, careful to avoid his neck.

"I'm sorry," he mumbled.

"No. You don't apologize for things you have no control over. Do you think you can go back to sleep?" Jack shook his head. "Okay. Try to rest and relax. Let your body find its equilibrium again." Jack nodded this time. Isaac did his best to ground himself on the even rhythm of Jack's warm breath across his chest.

"I really do like the ropes," Jack mumbled after a time. "It's just, it felt like they were crawling up."

"Can you tell me why you don't like things near your neck?" It was an easy thing for Isaac to avoid in a scene, but he knew it could be connected to bigger things or even a sign of something worse.

Jack rolled over onto his back and stared at the ceiling. "There was this guy in basic, big guy and that's me saying that. Damn near seven feet and a total asshole. I mean just a fucking bully." His words were hard with disgust. "Anyway, we were doing hand to hand training and I got him for a partner and he got me in a head lock. I was trying to get out of it the way we were taught, but he was just that much taller and stronger and I couldn't get the leverage. I remember he kept laughing and saying the 'enemy won't let you tap out'. I don't know if our training officer didn't notice or didn't care, but somewhere I blacked out. Woke up to our training officer giving me mouth to mouth, which was unpleasant for many reasons. They carted me off to medical and when I got back the asshole was gone. I don't know where, I didn't ask. I was just glad my neck wasn't broken and I didn't think about it. Next time we were practicing hand to hand I was paired up with this tiny guy. Must have stood on his toes to get past the height requirement, but he was going to be a computer tech so it didn't matter. He had to jump to get around my neck and the second those skinny little arms of his got near my neck I freaked out. Spun around and punched the poor kid in the face. Felt really bad about it." Isaac took Jack's hand and gave it a squeeze he hoped was comforting. "Few years later, first time someone tried to put a collar around my neck..." Jack shrugged.

"You freaked out again."

"Thing is, it's getting worse and I know it." There was a sharp edge to Jack's voice like he was trying to keep it from cracking. "I had to wear a tie for my full dress uniform and it wasn't a problem. Job interviews and weddings. I never liked it but... Now if I have to go to court, the tie goes on thirty seconds before I'm called up and comes off the second I'm off the stand, and I'm distracted by it the whole time. I mean I've been desperate. Totally, fucking, half out of my mind desperate and walked out of scenes when someone has tried to insist on a collar."

"I never will." Isaac's voice was firm but he tried to keep it reassuring.

Jack shook his head. "I get it. I mean, I get why people want them, the whole symbolism, or want to use them but... I know I should talk with someone. Find a shrink or a therapist. I don't want to go to the department and I really don't want to jump through VA hoops. They're overworked as is. So, I should find someone private, but that costs like two hundred an hour or something and explaining all this—"

"It's okay." Isaac squeezed his hand again. It was good that Jack was self-aware enough to acknowledge that he needed help. It was also good to know that even when desperate, there was at least one thing that could get Jack to walk out of a scene. "If you want, when you're ready, I'll help you find someone. I know people, who know people, who know people. And I know several people in the mental health profession who are understanding of certain lifestyles."

"You know a lot of people involved in—" Jack randomly gestured to the room as if it encapsulated the entire BDSM community. Where Isaac fit into the local community was complicated and not something they had discussed.

Isaac shrugged. "Sort of. I'm more known of than known."

"Known of?"

"I did fully train as a doctor. I don't regularly practice on live people, but I keep my licenses up to date because there are many members of the community, especially young ones, who can't afford health care, can't access it, are scared to, don't have a proper support network. Runaways, throwaways. I do a lot of handholding in doctors' offices. Sometimes it takes another doctor to explain 'those bruises are consensual, we're here about the bronchitis'." Jack smiled at that. It had been a strange conversation to have. "I know a few people and those few people are the kind of people who know everyone else and know how to send up the bat signal if I'm needed. Sometimes I'll go to events, but those are usually to give talks. I'm billed as The Doctor. Flogging demonstrations, Kinbaku models, and The Doctor giving a first aid lecture. I've got a friend who's certified to do first aid training. We have a double act. She brings the CPR dummies."

"You're really billed as The Doctor?"

"I show up in a suit, tie, lab coat, medical bag, the whole deal. People don't recognize me in normal clothes. I give a whole lecture called Since You're in the Neighborhood, which is all about recognizing problems with down there bits. I mean if you're going to be sticking fingers up peoples' butts you should know what a healthy prostate feels like."

Jack chuckled even though it wasn't particularly funny.

"Let me tell you it's much easier to find someone willing to have forty strangers stick a finger in their ass and fondle their balls at a bondage event than it is at a med school."

This time Jack fully laughed.

"I think it was the greatest night of that kid's life."

Jack rolled back over and wrapped his arms around Isaac.

"Thank you, sir," he whispered for a reason known only to him.

"My pleasure."

ISAAC HELD HIM CLOSE AS HIS BRAIN BEGAN TO SLIDE BACK INTO place. The shaking fear from the meth house explosion was gone. He'd never told anyone about the guy in basic. Only his training officer clued in about two seconds after he hit that poor computer tech. And it *was* getting worse and he didn't know why. He worried about having a panic attack in court. Isaac said he'd help him find help. Someone who wouldn't judge him for the other things he needed to do. That would be nice.

It wasn't the first time he'd had that snake dream either. He solidly blamed the army for that one as well. He'd been stationed at Fort Bliss in Texas for all of a month and week one he found a giant (from his point of view) snake in his boot. It was a nice modern building that should not have had snakes, and coming from Boston he was not used to having snakes crawling over his feet first thing in the morning, while still half asleep. The local guys thought it was hysterical and proceeded to stick rubber snakes in his boots for the rest of his time there.

There was still the worry about the leak. He wasn't sure if the explosion on Friday was linked to it or just bad luck. Isaac said he would talk to Lydia. Isaac said he'd take care of a lot of things. Leaks could be dangerous and he wouldn't want to see anyone get hurt trying to find it. He needed to keep his own ear closer to the ground. Proactive, not reactive as Clare always said, usually about 30 seconds before getting arrested for protesting something. He was pretty sure half the cafe's profits went to bail money. Still, proactive to keep his team safe.

Isaac ran fingers through his hair. He wanted to fall back asleep but he was hungry and his mouth was dry. He licked his lips a few times.

"How about if I go get us something to drink?"

"That would be nice."

"Think you can eat something?" Isaac asked.

"Yes, I think I worked off those waffles."

"I have no doubt about that." He put a kiss on his head before getting up. Jack felt colder for the loss of body heat, but it wasn't that bone deep chill that would hit if he'd been in a long scene. None of the nausea either that sometimes happened if he had to drag himself out quick. It hadn't been all bad. There had been some more like Isaac, who at least took time to make sure he was okay, but those had still been half anonymous. Fake names sometimes in distant cities. He knew those nights were particularly risky, but there was always that need under his skin.

Isaac returned with rehydration fluid in a large glass along with grapes, crackers, and some cheese. He insisted Jack only take little sips and small bites but he still finished the plate.

"Let's take a shower," Isaac suggested once the plates were cleared. "I'm going to clean you this time."

When they got to the bathroom Isaac took off the cuffs with as much ceremony as they went on. Jack wobbled as it hit him that those weren't going back on today. Possibly not for a while, not until their schedules matched up again and there was no way of knowing when that might be. That he'd gotten two days not on call, and only with a lie about going to the mountains, was a miracle. But he supposed on-call didn't matter as much anymore if he continued with Isaac. As long as he didn't come up too fast or too hard, he could get to work. It wasn't the most pleasant thing but he could manage it.

Isaac washed him gently and held him close, almost like a slow dance. He also inspected Jack's body carefully, going over every inch. He pressed some soothing cream into his ass that eased an ache he hadn't really noticed. It got him half hard again but in a lazy sort of way.

"You heal quickly. All that flogging and there's hardly a mark left." He put a small kiss on Jack's butt cheek. "One of these days you're going to take some real time off. I'm going to get you down nice and deep and absolutely paint your ass."

"Things seem to ease up after Thanksgiving for me."

"I guess even criminals fall into week long turkey comas."

Jack had a sudden flash of getting fed turkey on his knees. It got him properly hard. He usually spent Thanksgiving on call so family guys could be at home, and he'd have an excuse not to be in Boston. He wasn't an exhibitionist, he didn't like being on display, but spending the slightly depressing holiday season on his knees, maybe his head in Isaac's lap was a pleasant fantasy.

"What are you thinking about?"

"Eating out of your fingers." It was a half-truth but not a lie.

Isaac pressed himself against Jack's back then wrapped his hand around Jack's cock. "One more for the road."

Jack nodded. There was something to be said for an old-fashioned reach around. Like doing it yourself but with less effort. He didn't cry out as he came this time. It was more of a long and satisfied sigh.

Isaac rinsed him off and kissed him. "Let's get you out, you're getting wrinkly."

Isaac dried him just as carefully as Jack had dried him that morning, then helped him dress. The clothes felt strange again, the jeans restrictive. He was beginning to understand nudists.

Isaac led him into the front room and sat them down on the couch. The shadows through the high windows were getting long. Murrcat jumped into his lap. "How are you feeling? Honestly. Head to toe, but especially head."

He pet the cat who purred at a level that shook his whole body. It was nice. "Steadier. Clearer than I was. Focused, I think. Bit sore. Still a little—" he waved his hand trying to convey the idea that he still wanted to sink, but knew he could handle the world. "Tired. I think I could take another nap."

"Then you should." Isaac got up and patted the padded arm of the couch. "It's actually quite comfortable."

"Really?"

Isaac patted the arm again. Jack felt silly but he stretched out, Isaac draped a blanket over him, Murrcat jumped on him and began to purr, and he fell asleep.

CHAPTER 23

J ack settled into sleep, Murrcat purred, and Isaac watched
    from the side chair. He was tempted to fall asleep himself
    to the sound of purrs and Jack's steady breathing, but
    falling asleep in that chair always did a number on his
back. He was going to be sore for a week already.

Instead he got up as quietly as he could so he could pack a
few extra things into Jack's bag. He couldn't say he wanted Jack
to go home. Not just because he wanted Jack around, but
because he wasn't sure if Jack knew how well he truly was. If he
was used to running out the door and taking care of himself
after scenes, his guideline for 'fine' might not actually be fine, or
even good. He still seemed a hair unsteady on his feet, and there
was laziness in his blinking. That he went to sleep so easily, even
with Murrcat's chainsaw of a purr, said something as well.

He made a couple of sandwiches, one for Jack later, and
settled in with the whole 'what to do next' question? Amalie was
going to ask him the second she came through the door. There
had certainly been a few moments, usually when holding Jack
tight, when he'd felt something in that little spot under his
breastbone. It scared him, probably as much as the whole thing

scared Jack. He'd messed up before, he'd run before, he'd put his heart out before. And he came with the baggage that anyone who loved him back would be sharing him.

He knew Amalie loved him as much as she loved Lydia, and he'd known that before they got married. He never for one second asked her to choose, and he never would. And while he had nothing Lydia was even remotely interested in, she was still one of his closest friends. She kept rice milk in the fridge and a half dozen power suits in the closet. There was an open suggestion that she move in, but it was also well accepted between the three of them that it was her career and reputation in the Prosecutor's Office that was most at risk if everything came out.

There weren't many people who could handle that, even if they thought they could at the start. The time management and scheduling alone could be a nightmare. Jack obviously feared being outed as well but a stable relationship can't be built on sex, even really good sex. Getting him out the door for breakfast had been a mission and a half. A romantic dinner, a concert, a weekend away would take a hell of a lot of work. And that's assuming Jack even felt the same way. He might just be thankful for someone to submit to who won't kick him out if the phone rings.

Isaac rubbed the bridge of his nose. He could feel the start of a headache. One step at a time. Get Jack steady and back on his feet.

THE PINK-ORANGE OF SUNSET WAS PEAKING AROUND THE CURTAINS when Jack was finally awakened by the force of Murrcat jumping off him. Isaac set aside the journal he'd been reading. "Hey, sleepy head."

Jack sat up blinking at the orange light. "It's late."

"Heading that way. I made you a sandwich. Think you could eat?"

"Yeah, I'm a bit hungry."

Isaac grabbed the sandwich from the kitchen, glad he'd made it extra-large. He had a feeling 'a bit hungry' actually meant 'I could finish off a rack of ribs in about five minutes'.

He added half an extra avocado and another layer of ham before bringing it out. Jack finished it in about three minutes, along with extra glasses of orange juice and water.

"Feeling better?"

"Yeah. I'll eat avocado on just about anything though. I think it's half the reason I stay out west."

"I'll remember that." There was a sudden uncomfortable silence, the first of the weekend, and Jack's eyes darted to his bag waiting by the door. "You don't have to go home tonight. You can stay and have some dinner, take another night to sleep, relax, head out early tomorrow."

Jack didn't answer right away but eventually shook his head, to Isaac's disappointment. "I should get home. Check messages. See how much of the county burned down or blew up while I wasn't looking."

"Probably not much if I didn't get called in. But, before you go, I want you to stand on one foot, and touch your finger to your nose." Jack laughed. "I'm serious. Before I let you out of here I want to see physical and mental equilibrium."

Jack sighed and rolled his eyes. Isaac was tempted to threaten him with a spanking for being bratty about it. He stood on one leg, closed his eyes, and touched his finger to his nose repeatedly. "Would you like me to do the alphabet backward?"

"Most people I know can't do it sober."

Jack gestured to the perfectly ordered shelves then did the alphabet backward nearly as fast as Isaac could do it forwards.

"I am officially impressed."

Jack gave a bow.

"Okay, but, and I'm not being clingy here, I want you to give me a text when you get home so I know you made it. I want you to eat something. Preferably not microwaved, order delivery if you need to, and before you go to bed I want a SitRep, head to toe. I want to make sure I didn't break you."

Jack smiled softly. "You didn't break me."

"Sometimes it takes a while to tell." Isaac kissed him. He kept it soft but let it linger, collecting Jack's taste and the warmth of his body one last time. "Okay, you can go, but text me and eat something."

Jack grinned. "Yes, sir."

JACK PRESSED HIS HEAD TO THE STEERING WHEEL OF HIS TRUCK. THE bruising might be nearly gone but he could still feel it when he sat.

Stay another night. He wanted to, but it would be too tempting and too easy to go right back onto his knees. He had work in the morning. He had real life in the morning, where he would be looked at to lead. Despite saying the alphabet backward, which honestly, he could do while drunk, it was his party trick, he could still feel a faint haze of that lust fog pulling around the edges. He needed his own space to burn it off.

He turned on his truck and felt the twelve cylinders roar to life sending a heavy vibration through him. He pressed his forehead to the wheel again. Getting half a boner every time he turned on his truck was going to be a problem. Time to work on compartmentalizing.

He drove carefully on the way home. It felt almost like he was learning to drive again. For two days his body had not been fully his, and like his brain, it was taking a bit of extra focus to bring it all back together. He would also feel bad if he crashed on the way home, and left Isaac wondering what happened.

His bag felt heavier as he went through his front door. Isaac had said he'd put in a few books. He looked around his plain apartment and it truly felt plain. In two days he'd gotten used to the old wood, heavy furniture, and shelves of books. A lived-in coziness that he hadn't developed for himself.

He took out his phone and turned it on for the first time all weekend.

Made it home, he texted.

In less than thirty seconds his phone buzzed.

Good. Go eat something.

Before he could reply his phone buzzed again and again. A weekend worth of emails, voice mail notification, and a couple of texts came through. He swiped away the mailing list junk, ignored the texts from his sister about thanksgiving that year, and skim read the briefing on the Friday explosion. There were three people inside which made Jack think it wasn't connected to the leaks, but he couldn't rule it out entirely. His phone said he had three missed calls from Dan and one voicemail. He listened to his voicemail while he rummaged through the freezer. Isaac had said no microwave, but ravenous hunger caught up with him and he didn't want to wait for pizza to be delivered.

"Hey there. You are not picking up your phone and I know you don't like texts. I don't think you are as far out of town as you are saying you are. I'm at this party and there are three lovely and single people here and I am pretty sure at least one of them has got to be your type. So, call me back. And if you don't I'm going to assume you are with Kinky Married Complicated, in which case have a good time."

Kinky, married, complicated. That did sum it up. He also couldn't deny that he had a good time. He watched a Stouffer's lasagna spin around his microwave. He didn't like microwave meals, and he could always feel Clare's highly disapproving look in the back of his head, but after painfully long days, or weeks it was sometimes all he had the energy for.

The microwave dinged and he let it sit for the recommended three minutes. He'd been mocked for being the only person on earth who actually waited but he didn't care. He'd had enough steam burns in his life that he didn't put up with getting them from a microwaved lasagna.

Three minutes later he carefully pulled the film off the lasagna then sent a text.

Eating.

This time it was a good minute before he got a response.

We'll talk about the quality of your microwavable food at some point in the future.

Jack looked around. He was pretty sure there were no spy cameras in his apartment and it was simply a guess on Isaac's part, but it was still a little creepy.

Didn't want to wait for pizza.

Next time stay and I'll feed you.

CHAPTER 24

The street lights had blinked on and Isaac was stretched out on the couch, drifting in his own way when Amalie got home.

"How was your weekend?" she asked before Isaac could even say hello. "Dropping?"

He shook his head. "Nah, not hard, wafting gently downwards." She patted his feet and he lifted his legs so she could sit. "It was good, nice, he was good. And fucking hell is he amazing in rope"

She smiled at him. "I'm glad it was good. By the way, why are there yellow stickies on all our bookshelves?"

Isaac grandly waved his arm toward the shelves. "All our books are now arranged by the Library of Congress Catalogue system because my new boy has a bit of an obsessive streak and the LCC memorized."

"Neither of us has used the LCC since college. We'll never find anything in here."

"We couldn't find anything in here to begin with."

"That's true." Murrcat jumped onto Isaac's legs. He spread them to give the cat access to Amalie's lap. "So, your new boy makes excellent coffee, looks pretty in rope, organizes books, and judging by how relaxed and happy you look, I'm thinking he's a keeper."

He rubbed one of his feet along her leg. "I'm always happy."

"I know. But that happy is steadier when you've got someone that enables you to be your whole self. So, are you keeping him?"

Isaac gave a thumbs up. It wasn't even really a question. "If he's willing to let himself be kept."

Amalie reached over and tapped the center of his chest. "And how is this feeling?"

He knew she was going to ask and had been thinking on it, examining the stray thoughts and feelings he'd pushed down over the previous few days. "It's changing shape. Broader in some moments. It's scary," he answered honestly.

"These things usually are. And how's he feeling?"

"Not sure. I offered for him to spend another night, just relax, but I think he needed his space. Needed to get his own thoughts in order."

"For what it's worth, when it happens, I think being in love looks good on you."

He had been avoiding the word love. It was too big a word, too fast and if he went there he wasn't sure if Jack would follow. "I'm always in love."

Amalie smiled. "Yeah, but we're well-worn love. We've got some scuffs and scrapes and tread marks."

"I love how you compare our relationship to hardwood flooring."

"There's something to be said for shiny new love." Isaac stretched out and took her hand, giving it a squeeze. "I should probably get a chance to chat with him before you two get too much further and start admitting to feeling things."

Isaac knew that was going to be necessary, as necessary at their first long weekend together, but it wasn't going to be easy. That had always been the problem. A wife, even an incredibly supportive one, might be accepted in theory but not always in practice. He knew he was capable of loving equally, but he'd also never had the energy or will to put up with other's jealousies.

There had been a brief stint, hardly more than a day, many years earlier, when he had found himself jealous of Lydia, but he'd gotten over it when he accepted that Lydia loved Amalie as much as he did and it would be cruel to take or drive away that much love from someone's life.

"Be gentle. He's still skittish."

"I'm always gentle."

He snorted with laughter. Amalie lightly ran a single nail along the bottom of his foot. Isaac squealed and rolled from the couch flat onto his face.

"See, gentle."

THE MICROWAVE LASAGNA HAD NOT BEEN PARTICULARLY SATISFYING on a culinary level, but it provided enough carbs and protein to get Jack through until breakfast. Now fatigue was nipping at the edges of his mind but he didn't want to sleep, yet. Plus, he promised to text Isaac a SitRep.

He dropped his heavier than usual bag on his bed and opened it up. On top were a half dozen books each bristling with bookmarks. There was a yellow sticky on the top one.

One size doesn't fit all but there are bits and pieces you might find helpful.

He moved the books to his bedside table expecting to find his clothes and toiletries underneath. Instead there was a large dildo with a suction cup on one end. A second longer and narrower one. A pair of nipple clamps, a medium sized butt plug, and a cockring was also included. And tucked along the side, held together with red ribbon, were a half dozen thick

leather cuffs. His hands shook slightly as he took them out.
There was a note tied to the ribbon.

No matter what, these are yours.

There was of flash of something in his chest that felt like
pain then faded into something warm. He ran his fingers gently
across the leather and around the D rings. He'd never had his
own anything when it came to the life he tried not to live. It was
always things belonging to others, briefly on loan. He brought
the leather to his nose and breathed deep. There was the strong
smell of leather with a hint of sweat and sex. He'd have to look
up how to properly clean and care for them.

He was about to untie the ribbon when he felt the need to
stop and count. There were seven rings of leather. Two small
ones for the wrists, two larger ones for the ankles, two extra-
large for the thighs, then there was a seventh, thinner with only
one D ring at the front. It was a collar that must have come with
the set and Isaac was giving it to him to keep even if he couldn't
wear it.

He picked up his phone.

SitRep: Feel fine. Tired. Sore in good way. Will get some sleep.

He hit send and began unpacking the unused spare clothes
when his phone beeped.

Have you unpacked your bag?

Yes. Thank you for the books and other things.

That seemed innocuous enough.

You should let yourself enjoy them as often as possible.

Jack pictured sticking the dildo to the wall and fucking
himself on it as he had the night before. It was a strange
thought, arousing but he felt disconnected from it. He felt self-
conscious even though it would be something he'd do
completely alone. He ran the chain that connected the nipple
clamps through his fingers. He remembered the idea of wearing
them when he masturbated at home. At the time the thought
had sent lust screaming through his body, but now there was

again a disconnect as though those feelings and ideas belonged to someone else. Someone wild and uninhibited who lived with no doubts or responsibilities.

He knew he should reply to Isaac's last text.

Okay.

He hit send and instantly wished there was an unsend button. *Okay?!* That was about as unenthusiastic a reply as you could get. That was what a kid said after being told to take out the trash for the fiftieth time.

I'll do some reading tonight. He sent quickly hoping that sounded more engaged.

I hope you enjoy it. You don't have to take all or anything from those books but they might give you ideas or questions to ask. Get some sleep as well.

I will.

ISAAC PUT HIS PHONE ON HIS BEDSIDE TABLE.

"Your boy in one piece?" Amalie asked in the middle of her own text conversation with Lydia.

"So he says."

"You don't believe him?"

Isaac shrugged. "I'm not sure if he fully knows himself. I guess we'll find out."

JACK'S EYES SNAPPED OPEN A FEW SECONDS BEFORE HIS ALARM WAS due to sound. He stretched, his body twinging in a few places. He stretched again and it felt good. Better than a post workout stretch or even a standard post sex glow, he felt good. He padded to the bathroom, his mind already planning the day, at least as much as law enforcement days could ever be planned.

He stopped and looked at himself in the mirror. He'd slept naked, even his shorts feeling constrictive. He checked himself for marks and again only found ten tiny bruises at his hips. He closed his eyes, a shiver running through him, and a smile stretching his face. A laugh bubbled up in him. In the past he'd done his best to carefully conceal every possible mark on his body, even the ones no one would ever see. Isaac had been careful. So careful to respect his wishes, to keep his skin clear of any evidence of his desires, except for ten tiny little points on his hips where he'd held on a little too hard again.

His cock rose at the memory and he shivered as the touches of the weekend filled him. The night before he'd slid between his cold sheets, his mind still twisting with little threads of uncertainty and embarrassment at the new contents of his bookshelves.

He pressed his finger to one of the ten bruises, eyes still closed, face still stretched in a grin, he didn't need to see to find it. It hurt. More shivers but no fog of need or lust descended on him. Instead there was a clarity and a feeling that he was pretty sure was happiness.

CHAPTER 25

"Move, move, move!" Jack shouted waving his team out the back door, counting them as they went. Keeping low to avoid any more shots, he led his team across the open field of weeds and dry grass until they were safely behind the command station.

"Have we got everyone? Anyone hit?!"

His team spun around looking over themselves and each other. "Clear," they each reported back.

Jack grinned and turned to Dan and Gonzales. Dan had a welt coming up on his face under a splosh of yellow paint and Gonzales's uniform was painted in purple and green.

"Oh yeah! Team Beta for the win!" There were rounds of high-fives and dirty looks from the other teams.

"Okay everyone," their training officer cut into the celebrations. "Secure your weapons and get cleaned up, we'll debrief in twenty."

The teams moved to secure the realistic looking paintball guns. Dan stepped up close. "That was impressive."

Jack hadn't stopped grinning. "What can I say, feeling lucky."

"That was better than luck and you haven't stopped smiling all day."

"Must be the weather."

"Maybe. Maybe Kinky Married Complicated is treating you good. Getting your head in order.

Jack shrugged and kept smiling. "Maybe."

JACK DID HAVE A GOOD MEMORY FOR NUMBERS AND HAD memorized Isaac's number easily. He still put the number in his phone, and thanks to Dan listed it as KMC. Kinky Married Complicated.

He dialed the number from memory. It was Friday and it had been a good week. A court appearance where he didn't have a full panic attack over the tie. Two successful drug busts. Top marks in training. He'd managed to get off work and home before six and was feeling good and wanted to share. He thought about calling Clare and the coven, but they would be getting ready for the post theater crowd.

"Hello there." Isaac sounded happy but Jack suddenly felt self-conscious. Randomly calling was something boyfriends did, but he wasn't sure about repeat sex partners. It had felt right while he was dialing and Isaac had texted him to see how he was doing on Wednesday. "What's up?"

"Um... nothing. I just thought I'd call and... Is this a bad time?"

"This is a perfect time. I was just thinking about you. How have you been?"

"Good. It's been a good week. I'm... I've really been on my game this week. I think the weekend helped. Just, things have been clicking along this week. Got some actual victories. I wanted to tell you." It sounded lame to Jack's ears and he cringed.

"I'm glad to hear it." He could hear the smile in Isaac's voice and began to relax. "It's good that you're feeling good. I was worried I pushed you too far."

"No." Jack's answer was quick. "I think... I think it was finally just right."

"Porridge wasn't too hot or too cold?"

"Just right. How's your week been?" Jack asked quickly remembering basic manners.

"It's been good. Dead bodies and paperwork but I'm feeling pretty good. It's nice to have a good long stretch." Isaac let his words peter out into a warm and lazy sounding hum. It sent a wave of warmth through Jack. "Have a chance to do any reading this week?"

The warmth in Jack grew and began to settle low in his body. He sat down. "A little."

"Anything interesting?" Isaac's voice had shifted low and smooth.

"Some—" Jack's voice squeaked and he cleared his throat. "Some of the rope stuff is impressive." Jack had needed to close his eyes as it was too easy to picture himself in some of the designs.

"I have a friend who is more or less a professional. He has a studio for people who don't have enough space to do anything really complicated. He's even set up for suspensions."

Jack had seen a picture online once of a muscular man tied up in ropes and suspended to look liked the Hanged Man from the Tarot decks. He'd been hard in the picture and his eyes closed.

"Sounds interesting." Jack had to clear his throat again. "Have you ever done those, suspensions?"

"A few times. I prefer to have other people and a padded floor for safety sake. Doctor and all."

"Of course." Jack pictured other people viewing him as he dangled in a room. Looking him over more as a piece of art, an object. The trailing fear of recognition slid up but he knocked it down for a fantasy, of being bound and hard, the center of a web of rope, a valued thing. He must have made some noise.

"Do you like that thought? I like it."

"Yes."

"Are you home?"

"Yes," Jack answered, closing his eyes.

"Good. I don't know if I mentioned it enough but you look amazing in rope. That strong body of yours bound and still. You don't try to struggle. You become part of it. And every time I bind you your cock starts leaking at almost the first touch of rope. Are you leaking now?"

"I don't know." Jack was hard in his jeans. That he knew.

"Why don't you take it out and check?"

Jack unzipped and pushed down his jeans and briefs not even thinking about refusing. The air in his apartment was cool but soothing. A drop of pre-cum pushed its way to the already slick head of his cock.

"Well?"

"Yes."

"Good. Are you holding your cock?"

"Yes?"

"Let it go. I'll tell you when you can touch."

Jack moaned and pried his hand off his own dick. He could have left his hand and lied. Isaac would have never known but what would be the point of having someone like Isaac if he did. He felt his nipples harden and his ass squeeze around nothing.

"Good boy. I know you did as told. Tell me about the rest of your body. Your nipples?"

"Hard. They hurt."

"And your ass?"

Jack whimpered thinking about it. "Empty."

"A terrible state for an ass like yours to be in. Where are you in your apartment?"

"The living room."

"Go find that plug I gave you. Get it in you, no teasing yourself. Just get yourself filled and sit on the edge of your bed. Don't
take your jeans off all the way when you sit. Leave them around
your ankles."

"Yes, sir." Jack's legs wobbled as much as his voice. He was
surprised he could stand. He stumbled into his bedroom and
pulled the plug and some lube from his nightstand. He tried to
hold the phone between his cheek and shoulder while he
spread the lube.

"Put me on speaker phone. It'll be easier."

"Yes, sir."

"Now tell me what you're doing."

"Um... putting lube on the plug."

"Good. For you it will probably be easiest to simply reach
between your legs and slide it in. One good push should do it.
I've seen you take far more."

One of the dildos Isaac had put in his bag was at least twice
as thick as the plug. Still he took a deep breath before pushing it
in. He groaned and sat on the bed hard pushing it in further.

"I bet you feel more relaxed now."

"Yes, sir." And he did. Not that he had been truly tense
before, but now he felt boneless like he'd slipped into a hot bath.

"You should do that at the end of every day. Fill your ass,
make yourself cum. A nice shot of endorphins for your body
and mind."

It did, in that moment at least, sound like a good idea.

"Now where was I? Oh yes, you tied up. Mindless and
desperate. I have a bondage bench I haven't assembled in a
while, but it's strong enough to hold your weight. I could easily
strap you into it. It would leave you spread and exposed. I
could do whatever I wanted to that gorgeous ass of yours. Fill
it, flog it, fill it with something even larger. Fuck you over and
over. Make you cum as many times as I want until you are

simply wild. Desperate for me to stop but begging me for more."

Jack whimpered. He couldn't respond. His head was too full of the images Isaac was painting.

"Pinch your nipples through your shirt, hard. I want to hear you cry out."

Jack did, the desperate cry perhaps louder than he intended.

"Good boy." Now Isaac's voice was low and a growl. "Grab your cock now. Squeeze it tight but don't move your hand. Don't you dare cum. How does it feel, your cock in your hand?"

"Good," Jack squeaked out.

"I bet it does. I like the way it feels as well. Thick, hot, heavy. The way it twitches and swells right before you cum. Not that you'll get to feel it next time. Next time I put you in that nice steel tube the moment you're through the doors. Leave it on for at least a day. Maybe longer. Leave it until you don't even bother thinking about your dick anymore."

Jack whimpered again squeezing his cock that much tighter. He couldn't stop himself rocking back and forth pushing that plug in deeper.

"Maybe I'll send it home with you. Every night you come home and slide a plug deep into your body and your dick into a cage, locking it away until morning. I'll give you the vibrating plug so you can still cum, still drain yourself out. You'll just do it with the feel of steel in your hand instead of flesh."

Tears slid down Jack's cheeks and his whole body shook.

"Go ahead and cum for me now."

Jack moved his hand ever so slightly and came screaming.

THE SMALL COUCH IN ISAAC'S OFFICE WASN'T QUITE LARGE ENOUGH to properly stretch out on but he tried. He had listened to Jack simply breathe for several minutes after cumming with a shout that had Isaac jerking the phone away from his ear. Then he talked him through cleaning up and kept going until Jack sounded fully coherent again.

When Jack's number had popped up on the caller ID he hadn't planned for it to turn into phone sex, especially not a bout of it that intense. He couldn't say he was sorry though. It was nice to hear that Jack was in a good place after their weekend together. With any luck regular time together would keep him in that good and happy place.

Isaac had certainly felt extra pep in his step the last week.

There was a knock on his door and Amalie popped her head in. "Finished your little afternoon phone delight?" Her voice was light and teasing.

"Pot, kettle." Amalie had regular *special* conversations with Lydia when their work schedules got too complicated to spend time together.

"I wasn't complaining, only commenting. Though if you've gotten up to the naughty phone call stage then I think it's time for your boy and I to have a chat."

Isaac knew that was true but he still felt uneasy. "Can you wait until tomorrow to text him? I think he's still ... fragile."

"I'll be gentle. I promise."

CHAPTER 26

The sound of Jack's heart racing was deafening in his ears. Any training provided by either the military or the police in self-control was failing. Panic gripped him, his hands shook, and he felt like he might puke.

You knew this was going to happen, a dark, lonely part of himself scolded.

He read over the text again. *...maybe grab some coffee.*

It sounded polite and reasonable but why wouldn't it be. Isaac had always said his wife was fine with it. They'd had a perfectly nice breakfast once, the three of them, but she was still his wife and he was...

A nice dumb convenient fucktoy, a pet, that part of him snarled again. *What did you think you were? Lover? Boyfriend? You think you can just call him randomly because you want to talk? This is what happens when you start getting ideas above your station and that is what she is going to tell you.*

Jack ran to his bathroom barely making it to the toilet before he lost his dinner in great heaves. He gripped the porcelain as if he could drive his nails into it and told himself that the tears in the corner of his eyes were from vomiting.

He forced his way to his feet and stumbled to the sink. He tried not to look in the mirror as he ferociously brushed his teeth.

Coward. He looked up at himself with his regulation haircut, broad chest, and his blue eyes. *Dumbass coward.*

He dropped the lid on the toilet seat and sat down, his hands still shaking as he considered what to text back.

He swiped over to the phone and dialed Isaac's number, wanting to hear his soothing voice and at the same time not wanting him to pick up and confirm all of Jack's dark thoughts.

"Hello?"

"Hey." Jack heard the rough cracks in his own voice.

"Breathe. Deep slow breaths."

Jack tried to obey but each breath was shaky.

"Keep breathing. It's okay. Five seconds in, seven seconds out. Keep breathing." Jack tried to count in his head. "When you can breathe clear tell me what's wrong." Jack tried to calm himself but it wasn't working. "Do you need me to come over?"

Jack shook his head forgetting for moment that Isaac couldn't see him. "No," he croaked out.

"Okay. Did something happen at work?"

"No."

"Is this about the text you probably got from Amalie about five minutes ago?"

Jack nodded again like an idiot then made a sound he hoped was in the affirmative.

"Okay. You need to keep breathing, and I know you shouldn't say this to someone who is panicking but you don't need to panic about anything."

Jack made a noise between a squeak and a whimper.

"She just wants to get to know you without me hovering around. That's it. Nothing aggressive. It's not a pissing match. She knows I like you and if you're going to be around she wants to get to know you. You don't have to. You don't have to do anything you don't want. Is that okay?"

Jack made another affirmative noise unable to get the word yes past his lips despite the calming effect Isaac's voice was having.

"Keep breathing for me. Five in, seven out."

Jack moved his lips slightly as he breathed forcing himself to stick to the count.

"She doesn't bite. I promise. She just wants to get to know you. Tell her about your coven in Boston."

Jack's breath lost its rhythm. "I was never officially a member."

"And yet they had you dancing around a maypole. Tell me there are pictures of that somewhere."

"Probably," Jack lied. There was a half dozen of them stuck on the wall in the break room at Coffea Contenuto. They were right next to the ones from the time he accidentally ingested a special brownie and thought it would be a great idea to strip naked and paint himself green.

"You honestly have nothing to worry about. Amalie likes you. She is very impressed by both your coffee making and library skills, and she knows you make me happy."

"Okay." Jack still didn't feel particularly calm but he felt less likely to throw up his stomach lining.

"It will be okay. I promise. She already likes you and I like you."

"Okay," Jack answered only because he felt like some words should be coming out of his mouth, though only about half of what Isaac was saying was sinking in.

"You are already important to me."

That did get through. "I am?" Important was good. People took care of things that were important.

"Yes, Jack. You are."

Isaac hung up the phone with a long sigh after nearly twenty minutes of calming Jack down.

"Was that Jack?" Amalie asked, deep furrows of worry on her brow.

"In a dead panic."

"I thought I'd been pretty pleasant. You saw the text."

"It wasn't you, really. I think someone, somewhere, fucked with his head, hard. My money is on family."

"That's usually a safe bet." Amalie sat down next to him and Murrcat followed. "I don't have to talk to him if you don't think he'll handle it well. You did say he was fragile."

A part of him wanted to keep Jack wrapped up safe and away from everyone, but he couldn't see how that wouldn't lead to Jack feeling like a bit on the side as opposed to an equal partner. "No," he said after a long sigh. "He's going to need to hear he's welcome from you. Besides you're usually better at expressing my emotions than I am."

"I'd accuse you of gender stereotyping if it wasn't painfully true in our case. How *are* you feeling? Just so I can know what to tell him."

When Isaac had been in med school there had been long lectures about putting aside feelings. When he'd shifted into law enforcement there was even more emphasis on setting aside feelings and looking at facts. Sometimes it could be hard to lure those feelings back. Sometimes he was scared to let them back. Sometimes they broke down the door and grabbed him hard. "If I let myself... Yeah, it won't take much if I let myself. He's smart, smarter than he lets himself believe. And he's kind. I've seen him on the stand a few times. Even when he's testifying against very bad people, there's not the anger or hate you get from others. More, sadness from it. I think that speaks to something kind in him. Strong. Stronger than he thinks. So, yeah." Isaac tapped his chest where he knew there was a Jack sized empty space forming. "Won't take much."

⚜

AMALIE HAD SUGGESTED THAT JACK PICK THEIR MEETING PLACE. He knew she was trying to make him feel at ease by letting him choose the field. He kept telling himself this wasn't a battle. This was coffee with someone who, if he continued with Isaac, would be at least by extension part of his life. He still rolled a bottle of honey between his hands with nervous energy. Amalie sat down across from him and he put down the honey.

"I hear it's becoming quite trendy to put honey in coffee," she said as an opener.

"Hides the flavor of the coffee. If the coffee is any good and you want it sweet, stick to cane sugar."

"And if the coffee isn't any good?"

Jack shrugged. "Then why drink it."

Amalie grinned. It was pleasant, much like Isaac's. "You're a cop. You can't tell me you've never drunk bad coffee."

"I've drunken lots of bad coffee. Let it cool then chug. Try not to taste it." Jack looked down at his hands and found he was twisting a napkin into knots.

"I'm just here to talk, not give you a talking to. Big difference." Her voice was calm and soothing, again much like Isaac's. He could see how they worked.

A waitress came over to take their orders. He knew he shouldn't order anything that would make him even more jittery, but they were at one of his favorite coffee shops which was unfortunately a trek from his apartment or work. "Cafe Del Tiempo." The waitress gave him a sideways look. It wasn't a common order. Then she turned to Amalie.

"Why don't you order for me?"

"Um..." He wondered if this was some sort of weird test. She had liked the latte he'd made but that was generic considering where they were. "Double Con Panna." The waitress made a note then left.

"I don't think I've ever had a Double Con Panna."

Jack shrugged. "It's just a double shot espresso with whipped cream, but they do the cream here fresh with virtually no sugar, so it doesn't overwhelm the flavor of the coffee."

"Sounds good." There was a silence and Jack was aware of being watched. "Isaac likes you."

Jack's head shot up. "I... I like him too."

Like? What are you, ten? Like is a pretty sad term for what you know you've been feeling.

"That's good to hear. He isn't always easy to like. He has a history of being an oblivious idiot, occasionally a jerk. Closing himself off when he should open up." Jack nodded, not entirely sure what to say. "Though, for all the times he plays the detached doctor, and all the horrible things he's seen people do to each other, he does not believe that the human capacity for love is a finite thing. Neither do I. But that's a rare belief."

"I've..." It was the first-time love had been mentioned and it sent his pulse racing. She had said *like* before. Isaac *liked* him. "I've never..."

"Been in love?"

Jack shook his head and began twisting the napkin around his fingers again. His hands had always felt too large, his fingers too thick. He hadn't noticed as he'd been growing up, but could still remember how tiny the espresso cups looked in his hands when he'd done a shift on his first leave from the army. He took a deep breath and tried to find that place of calm under fire. He looked up and properly met Amalie's gaze.

"That's better," she said, smiling again. "You should be able to look your boyfriend's wife in the eye. I can understand the need for privacy but there's no need for shame."

"Boyfriend?" Jack's voice squeaked and his brain froze on that word.

"That's how he thinks of you. Or at least wants to if you'll let him. How do you think of him?"

For the first time her voice had a hint of an edge to it.

"I just thought—" Jack's brain was scrambling for words. He knew he sounded like an idiot and it was making it worse. It always did. "I figured—" He shrugged, his eyes once again firmly locked on the table.

"That he was going to keep you in the back room like one of his toys?"

He shrugged again even as her words rang painfully true. She reached across the table and settled her hand over his. It was light, like one of the chickadees hopping around the table looking for crumbs, but her skin was liberally sprinkled with, what to Jack looked like splash burns, probably from chemicals from her life as a scientist.

"He's better than that." Her voice was soft. "If you want him to be. If you just want this to be a relationship of convenience, something physical when you need it, he'll accept that, but I know he's making a place for more." Jack nodded, now truly unsure what to say. "I won't lie, he comes with as much baggage as anyone else, and far more complexities than others you could find, and that's not going to change, but he won't lie to you, he will respect you, and he'll do his best for you."

Their waitress put their orders down on the small table forcing Amalie to move her hand from his. Jack decided to leave the waitress an extra-large tip. If she hadn't come he might have cracked right there in public. It still felt like something in him had just been stripped raw.

"Lemon in coffee?"

He looked at his Cafe Del Tiempo with the espresso in a small cup next to a glass filled with ice and a lemon wedge. "The lemon can bump up certain flavors in particular beans. Not many places serve it though."

"I'll try it next time." She took a sip of her Con Panna getting whipped cream on her nose. She wiped it off. "This is pretty good too."

TEXT WASN'T THE BEST WAY TO CONDUCT A RELATIONSHIP BUT AFTER coffee with Amalie, Isaac didn't want Jack to feel crowded or badgered. He'd gotten her report on the conversation a few hours earlier. They'd discussed coffee, Isaac's emotions and relationship skills, more about coffee, how she and Isaac had met (at a party where he had stopped her from drunk dialing her parents in anger), skimmed Jack's sexual history, and she generally agreed that someone needed to wrap him up, feed him soup, and tell him he's loved on a regular basis. The discussion of Isaac's emotions had led to some emotion on Jack's part and her thinking the feelings are reciprocal, but she'd done her bit and it was his turn to figure out the rest. Also, apparently, there are people who put lemon in coffee.

How are you doing? He figured that was neutral and not too pushy, and text would give Jack the time to think over his answer instead of letting silence hang on the phone.

Isaac was two pages into a paper on the accuracy of projectiles when used from a moving vehicle when his phone buzzed.

I'm okay. There was a second buzz. *How are you?*

Good. Was thinking about you. Isaac looked at the text and made a decision. *Would you like to go out later this week? Get dinner, maybe catch a movie?* He hit send and carefully put his phone on the desk. He wondered what Jack was doing, where he was. Was he at home? Had he gone to the gym? Was he hanging out with other friends? It was a minute but it felt like an hour.

Yes.

CHAPTER 27

Sitting in front of the Dog Box Bar at three in the morning was something Jack never thought he'd do again, until his team landed a new assignment. He'd been feeling good. He had a proper date with Isaac that was fun. He hadn't freaked out. They had talked a few times since. Had phone sex and made tentative plans for a 'back to nature' camping trip that would probably leave them with bug bites, poison oak, and memories they could laugh about later. Dan said he was positively glowing. Now he was back in front of the Dog Box.

"As far as we can tell the bar end of the place is legit but that'll really be up to the accountants to untangle." Jack focused as hard as he could on his CO and the detective who was doing the briefing, and tried to compartmentalize his brain while his team and Dan's was shown a layout of the bar and adjoining buildings. "However, we believe half the E in the city is being moved through the back rooms. The Feds think this is their case but screw them. We've got better intel and that intel is that one of the main money men is going to be there tonight." Jack heard one of his men give a dismissive snort and he gave him a hard look. Everyone on SWAT had become suspicious of drug related 'intel'. "This is a leather bar with a bunch of really disturbing kinky ass shit going down in the back rooms. People rent them out and do fuck knows what."

I've seen kinkier. The Dog Box was not known as a top-quality establishment, certainly not the worst but there were better.

"We can pretty much assume anyone tied up isn't going to be our money guy." The men laughed and Jack gave them all hard looks. "We've got descriptions and surveillance photos so just round up anyone who's moving and stick them in the main room."

Jack gripped his hands in to fists to keep them from shaking. This was going to be bad. He could just feel it.

"This is technically delivering search and arrest warrants. Try not to shoot anyone or crack any heads. We don't want the ACLU up our ass on this one."

People laughed. Jack swallowed hard. He wanted to vomit.

Now his palms were sweating. He wanted to rub them dry on his pants, but his team was watching him as they prepared to leave the van and rush the front doors. Dan's team was taking the back, which would put his team as the ones going room to room. He was glad for that. Dan obviously knew something about what he needed and was maybe less likely to judge the things they found and Jack could hopefully hide in the crowd of the main room and not encounter anyone who might recognize him.

Their CO received a signal from someone inside and they were given the go.

The bouncer at the door was the first to freeze. Some of the patrons ran, they were tackled. Some dropped to the floor with their hands up. More than a few pulled-out cell phones and yelled about calling their lawyers. The naked boys in leather dog masks in small cages were left where they were. The first-time Jack had seen it, his thought was that it constituted a major safety hazard in case of fire or earthquake. Now they were simply people who were contained. His team was usually pretty good at sorting out legitimate threats from people in the wrong place at the wrong time, but they hadn't been given nearly enough intel, people were yelling, there was gear that could be used as weapons, there were too many civilians. Dan was driving people from the back rooms to the main one, and Jack could feel it about to go to shit, just because someone wanted to get one up on the feds.

So much for hiding.

Jack stepped up onto the small stage that was sometimes used for demonstrations aware that there were several phones still pointed at him.

"Quiet!" he yelled as loud and deep as he could while trying to channel his third-grade teacher who could silence an entire yard with a single word. "We are looking for *one* person. If you are not that *one* person you will be free to go as soon as we find that *one* person." Dan's team came through the back door of the main room driving men dressed in heavy leather, as well as scantily clad to naked men ahead of them. The detectives followed pulling off masks and holding up pictures. "If you happen to be the person pushing quantities of E through the city, would you please raise your hand and save everyone a lot of time." Anyone who had their hands up quickly put them down.

Jack pointed at the bartender who had left his hands up. "You."

He slammed his arms down. "It's my first night here I swear I don't know shit really, please believe me!"

"Open the cages before we write you up on fire code violations."

"Yes, sir." The bartender squeaked and Jack wanted to laugh.

A patron near the stage had his mask pulled off. It was black silk and out of place with the general leather motif. A detective held up a picture. "Got him."

The suspect was whipped around, facing the stage as the

cuffs were slapped on. He looked familiar to Jack, familiar and as out of place as the mask. Something about the way he held himself. He looked up at Jack and Jack recognized him. Hugh Lancing. His stomach clenched. The whole room seemed to condense down around him then tilt. Hugh looked at him, squinting while his rights were read. Then he smiled. A slow grin stretched his face.

'Jack,' he mouthed silently before being dragged out the front door.

Jack didn't move. He couldn't move. He couldn't hear. He wasn't sure if he was breathing. Someone was moving close to him but his vision refused to clear. Someone touched his shoulder. He sprinted outside having never moved so fast in his life. He knelt over the gutter and puked. It was blinding, shaking and spasming his whole body. It felt like it might never end. He felt a hand on his shoulder again. He turned his head enough to see Dan looking at him face full of concern. Jack heaved again. When it finally stopped, he looked up at Dan.

"I'd ask if you're okay."

Lie, lie, lie, lie.

"Think I need to find a new favorite food truck."

KMC FLASHED ON THE SCREEN OF JACK'S PHONE. HE'D BEEN GIVEN a day off to switch over from the night raid and he'd taken a day off to be sick, then he'd crawled his way back to work forcing a smile and jumping at shadows. Isaac had called. He'd called and he'd texted and he'd called again. He'd left a few messages but Jack hadn't listened to them. He'd only read the first few texts. He went to answer them but each time his fingers froze thinking of Hugh's long thin smile.

How are you doing?
How was your day?

Would you like to grab dinner?

Jack had stopped reading them after that. Dinner, after what happened. He'd hardly eaten in two days. He'd known it was going to happen at some point. Known his luck would run out. He'd thought it was going to happen in the army really, that he'd be sent home in disgrace. This was worse. He had respect now, authority. His men looked up to him, expected him to lead. Every time the phone rang his heart stopped in panic. He was waiting for the call from Internal Affairs. It would only be a matter of time, he was sure. Hugh seemed the type to name names, make deals. There would be a call. 'What is the nature of your relationship with Hugh Lancing,' they would ask. 'None,' he'd answer truthfully. But that a man like Hugh even knew his name would send IA digging. Club fees for the Windsor, secret email addresses to get him into dark corners of the Internet. And they'd follow him to Isaac, then Amalie, then Lydia.

Jack started deleting texts and call logs. He tried to remember if Isaac had ever called his land line.

Another text came through telling him he had a message.

Idiot. How was he supposed to protect them if Isaac kept leaving messages? He could say stop. Just text stop. Isaac would stop but he'd want to know why. That was the thing. He had no way of breaking this off without leaving more of a trail.

Jack took a breath and listened to the most recent message.

"Hi, it's me. I'm afraid I'm coming across all clingy. It's just you haven't answered any of my messages or texts or anything. You're usually really good about that so I'm worried. I'm legitimately worried. And I'm sorry. If I came on too strong or moved too fast or just not giving you what you need, then I'm sorry. Please call, text, smoke signal. I just want to know if you're alright. Or if you're not alright, I want to know why and what I can do to make it better. I'm sorry, for whatever it is. I'm sorry."

He clamped his jaw tight trying not to cry then pressed three to delete the message.

Isaac rubbed at his face. It wasn't that late but he hadn't slept well. The first night he figured Jack had been busy. Maybe he was on the night shift. But then he'd gotten another day of silence, then another.

He thought it had been going well. It felt like it. They had a proper date which Jack seemed to enjoy. Talked a few times. There was even phone sex. They'd made other plans. Then there was nothing, and as the radio silence continued all the feelings he'd been holding at bay managed to break through. And it hurt.

Amalie sat beside him and put a cup of coffee in his hands. He knew it was the cheap stuff they put in the old coffeemaker. The good stuff was still sitting next to the espresso machine. "Still nothing?"

He shook his head. "I don't know what I did."

She put her arm around him and he leaned into her side. "There's nothing to say you did anything."

"I must have done something." It was always something he did. He moved too fast, or not fast enough. Didn't show enough emotion but insisted on acceptance of his life.

"It could have been me. I don't like sugar coating things. I could have scared him off."

"No. He was good. We talked, we made plans. It had to have been..." He sipped his coffee. It tasted flat.

"Hey, he could have lost his phone and there's some asshole reading your messages to his friends and laughing their asses off."

Isaac chuckled even though he knew that wasn't what happened.

"Are you willing to consider finding him in person? You know where he works."

Isaac shook his head even though he'd been contemplating

walking into the County Sheriff's Office and demanding to see Jack. "No. His privacy is important to him. Plus, you know, creepy."

"Yeah." She took the coffee from his hands and put it on the table before pulling him into a hug.

"I thought he was it," He mumbled into the skin of her neck. "I really thought so."

"So, did I." He raised his head to look at her. Her face was full of empathy and that somehow made it hurt more. "We still don't know what happened. And if he's not the one then I still believe you have someone out there waiting for you. I really do."

CHAPTER 28

The industrial strength coffee cup easily withstood Jack drumming his fingers along the rim. He didn't drink the coffee inside. Dan sat across from him eating his lunch. They decided that it looked weird if all three of the team leads met together outside work on a regular basis without the cover of group or social events. They all knew it was spy movie paranoia and probably absolutely no one was paying attention to them, but after two more duds and an abandoned meth house blowing up on Gonzales, they needed to do something.

"We need to get into the paper work. There's got to be some trail about where those tips are coming from. Even if it's an anonymous source they have to be landing somewhere. It's either that or go right to IA."

Jack did not want to deal with IA. And it wasn't for 'I'm not a rat' reasons. He was willing to rat like hell if it kept his guys from getting blown sky high, but their evidence was all still circumstantial.

"We can do IA but if I'm going to be spotted walking into their offices, I want to bring them something other than vague theories."

Dan sighed. "We need more friends. No, I've got lots of friends, we need connections."

"We wouldn't be in SWAT if we were politically minded enough to make the kind of connections that would be useful here."

"That's true."

Jack knew he had one connection, sort of. Someone no one would expect him to know. Isaac said he'd talk to Lydia, but he never mentioned if he had and she had never contacted him. He could ask. It had been a month with no calls from IA or lawyers involved in the Hugh Lancing case. His phone was heavy in his pocket. A month since the raid on the Dog Box and three weeks since Isaac had stopped trying to contact him. His last message had been 'for whatever I've done, I'm sorry'.

"Uh-oh. You're making that face."

Jack looked up. He'd been staring into his cooling coffee, not really seeing it. "What face?"

"That thinking about whatever it is that went wrong to put you in a shitty mood for the last month."

"I haven't been—"

"You've been incredibly shitty. Not asshole shitty. Shitty with yourself shitty. You spend every free minute in the gym trying to burn yourself out or something. Not healthy. I can only assume things went wrong with KMC which is a shame because you had that whole 'I'm in love' vibe going, but you shouldn't be damaging yourself over it."

Jack didn't so much as blink through Dan's little monologue. He wanted to argue that he was fine and did not need to defend his workout schedule.

"I wasn't in love."

"Keep telling yourself that. Maybe you'll believe it."

THE PARAGRAPH ISAAC HAD BEEN TRYING TO READ FOR THE LAST five minutes made no sense. Actually, it probably made perfect sense as it was the cover article in that month's *Lancet*. His brain just didn't want to focus on it. The house was too quiet. Amalie was working late at the lab, trying to force a breakthrough before a venture capital meeting. Murrcat had wandered off somewhere. He was half tempted to go to bed early but it was barely seven and he knew he wouldn't sleep. He considered doing something like jogging but he hadn't run since high school gym and he wasn't about to start. It wouldn't help anyway.

The sparking energy in his body and mind wanted a very specific outlet. Two months and he'd expected some word from Jack after whatever the crisis had been passed. He was hoping for at least an 'I'm okay' text. Even a 'leave me alone' would at least be some acknowledgment.

He considered rearranging some of the books. Maybe Jack's librarian senses would tingle and he'd show up at the door with a cute little scowl that Isaac could kiss away.

He mentally slapped himself. Getting sappy over ex-subs wouldn't do him any good. It never had in the past and it wouldn't now. Jack was probably sinking back into a pattern of complete self-denial. Hopefully what little time he'd had with Isaac showed him he could do better than whatever he'd been getting before. Isaac grabbed his keys and shoes. He wasn't about to go running, but maybe if he stomped around the block fifty or so times he'd be tired enough to sleep.

JACK YANKED THE TIE FROM AROUND HIS NECK AS HE PUSHED through the courtroom doors. He checked his watch. It hadn't even been twenty minutes but he'd spent most of it sure he was about to blackout. He couldn't have come across well. Even the judge asked him if he was okay. "Flu," he'd lied smoothly and everyone in the courtroom had leaned away. There was a bad flu going around, it kept taking out whole juries, so people believed him. It had been an easy lie. Breathing had become harder over the previous three months, along with focusing, but lying had grown easier.

He pressed his head against the cool unfinished concrete of the courthouse halls. He knew what he needed to do. He had a whole list of things he needed to do. The priorities kept shifting around but the items stayed consistent. 'Get a therapist' floated to the top after every court day where he felt like he was about to be strangled by his own clothing. That was hard though. Hard and expensive. Find a new Dom. But that was even worse than a therapist. Normally it had taken longer than three months before his head got to a place where he needed it but he'd gotten used to Isaac, how he did it, what it did to him. Hardly two months they had known each other but it had ruined him. It wasn't hitting his job, yet. He could split his mind. Keep the part that kicked in doors cold and logical while the rest of him screamed and craved.

Just quit your job. It kept sounding like a more and more reasonable idea. The coven would have him back. They could probably even find him someone in the lifestyle. He'd have to face his family but it would be better than the day he froze up or zoned out during an operation and got someone killed.

"Jack?"

He spun around blinking hard a couple of times just in case he *had* finally cracked and was hallucinating or something.

"Hi." Isaac's voice was quiet and his face serious.

"Hi."

"How have you been?"

"Fine," Jack said, the lie feeling unbearably blatant.

"Um... Look before anything else, I just want to say I'm sorry. I know you have your reasons. I know my life is complicated, and it's more to ask of anyone and I'm sorry. And, please, just—" Isaac stammered. "I know there is someone out there who is perfect for you and when you find them you are going to be so happy but please, please don't undervalue yourself. You are so amazing and what you have to give is just spectacular. Please just make sure whomever you find is worthy of you."

Jack blinked at Isaac. He didn't know what to say. He wanted to tell Isaac it wasn't his fault. It was nothing he did or didn't do. He wanted to say he had been happy. Happier than he'd ever been. He was trying to protect him, protect all of them. He opened his mouth but no words came out. Not so much as a squeak. He tried to move. To grab Isaac and pull him close. He wanted to drop to the floor but his knees locked tight.

Isaac reached out and lay a hand on his chest for a fraction of a second before rushing off.

THE HEAVY DOOR TO ISAAC'S OFFICE CLOSED WITH A SOFT CLICK. He leaned against it before sliding to the floor. It was going to happen sooner or later. They went to work in the same complex of buildings. They were in court at least once a week. He had told himself that when it happened he would let Jack take the lead but when he saw Jack, face pressed to the wall, a tie dangling from his fingers he couldn't walk away.

He'd tried to forget Jack. Tried to move on. He even went back to the Windsor Club but only ended up finishing a bottle of wine on his own and getting a cab home. He knew he could have confronted Jack face to face long before running into him but Jack had been so afraid of people knowing it didn't seem right to lurk outside of the station waiting for him.

He wanted to snatch that tie from his hands and burn it. It was ugly and would be no loss. He wanted to bundle Jack up, take him home, take care of him, give him peace. Jack's silence had made it clear that was no longer his place and it hurt. Three months and all it took was a minute to make it hurt like new.

CHAPTER 29

J ack felt the slither around his body in the dim light. He knew he should be panicking, ripping away the serpents that would try to crush him, but he wasn't, he wasn't sure why. He looked down at himself. Colors were winding their way around his body and down his limbs. They twisted into ropes, pulling around him tightly, holding his limbs spread and his body still. Then he was flying. He dangled there in a room of nothing. Upside down, one leg tucked behind the other, arms spread like the Hanged Man.

Isaac was there now. He was in black and slid in and out of the darkness of the room. His hands roamed over the skin not covered in rope. Words were whispered in his ear so faintly he couldn't understand.

Isaac kissed him deep, tasting of green tea. Then he woke up.

It was too late or too early, and there was a burn between his legs and low in his stomach. He wanted to cry in annoyance. He grabbed his erect cock and stroked it as fast and as hard as he could, just wanting it over with quickly. It refused to happen though. It hurt and that edge was just out of reach. His ass squeezed on nothing and he felt so empty. He had things now. A drawer that he never opened, with things that would at least give him a momentary shadow of what he wanted. He sucked two fingers of his other hand and reached behind himself. It hurt, his fingers not nearly wet enough but he pretended that bit of hurt was coming from someone else, there for a reason he actually wanted. It was enough and he came on his clean sheets with a frustrated scream.

❦

HE'D ONLY DRIFTED BACK TO SLEEP WHEN HIS PHONE WENT OFF. IT was the special, extra loud, not to be ignored, emergency ring.

"Hello." His heart was already racing and he was halfway to the bathroom. He needed to wash the cum off his legs if nothing else.

"All teams in, full briefing, half hour," his CO said before hanging up without an extra word.

❦

USUALLY IF THERE WAS AN ALL-IN IN THE MIDDLE OF THE NIGHT, IT was for a riot or disaster. Jack flipped through the news radio stations as he drove in using his light bar to speed, but the city seemed quiet and all the disasters on the radio were far from his jurisdiction.

He ran into Gonzales at the door. They exchanged questioning looks but said nothing. Dan was already in the briefing room. There were more questioning looks and shrugs. It only took another five minutes for the rest of the team members to arrive.

Their CO stepped to the front of the room. "I'm sorry for the early morning wakeup call but this is going to be a hard one. We're going in after one of our own." There was a murmur around the room. Dread filled Jack. Normally if you arrest another cop you do it quietly after work if you want to keep it quiet, or publicly in the middle of the day if you're making a statement. Three full SWAT teams in the middle of the night means you are expecting it to get ugly.

"Some of you may have noticed a problem with drug related tips over the last few months."

Jack bit back the urge to say something incredibly sarcastic.

"This department has sadly had a leak. That leak has been traced back to an Officer Jones in Narcotics. Unfortunately, the leak has been the least of his bad behavior. He has been keeping some bad company and doing some bad things with them. Ideally, we will be picking up some of his associates with him tonight. They will be armed. They will be dangerous. And as it's four in the morning they will hopefully be asleep. We gave you minimal warning in case there's another leak. We don't believe so but it's always a risk. You are to maintain full radio silence until you go in. Understood?" There were nods and a chorus of yesses, but Jack had a bad feeling about the night and glancing around at the others he was sure he wasn't the only one.

GUNSHOTS DON'T SOUND LIKE THEY DO IN THE MOVIES. JACK winced in pain at the high-pitched crack of a bullet flying past, like the crack of a whip but worse. The ringing in his ears would last the rest of the night. Officer Jones had indeed been keeping some spectacularly bad company, and instead of spending the night at his little condo, he'd taken to spending it with an unsavory woman and her heavily armed colleagues, in a much nicer house. Most of the house had been quickly secured but it only took one light sleeper with a voice that carried to wake up the rest.

Jack threw himself around a corner then pressed himself against a wall. There was the slice of shattered glass across his cheek as a bullet from a department issued weapon shattered a mirror. Blood ran down his cheek but he didn't feel any pain. The adrenalin and endorphins where taking care of that. He'd feel the pain later when he had the time.

"Officer Jones," the Internal Affairs investigator shouted down the hall. "Jones, you know how this works. You know there's only a couple of ways for this to end."

There was another shot, sharp and loud, with a small thump as the bullet sunk into the drywall. Jack crouched low.

There was a shot from somewhere else in the house and the sound of furniture breaking.

"Living room secure," came a breathless voice over the radio. "Jones is the only one left."

"Confirm."

"Did you hear that shot, Jones?" the IA man called out. "That was the last of them. You're the last one left. Just put your gun in the hall and come on out. This night doesn't have to get any uglier than it already has."

There was quiet. The whole house was quiet. Jack heard a dog bark in the distance and a garbage truck a few blocks away.

There was a single gunshot, then silence.

JACK WAS THE LAST TO DRAG HIMSELF FROM THE HOUSE, DOING ONE final sweep. The paramedics saw the blood on his face and descended. He did his best to shoo them away while he checked over all his men. One had dislocated a shoulder trying to wrestle a far larger suspect to the ground. Another had gotten a bullet in the chest, stopped by his vest. He'd probably cracked a few ribs but he was lucky. There were plenty of rounds that could go right through Kevlar these days. There were two bodies in the house. Jones and another who didn't want to go easy.

A paramedic finally caught up to him to clean his cheek.

There was going to be so much paperwork and the debriefing was going to be epically long. His team was alive though. He closed his eyes as the tiny bandages were place on his cheek, holding the fine cut together. Adrenaline was still swimming through his system but he knew a crash was coming. A proper one had been coming for a while but this wasn't going to help.

"Okay everyone." his CO's voice rose above the scene. "If you've been cleared by the paramedics then you're heading back to base to debrief."

Jack turned to the paramedic still working on him. "I don't suppose you could tell them I have a punctured lung or something?"

"Only if you let me jab a tube between your ribs. I could use the practice."

"I'll think about it."

THE OLD-STYLE SCHOOL CLOCK ON THE LOCKER ROOM WALL TOLD Jack it was nearly three in the afternoon. He'd lost track of how many different people had debriefed him. Their prime target had shot himself, and a secondary target had been shot by someone on Dan's team. He'd heard one and hadn't been in the room for the other. He'd played up the dried blood on his face and neck to get a shower before filling out paperwork repeating what he'd already told a dozen or more people.

He needed more than a shower. Technically he hadn't been awake that long. Technically he'd even gotten enough sleep to be functional. He listened to the drip from one of the showers, ever so slightly out of sync with the tick of the clock. He'd put in a request to have that fixed. He was an east coast boy, but he'd been out west long enough to know how much water that drip was wasting. He supposed he could get a wrench and fix it himself. He'd never done it before but there was almost certainly something on YouTube. It couldn't be that hard. He supposed he should do that.

He sat, the towel still around his waist, drips of water rolling occasionally down his back. Now that he was alone, his uniform sitting in the laundry, his mind slipped to the dreams that had interrupted his sleep. He could feel the ropes, the catch of his own breath, the heat of hands on his body, remembering reality now more than any dream, breath against his skin, a voice in his ear. His vision narrowed down to just his locker in front of him.

A hand landed on his bare shoulder. It was warm and strong. So, good. He straightened his back his head dropping.

"Jack?"

Jack felt his lips move but he wasn't sure what he said. The hand squeezed his shoulder, then someone was crouched in front of him. He recognized that face. It wasn't the one he expected, or the one wanted, but the warmth of the hand on his shoulder sunk into him and held him in place.

"Jack, I need you to listen to me." Jack listened. He always listened. "You need to come up from where ever you are. Take a deep breath for me. This isn't the time and *really* not the place, so you need to come up. Deep breath."

Jack breathed deep as he was told.

"That's right. Deep breath. You know who I am?"

"Dan." Jack answered but he felt confused. Parts of his head didn't seem to be lining up with others the way they should. He needed to get up. He had things that needed to get done before... He wasn't sure before what, but before.

"I need you to try to focus on what I'm saying." Jack watched Dan's lips move and tried to focus. "You are really bottomed out right now and not in a way a cup of coffee and a nap is going to fix, and I think you know that. Nod if you agree."

Jack nodded.

"Do you have someone maybe I can call for you? Take you home?"

Jack wanted to nod. Wanted to call Isaac to come and get him. To apologize. To tell him he had nothing to apologize for. Ask forgiveness for being a coward, for running. He shook his head.

Dan rubbed his face. "Okay, I know all kinds, and I can probably make some calls and get you what you need but it's going to take a few days, which doesn't do you any good now and I don't think it's what you want." Jack twitched. He felt like he should maybe be screaming. "Fuck. I don't suppose you're in a place where you can tell me what you need 'cause I know if I do this wrong, you're likely to puke on me or go into shock or some shit like that."

An alarm went off, blaring through the building. Jack slapped his hands over his ears as adrenalin slammed into his body, slowing down time and snapping the world into sharp focus. Someone banged open the locker room door.

"Across the street, someone is shooting up the courthouse."

Jack grabbed his pants, pulling them on as he ran.

CHAPTER 30

The courthouse was technically across the street and around the corner, part of a collection of cinder block county buildings housing most of the local bureaucracy. It was chaos in front of the courthouse. People screamed as they ran. Others collapsed, weeping. Someone had pulled an alarm and there was blaring from the other side of the reinforced doors, punctuated by the occasional crack of gunfire. Court bailiffs were yanking people out through broken windows, the individuals not seeming to care about the shards of glass. Some people ran from surrounding buildings while others were locked down. There appeared to be inconsistency in active shooter response training.

Jack looked around for anyone in charge but it was chaos. He grabbed a city cop who was running past. He looked about fourteen and his eyes were wide with terror. "Cordon off this area. Everyone two blocks, no civilians within five. Grab anyone in a uniform to help." Jack knew he had no authority in the situation and the kid probably knew that as well, but he looked grateful to be told what to do.

The cop turned around. "Everyone, away from the building," he shouted. No one argued.

Gonzales jogged up, a few of his team in tow. "What the fuck is going on?" He shouted over the blare of the alarm.

"I don't know," Jack shouted back.

"Don't we have staging drills for just this sort of shit?" Dan yelled with heavy sarcasm.

There was a rattle of automatic gunfire and a crash of glass hitting the street. All three of them dove behind a gray sedan then looked up. From a broken third floor window, a yellow flag with a coiled snake was flown.

Dan put his hand to his face. There was a long string of angry mumbles. The only words Jack caught clearly were fuck and rednecks.

Someone cut the alarm. Dan stood up, fully exposing himself to anyone standing at the windows. "The tax offices are on the other fucking side of town!" he shouted in the fresh silence.

Jack yanked him back down behind a car.

"It's always fucking taxes with yahoos like that! And they're all bible thumpers. Mark 12:17 Render to Caesar what belongs to Caesar. Even Jesus knew to shut up and just pay his damn taxes like the rest of us!"

"You better believe it." Gonzales had been gifted the first name of Jesús, giving him nearly never ending opportunities for weird comebacks and random comments. "They're probably wearing polycotton blends as well."

There was the sound of another window being broken and Jack didn't feel like getting cut open twice in twelve hours. "Let's get people out of here and figure out who's in charge.

THEY HAD TAKEN THE CORONERS' OFFICE OFF LOCKDOWN ONCE IT

was determined there was no direct threat. Isaac found morbid lookie loos trying to sneak past the police barriers, while others complained about the fact that they couldn't get to their cars, and wherever it was they needed to be was far more important than everything else going on. News helicopters circled above trying to get a shot of what was now considered a hostage situation, only to be pushed back by choppers from various departments and agencies. Isaac leaned against the outer wall of a deli, already reopened, he looked up the street then back down at the message on his phone.

'Lydia had court today,' was what Amalie had sent him. He had messaged her to say he was fine before everything got all over the news. He heard the slap of flat shoes on cement as someone sprinted in his direction. He looked up to see Amalie making a mad dash for the police barricade, her face set in determined lines. He stepped out and wrapped his arms around her as tight as he could before she crashed right into the cops. She beat at his back with her fists but didn't try to pull away.

"It'll be okay. I'm sure she's fine, there are a lot of people—"

"She messaged me." Amalie's voice was rough as if she'd been screaming. She held Isaac as tight as he was holding her. "She's pinned down in a courtroom, hiding under some benches, while a bunch of armed fuckers are roaming the halls rounding people up." She shook and he could hear the anger in her voice.

"She'll be okay," Isaac said because that was what he was supposed to say. He was amazed the words came out. His throat had tightened and he could feel his own heart pounding in his chest. "She has glared worse men than those into submission."

Amalie nodded, her chin bumping into his shoulder.

"I didn't say I love you the last time we talked. It was just bye, talk to you later." Isaac's heart clenched. He tried to remember what the last thing he said to Lydia was. It was probably just a wave and I'll see you later as she walked out the door.

"Hey, this is Lydia Vega we are talking about. She's going to walk out the front door of that courthouse without a hair out of place and some asshole's head on a pike. And when she does you're going to tell her you love her and give her a kiss that'll melt down the internet."

Amalie laughed but it sounded more like a sob. Isaac grit his teeth together wanting to cry at the unfairness and waste and full on stupidity of it all.

He stood there holding Amalie, his mind running through best and worst case scenarios, trying to plan for disaster he didn't even want to contemplate. After long minutes, she pulled away and wiped at her eyes.

"Do you know how Jack is?"

Isaac shook his head. He knew, most likely, Jack was fine and if Jack hadn't wanted to hear from him on a day to day basis, then having your ex sort of boyfriend text in the middle of a crisis situation was a distraction he didn't need. That was what the rational part of his mind had been pointing out for the last hour.

"You should text him. Just 'are you okay'."

Isaac took out his phone. It was permission, or at least support.

Are you okay?

"He's probably in the middle of a briefing and there are probably rules about communication blackouts during crisis." His phone buzzed. There was a one word reply.

Yes.

FOR MOST OF THE YEAR JACK HATED THAT THE SWAT GEAR was black, but the evenings were becoming cooler, verging on crisp. He leaned against the outside of one of the vans and closed his eyes letting a few last rays of the sunset fall on his face. Someone leaned against the van next to him.

He cracked open one eye, saw it was Dan, and closed it again.

"And now we hurry up and wait," he mumbled.

"I'd be surprised if anything happens before morning," Dan replied. "You should find a corner, get some sleep."

Jack shook his head. "I'm fine."

"Yeah, that's a lie. You are running on adrenalin, coffee, more adrenalin, and stubbornness. Mostly stubbornness and when you crash from that it's going to be ugly."

Crashing was not something Jack wanted to think about. There were a lot of things he didn't want to think about, like the hazy state he'd been in before the alarm had gone off, or the three word message that was sitting on his phone, answered and not deleted like all the ones before. He didn't reply to Dan. Just focused on the last of the warm light and compartmentalizing the shit out of his brain. The pressure of the Kevlar vest and the weight of the weapons strapped to his body all helped anchor him to the moment and the job.

Dan allowed for the quiet until the sun finished dipping below a distant set of office buildings. "So, Kinky Married Complicated?"

"I don't particularly want to discuss it. Especially here and now." Jack was proud at how steady his voice was.

"Good for you, but there are good odds you are going to be within five feet of me in a live fire situation soon so I am going to talk about it." Jack pushed himself away from the van. "And if you walk away from me, I will follow and keep talking and my voice can carry."

He froze. He wasn't sure if Dan would follow through on a threat like that but he wasn't sure if he wanted to risk it.

"Good. Now whatever you had going on with Kinky Married Complicated was good for you, and *exactly* what you needed. I don't know what went wrong but you either need to try to fix that, or you need to start looking for someone else. I can give you a little help there, but I know it's a Goldilocks thing and I'm betting whatever you had was just right."

Jack sighed. He didn't want to think about it. He was tired. More tired than he should be. Over the past few months it had sunk into his bones and every hit of adrenaline made it worse. "When I was a teenager I was a barista at a coffee shop run by a coven of pagan lesbians."

Dan blinked at him. "What does that have to do with anything?"

"They were really pissed when I became a cop. Got an hour long lecture on militarization and the oppression by the patriarchy, and at the end of it Clare gave me a kiss on the head and told me I could always come back because they still liked me, and the gluten intolerant customers really liked my scones. They just texted me offering to pay for my plane ticket back to Boston."

Dan nodded. "Your head is scrambled right now but frankly you'd have to get a fuck load worse before you're not doing the job better than most."

Jack shrugged. He was tired.

Gonzales came over with three cups of coffee. "I got a joke for you." He started passing around the cups. "A white guy, a black guy, and a Mexican who are all SWAT commanders go into a court house filled with heavily armed rednecks."

"I like the set up." Dan sipped his coffee. "What's the punch line?"

"I don't know but I think we're going to find out. I just overheard some of the negotiations. Aside from the fact that these yahoos need a major refresher on constitutional law, there is no way they are coming out without us going in."

"Yippy." Jack let the warmth of the coffee slip into his hands but couldn't bring himself to drink it, even for the caffeine hit.

"And the feds want to take point on domestic terrorism grounds."

"'Cause that always works out great." Dan's sarcasm was thick. "Any idea when we might be moving?"

"If I had to guess, not until morning but who the fuck knows."

Jack sighed and chugged the coffee trying not to taste it. It was going to be a long night.

THE BRIGHT BLUE CASE OF AMALIE'S PHONE WAS STRANGELY hypnotic as she spun it over and over on Isaac's desktop. Isaac had only suggested she try to sleep or go home once. He'd done that mostly for show then they'd moved to his office. The night shift hadn't commented and one of his assistants even brought some Oreos from the vending machine. Most everyone knew someone who was either stuck in the courthouse or was camped outside of it waiting for the next move. And those were the lucky ones.

It was after midnight. The last message they had gotten from Lydia was that the battery on her phone was going, and that she loved them. Amalie cried for twenty minutes, cussing the whole time, while Isaac kept up the platitudes. He stared at his own phone, not expecting a message but quietly hoping for one. It hadn't taken long for the world to know what was going on. People had flooded social media with reports almost as soon as the first shots were fired. There were people stuck in offices and closets still posting updates. He'd sent quick messages to his parents and siblings that he was fine. His sister sent him a link to a video 'manifesto' declaring the evils of the federal government and how everything was all one big conspiracy. Isaac didn't watch, only wondered if someone had pointed out that the idiots had stormed a bunch of county offices not federal ones.

"Do you think they'll need to send someone in?" Amalie's

voice was flat and she didn't look up from spinning her phone around and around.

"I don't know. But they're trained to do stuff like that." Isaac had little doubt that he'd be signing more death certificates by the end. It wasn't like these were some yahoos on a ranch in the middle of nowhere and could be waited out. No one in any organization or branch of government could afford to let this one drag. Every piece of evidence left in the building now had a tainted chain of custody. Every jury was now compromised. And if any one of those nuts had any computer skills they could access huge amounts of private data.

He stared at his own phone. He hadn't been expecting that one word reply from Jack and until it had arrived he didn't realize how grateful he was for it. If Jack was stuck inside or worse, with the ends between them still ragged, Isaac wasn't sure how he'd be coping.

The clock on his desk flipped over to one.

"You should try to sleep," he said.

"I know."

"DID YOU SLEEP AT ALL?" DAN ASKED.

The early morning sun was pushing its way through the white plastic walls of one of the staging area tents, painting it slightly pink. Jack had sat down in one of the folding chairs in the middle of the night. He was pretty sure he hadn't slept but he didn't think he'd been properly awake either.

"Did you?" he asked in return.

"Grabbed a couple of hours on a stretcher. I think I feel worse for it."

He pushed himself to his feet and nearly fell as the muscles in his back and legs protested the extended lack of movement without accompanying rest. "Fuck."

"Think anyone tried just saying please? Maybe they'll come out nicely."

He bent back and felt something in his lower back pop. "I can do this," Jack said mostly to himself. "Another cup of coffee, a little adrenalin."

"That how you got through combat? Coffee and adrenalin?"

Jack froze mid-stretch. "What?"

"You never talk about it but rumor is you were special forces or something badass."

Jack didn't move. He wanted to laugh. He knew that rumor was going around but there was an unwritten rule that you don't bring up the military with the ex-military guys, unless they bring it up first. Some of them had better runs than others and you didn't want an offhand question to turn into an hour-long story about mass graves that you had no polite way of extracting yourself from.

The tent flap was pulled aside, the heavy plastic slapping against itself. "Hey, everyone to the briefing tent," some guy in an FBI windbreaker said.

Dan looked at him. "Coffee and adrenalin."

PROVING THAT ONLY COPS ON TV GOT COOL TOYS, THE BRIEFING tent was lined with blueprints and hand drawn maps instead of some 3D projector system. The FBI counter terrorism agent who had taken over was pointing to one of the large hand drawn maps. It was covered with driver's license photos. "We lost contact with most of these people during the night as their phone batteries ran out, but before that we were able to gain a pretty clear image as to patterns of movement, numbers, and armaments. And they are heavily armed. They are also unwilling to engage in any reasonable negotiation. Due to the heroic work of one of the IT support staff we now have access to the interior security cameras."

For a brief second Jack felt the occupants of the tent relax.

"Unfortunately, many of the cameras have been blacked out or destroyed. Not all, but at least by knowing where they aren't we can get a better idea of where they are. What we do know for sure is that hostages are being kept in the 2nd floor cafeteria. Everyone else in the building has spent the night hiding. They are tired, hungry, and probably have to pee so we're going to go in and get them out."

Jack was sure that was supposed to be some sort of rallying speech but frankly he was tired, hungry, and had to pee. The rest of the briefing became a list of who was going where. Some borrowed special ops teams were going to drop in from helicopters onto the roof. A dozen or so snipers were going to do their thing. The feds were going to go through the front and side doors, which would look great on the news. And county SWAT got to sneak in through maintenance doors in the underground parking lot.

Go County.

"Okay everyone, suit up."

Jack turned to his team. "You heard the man. Let's go be heroes." There were no cheers, but everyone headed to the equipment vans to get dressed and armed. Dan fell into step beside him.

"How are you feeling about this plan?" Jack asked quietly.

"Do your pagan lesbian coffee shop friends need a waiter, busboy maybe?"

"Yeah, that's about how I'm feeling."

THE BUZZ OF HIS PHONE ON THE METAL DESK JOLTED ISAAC AWAKE. He'd managed to fall asleep in his office chair at some point. He fumbled it around in his hands squinting at the screen that seemed far too bright. There was one text message.

You have nothing to apologize for. You did nothing wrong. All on me. I'm sorry. Thank you.

"What is it?" Amalie asked from her place in the office guest chair, her voice anxious.

"It's from Jack. I think somethings going to happen."

JACK WAS PRESSED SHOULDER TO SHOULDER WITH DAN AND Gonzales as they crept through a small maintenance hall originally designed for utility access. In theory, they would get to the end of the hall then the teams would split up and start going room by room clearing everyone out. Even with them, and the feds, it was a six-story building with numerous little offices and closets to rummage through. Before going in Jack had sent one simple text and felt lighter for it.

The adrenaline had been slow dripping into his system, just enough to keep him standing, but he'd been waiting for the big hit. He wondered if this is what junkies felt like the second before the drugs hit their brain. Fear, hope, hate, bracing for the inevitable. But like drugs, the more you took the less it worked. Jack took a breath. One more solid hit to get through this. His hands tightened around his weapon. If the take down of Detective Jones had been a cluster fuck, this was going to be a complete disaster. There was no way everyone in the building was getting out alive. His team and the civilians he encountered had to be his priority. Anyone after that was a bonus.

The Go signal came over the radio and one more flash of chemicals hit his overtired brain, and once again he was clear and focused. The briefing told him these lower halls were probably currently clear. They didn't have enough people to patrol so large a building but that didn't mean they hadn't been down there earlier and left some presents. There was an urge to move fast, to simply run through the building like a video game level but that was a good way to get blown to bits. Quietly they crept into the wide basement hall. His team went left. Dan's went right. Gonzales spread out their goal to provide a human chain to lead civilians out of the building to safety.

There were booms from flash bangs and smoke bombs, and the rattle of automatic weapons fire but it was muffled and distant coming from above. They crept on carefully opening closets and storage rooms.

They found their first civilian in a storage closet. An older man in maintenance overalls. He tossed them a key ring and an all access swipe card before being gladly shown the way out.

They found their first body around the corner from that. A bailiff with his weapon drawn. The wall behind him was pock-marked in a dozen places. He cast a quick glance to a few of the younger members of his team. SWAT didn't actually deal with many dead bodies. Everyone had solid masks of calm and focus and that was as much as Jack could ask for in the moment.

They cleared out the floor with no more encounters, but there were still bursts of weapons fire in the distance.

"Sub-basement clear," he radioed in.

"Copy. Proceed up."

"Copy."

There was another body in the stairwell. No blood, but twisted around. Jack radioed in the location and pushed on.

From there it did start looking like a video game level. There were half built barricades of tables and chairs. An office where a few bailiffs had put up a fight and failed. Reports were coming over the radio that the suspects had scattered into the rabbit warren of 80's government architecture. They were finding more survivors though. Ones who hid through the night, texting in their locations and messages of love to their families.

Someone back at the staging area was checking them off a list of missing and unaccounted for.

Jack knocked on the double doors to Courtroom B-27. "SWAT, coming in," he yelled out. He'd been told to expect a half dozen people, including a bailiff who was still armed. He slowly pushed the door open not wanting to spook someone overtired and undertrained who might be in there. The room was dark and he turned on a flashlight. "SWAT," he said again.

There was movement and he turned his weapon toward it. A middle-aged man, a judge by the look of the robes, stood from behind his desk. The bailiff, his weapon drawn but lowered stood next to him.

"Turning on the lights," someone said behind him and the fluorescents thrummed to life.

The occupants blinked in the light.

"Hey. SWAT boy." Jack turned to the exhausted sounding voice.

"Ms. Vega." She smiled at him while brushing the dust from her suit. "Anyone injured?"

"We're all fine, Jack, thank you." Time slowed and shifted as Jack turned toward the speaker who had put an oily sheen on the polite words. Still handcuffed but perfectly dressed, Hugh Lancing smiled at him.

No. Jack's pulse sped up and his vision narrowed. He felt his finger move like someone else was controlling him. It slid slowly down, following the curve of the trigger. Maybe not so slowly, as it happened between one breath and the next but that space felt nearly infinite. Lancing's smile broadened.

The concussing crack of a shotgun came from down the hall and everyone hit the floor again.

Time returned to normal. It took a whole two minutes to neutralize the man with the shotgun before the occupants of courtroom B-27 were ushered down the hall and hopefully out of the building. From there they moved to courtroom B-25 then

B-23. Room after room, hall after hall, they worked up the building while others worked down. There were bodies, survivors, some who resisted, and some who surrendered. Jack tried to forget the moments as they passed, not wanting them burned into his memory. He knew it would be futile but he could try. At one point, he felt blood on his cheek. He wasn't sure if it was fresh or if he'd reopen the cut from the botched Jones arrest.

They crossed over with the fed teams and were double checking floor five when the all clear came in and the orders to report back. One of his men sat down hard on a bench. "Nope." He pulled the young man up by his arm. "Keep moving. You sit down for more than twenty seconds and you're not getting back up, so let's get somewhere where we can collapse first."

The fed who had briefed them, in his nice clean FBI windbreaker, was the one to greet them as they stepped out into the offensively bright afternoon sun. The warmth of it made him aware of how gritty his face and eyes felt. Sweat was drying on his body and his mouth tasted like he was waking up from a bad fever.

"Good work everyone; we'll need to debrief you—"

"No." Gonzales stepped forward just as Jack contemplated hitting the agent. "The only members of County SWAT who have properly slept in the last 36 hours, are the ones who are still in the hospital from the cluster fuck that was our operation *two* nights ago. These men, all these men, are going home, sleeping for twelve hours, getting some breakfast and then, *if* they're feeling up to it, you will be allowed to debrief them, and if you try to stop us from that plan I will let Jack hit you and everyone here will swear under oath you walked into a wall."

"So spake Jesus," Dan said leaving the agent to blink in confusion as County SWAT stumbled past.

CHAPTER 31

The message from Lydia had arrived from someone else's phone. It was just a quick one. She was safe, she was fine. Amalie had cried. Isaac cried as well, not aware until that moment how much he'd been holding in. Lydia had been in his life as long as Amalie and while their relationship would never be romantic or physical, he'd spent the night contemplating how large her place in his life was.

Her message had come in hours earlier. Isaac managed to use his ID to get closer to where the medics were treating the injured, and the survivors were being interviewed. The press was still hovering around the barriers eager to shove a camera in the face of the first person to get out.

Amalie was leaning against a light pole, drumming her nails on the rough metal. Every thirty seconds or so she would check her phone, then go back to drumming her fingers.

"She's fine, you know she's fine. She just has to go through the bureaucracy."

"She almost dies, and they're making her do paperwork."

Every so often a tent flap would open and a haggard looking individual would step out, blinking in the sunlight. Half the time they were wrapped in a Red Cross emergency blanket and clutching a paper cup of weak coffee. Every lawyer Isaac had ever met lived off gallons of coffee. Once the adrenaline was done draining out of peoples' systems the caffeine withdrawal headaches were going to be ugly.

The tent opened again and Lydia stepped out. Her suit was dusty, and her makeup smudged, but her back was straight and there wasn't a hair out of place. Amalie ran to her and the kiss would have melted the internet if anyone nearby had cared enough to lift up their phones.

Isaac hugged her next, holding her tight. She squeezed him right back. "Let's get you home."

"Yeah." He let her go but she put a hand back on his arm.

"Wait. Hold on." She squeezed her eyes shut and tilted her head back making the 'trying really hard to remember something important' face. "How does your SWAT boy know Hugh Lancing?"

"What?" It was a complete non-sequitur to the situation and his brain stalled.

"I'm prosecuting this asshole called Hugh Lancing."

"I've encountered him. He's an asshole. I heard he'd gotten arrested but I didn't hear for what."

"Pushing a metric shit-load of E through town. We were in a pretrial hearing when shit went down. Then this morning SWAT boy comes through the door looking like a big damn hero, then Lancing calls him by name and I swear to god I saw his finger get really close to the trigger on that gun of his."

Shit. Some things clicked into place.

"When was he arrested?"

"Few months back. Picked him up at some nasty leather bar."

"Any idea if Jack was part of the arresting team?"

Lydia shrugged. "Maybe. They sent in SWAT."

Isaac rubbed his face as things clicked into place. Jack goes in to help arrest someone, Lancing recognizes him, Jack freaks out, Isaac assumes it was something he did, and there they were three months later, not talking and miserable.

"Fuck," he muttered into his own hands feeling like both an idiot and an asshole for not making more of an effort to confront Jack.

"Go get your boy," Amalie said patting his arm. "I'll drive Lydia home, you get your own car."

"He's not my—"

"Go. Find. Jack." Her look was hard and bore no argument.

"I'll go find Jack."

๛

No one at the Sheriffs' Office asked questions when Isaac flashed his ID and asked for directions towards where SWAT members might be. They all looked exhausted. He knew he could text Jack and ask where he was but it didn't seem right. They needed to talk face to face without either of them running. He saw a few men in SWAT t-shirts who looked even worse. They didn't ask what he wanted either, just pointed him to the locker room. He knocked softly before stepping in. He didn't see Jack right off, so began walking down the rows of lockers. At the third one he saw Jack slumped on a bench a large man standing next to him, hand on his shoulder.

"Jack?"

Jack's head snapped up. There were dark rings under his eyes and a cut on his cheek. He looked thinner and drawn. He didn't say anything.

"Are you KMC?" The large man asked.

"Who?"

"Kinky Married Complicated."

Isaac laughed in exhaustion though it wasn't funny. "Yeah. I guess that's me."

"He's not fine," the man said.

"I'm fine," Jack mumbled.

"He hasn't slept in 36 hours."

"I'm fine."

"He's been in *two* active shooter situations with fatalities in that time."

"I'm fine."

"And he's been going downhill the last three months. Under eating, over exercising."

"I'm fine." Jack dragged out the last word.

Isaac's stomach twisted in guilt. He should have gone after Jack, should have followed up, asked for a real explanation instead of making assumptions about the silence, and running away like the coward he was.

"Take him home, fix whatever went wrong. Put him back together."

"I'm—" Jack started again.

"I talked to Lydia," Isaac cut off Jack. "She told me about... stuff. I get what... I *think* I get what happened."

Jack slumped further into himself.

"Let me take you home. If nothing else, you're not fit to drive." He held out his hand and held his breath. "Please."

Jack stared at it for a long time, then slowly and stiffly, like an old man, rose to his feet.

JACK WAS ASLEEP ALMOST AS SOON AS HIS SEATBELT WAS CLICKED into place and slept all the way back to the house. Isaac drove carefully, short on sleep himself, though not to the same extent. It occurred to him on the way, that he didn't know where Jack's apartment was. Not that he would have taken Jack there but it felt like one more oversight on his part.

"Jack," he said softly not wanting to jolt him awake when he could still be on a hair trigger. He'd signed off on bodies from a botched arrest of a dirty officer from a couple of nights before. The debrief must have run into the courthouse mess if Jack was involved in that.

"Jack, time to wake up." He settled his hand onto Jack's shoulder. "Jack."

Jack snapped awake clawing at his seatbelt.

"It's okay, it's okay. We're home. There is a shower and a bed waiting for you. It's okay." Isaac slowly reached over and unclipped Jack's seatbelt before rushing around the car, barely keeping Jack from falling out.

Inside, Amalie was sitting on the couch, Lydia stretched out with her head in her lap. "We didn't make it upstairs," Amalie said in a loud whisper. "Murrcat peed in the kitchen. He's mad at us. Hi, Jack."

"Hi." He gave a small wave.

"I'm going to take him to bed."

"Good idea."

If Jack had any objection to being talked about instead of to, he didn't voice them. He didn't comment as Isaac led him to the extra bedroom, took off his shoes and his clothes, and helped him into bed.

"You're staying?" he did ask as Isaac began to undress.

"I'm not leaving you alone and I could use some sleep myself."

Jack nodded and was asleep before Isaac even finished undressing.

It hadn't been more than a few hours when Jack opened his eyes. He wanted to be asleep. He *needed* to be asleep. Instead his head churned, sorting the memories of the last two days, twisting and meshing them, trying to fill in gaps. He prayed to his mother's god and Clare's goddess for sleep, but it refused to come. A small sob of exhaustion pushed its way from his lips. Isaac stirred and he tried to fight back any more sounds, but failed.

Isaac opened his eyes full of too much kindness and Jack broke. The last two days, the last three months, his whole life came out in choking sobs. He tried to curl up, tried to turn away but Isaac held him close and tight. He was such a coward and such a fraud. He wasn't sure how long he cried. Every time he managed to force it back, he'd hear his father's voice in his head or feel Lancing's eyes on his body. He pictured himself pulling the trigger like the coward he was. The whole time Isaac held him, making little soothing noises which made it worse.

When his head was pounding and his eyes felt like they were on fire, he managed to choke out three words. "I'm a coward."

"No, you're not."

He shook his head. Isaac didn't understand. "I almost killed someone. Someone I was supposed to be trying to save."

"Almost is the key word there. Almost. There is a vast difference between did and almost. You came out of one bad situation and went into another. You led your team. You saved people. You took your training and experience and made good use of it."

"I was never in combat," Jack confessed, his head was throbbing but his mind felt numb, flayed down past any emotional nerves. "Outside of basic I was never even trained for it. People see army on my resume and a bunch of acronyms they don't understand, and they look at my body and make assumptions. I've never lied. Never confirmed but I don't correct. And I should but—" Jack tried to take a deep breath but it was ragged and left him coughing.

"It's okay, slow easy breath."

There were things he didn't like to talk about, things no one ever talked about. But someone needed to know. Someone needed to understand, if they could.

"My father is head librarian at one of the largest libraries in the country. I could recite the better part of the LCC by the third grade. My mother is from... money. Blue blood. She does lots of volunteer work. Friends of the opera, veterans support fundraising, historical building preservation. Stuff like that." Jack stared at a point over Isaac's shoulder, unable to meet his eyes. "I'm eight inches taller than my dad. Seven taller than my brother, a solid foot taller than my sister, and my eyes aren't the color they should be." Isaac nodded and Jack was sure he understood. "My sister went to Yale; my brother went to Harvard. I worked at a coffee shop, had a 3.8 GPA, and only 14 hundred on my SATs. I could have gotten into perfectly good state schools, but if you weren't going ivy league..." Jack had fought with his school counselor over that as she shoved college applications at him. "Year after high school I made coffee and hung out with the coven, went to concerts and protests. Lost my virginity against a tree at a Mayday bonfire. That was fun."

"Sounds like it."

Jack could still remember the way the bark had scraped against his back as the girl wrapped her legs around him.

"I was happy, I think, that year. I think that was the last time I was happy. After a year, my *father* came into the shop and we had a fight. Nineteen years of passive aggressive bullshit turned into a screaming match. He told me what I was good for, where I probably came from, and exactly where I should go."

It had been late and Jack had been closing up, the shop empty. Someone who popped their head in hoping for a coffee called the police, so sure the screaming was going to turn violent.

"I spent the next few days just wandering around town, thinking, then stumbled into a recruiting office. Do something, be something, do something with this." He gestured vaguely at his body. Isaac stroked his head. "After basic you can apply to go into extra training, medical, engineering, whatever. I tried to get into special forces, airborne, something like that, except they make you take this test called ASVAB and something pinged on that test, and then they found out I could type 98 words a minute and—"

"You didn't get into special forces."

Jack had been sure there was an error when he was handed his assignment for further training. It made no sense to him. He'd been the second-best shot, never needed to be disciplined, excelled at all the physical tests and requirements. "I had a full four-star general tell me that he could walk down the street and find ten people willing to shoot at other people, but only one in a thousand that could handle the personnel database, which is stupid because, yes it's a little counterintuitive but not *that* hard, especially up against the Table of Organization and Equipment. My safe word is ROWPU because the first time I was asked I'd just spent three days dealing with a Reverse Osmosis Water Purification Unit that had been shipped to a training unit outside of Seattle instead of a support unit in Afghanistan, and it was the first thing that popped into my head."

"It is one of the more interesting ones I've encountered." Isaac's voice was light but soft. "Most people just use Red or something like that."

Jack shrugged. He'd never really used it. "When I got out of the army, I swore I'd never do that much paperwork again. I applied to the force, then SWAT. I figured I could be useful there. I didn't think I'd make commander. Didn't even really try. I just sort of floated up into it. I'm not a leader, I'm..."

"That's not true. Not in the slightest." Isaac's words were forceful enough to startle Jack.

"A leader wouldn't have frozen, I froze, wouldn't have even—"

"No." Isaac cut him off. "You are a leader and a good one. Bad people put you into a bad situation. You think combat experience would have made yesterday easier? I can bury you in neural science research on what any stressful situation can do to the brain, in both the long and short term. Hugh being there was bad luck."

"I thought about shooting him," Jack confessed.

"And a lesser man might have, but you are not a lesser man."

"He could still talk."

"And? He likes fucking with people's heads. *That's* what he gets off on." Isaac's voice was full of enough venom to catch Jack off guard. "And not to bruise your ego, but there are federal judges on the roll at the Windsor Club. If Hugh wanted to drop names you'd be at the bottom of the list." Jack nodded even if he still felt rattled right down to his teeth.

"I still feel like a fraud." It wasn't an exaggeration. It was possibly the truest fact in his life.

Isaac gave the longest sigh Jack had ever heard. "Do you know why I work on dead people instead of live ones?" Isaac asked.

"No."

"Because I couldn't handle not being a god."

Jack looked at him not sure what to say.

"You want to talk about feeling like a fraud? My parents are doctors, my grandparents are doctors, my siblings are doctors. I cut up dead people. In med school you get lectures about how you won't be able to save everyone. There will always be people who are too sick or too injured or just don't want to be saved, and they will die. And we all nod our heads and say we understand, but somewhere in the back of our minds we all think that we're going to be different. We're going to be the special one who saves everyone. And I lost a few while I was training, mostly old people with long lives, junkies who ODed for the fifth time, homeless who just died. People I could mentally brush aside, but there was the first night I flew solo, but I shouldn't have had to."

Isaac looked away from Jack focusing instead on a blank patch of wall.

"It was four hours into shift and the senior doctor hadn't shown up, no one could get a hold of him. Middle of the night, shithole of an ER, just interns and trainees begging the nurses to tell us what to do. We got told there was a patient coming in with a collapsed lung, a child. Also, some victims of a drive-by shooting, but we weren't told they were part of the same incident. I took the collapsed lung, which isn't really that hard. Yes, it's bad but survivable if you're quick. Got the kid on the table, nine maybe, nurses cut off his shirt and it wasn't a collapsed lung it was a punctured lung. Little tiny hole, no exit wound, no one told me it might have been a bullet. It looked like he was running with a sharp pencil and tripped and I'd seen that before. Then—" Isaac's voice cracked and he rolled away from Jack. "Fuck. It all went to hell. It was a bullet, tiny, slow, already gone through a wall, it ricocheted into his abdomen and—"

Isaac clenched his teeth and looked like he was trying not to cry. Jack reached out and took his hand. It was several seconds before Isaac gave it a squeeze.

"I screamed for another doctor," he continued, his voice hardly more than a whisper. "I needed help and no one came. When it was all over I stumbled into this little utility closet, got sick in the sink. This orderly in his sixties came in and slapped me, yelled for five minutes in some language I didn't recognize, slapped me again, then literally threw me back out onto the floor just in time to watch one patient pull a knife on another. Had a... crisis after that. I let it affect every aspect of who I was and I turned into, to be blunt, a complete asshole for a while. I was with a man called Ricky at the time. I drove him away. Drove him into the arms of—"

Isaac pinched his lips closed and Jack was willing to guess a name.

"Someone not good. I pushed away my family. I nearly drove Amalie away but she is stubborn as hell. I realized somewhere in the middle of being a complete asshole to everyone who cared for me that you can't disappoint the dead. You can't fail them, at least not to the same extent you can fail the living. Want to talk about being a coward? I ran to the dead because I was afraid I'd have to face my own weaknesses if I had to deal with the living. Still am. And you better believe my mother finds some way to drop it into conversation every fucking chance she gets. I mean mostly we're on good terms but—"

"Parents suck sometimes."

"They do."

Jack gave a gentle tug on Isaac's hand and he rolled back close. Jack was aware that he must smell but he didn't want to move from Isaac's warmth.

"I'm thinking about quitting the force." The words spilled out. Jack had joked about it, and thought about it a lot, but that was the first time he'd said those exact words out loud. "I was happy, before. Making coffee and scones and going to bonfires. I don't know if it was a useful life but I remember being happy."

Isaac kissed him on the head. "You can do that if you want. You should be happy. I would miss you if you left town." He pulled away and looked at Isaac. His face was open and honest. "I've been missing you, but I'll support what you think you need to do for you. For what it's worth, you are good at your job even if you're not feeling it right now. Also, you shouldn't make major life decisions while exhausted and in the middle of an emotional crisis. Just speaking from experience here."

Jack pressed his face to Isaac's chest, feeling tears and emotions threaten to overwhelm him again. "I should have told you. I should have just—"

"Yes, you should have. And I should have come after you. I shouldn't have made assumptions. I should have insisted on answers. We both messed up. Though as the more experienced member of this relationship, I fucked up more."

"Can we put it back together?" he didn't want to sound like he was pleading but all he wanted was to be back in Isaac's life where he had felt peaceful and happy and cared for. He wasn't sure if he deserved it but he wanted it more than anything.

"Absolutely." Isaac replied instantly and before he could say anything Isaac kissed him. It was soft, hardly more than a brush of lips, but it shook him to the core and the last of the madness of the previous days fell away.

"Maybe Coffea Contenuto could open a west coast branch," Isaac suggested.

Jack would have smiled if he wasn't so exhausted. He still had his gluten free orange scone recipe memorized and could make a good cup of coffee. Plus, fewer people shooting at him. In theory, at least. "I can still roast beans. Not that hard."

"That's good to know. You should sleep first. We both need to sleep."

Jack nodded. His head was full but quieter. "Okay."

"I might need to get up later but I'll come back. I Promise."

※

ISAAC WAITED UNTIL JACK WAS DEEP INTO SLEEP BEFORE SLIDING from his bed. The truth was he was hungry and thirsty, and there was at least one slice of cold, probably rock hard pizza in the fridge calling his name.

He was halfway through it when Amalie came into the kitchen. "I was going to have that."

He handed over the rest of the slice without comment. "How's Lydia?"

"Asleep. A bit messed up." She took a bite of the pizza and chewed it slowly. "How's Jack?"

"Asleep. A bit messed up." Amalie just nodded.

"Staying?"

"I think so."

She nodded again. He poured himself a half cup of the cold coffee in the pot. It wasn't enough to wake him up but it gave him something to do with his hands. Amalie finished her pizza then slowly leaned into his shoulder. He pulled her into a hug and they stood like that for a long time. At some point Murrcat twisted around their ankles but wandered off when he realized he wouldn't be getting attention soon.

"We should get a bigger bed," she finally said, not breaking the hug.

"How big?" He was too tired to question such a random sounding comment.

"Big enough for four."

"Really?" There had never been a lot of co-sleeping between the three of them except in cases of exhaustion or occasional drunkenness.

"Not for every night but for these kinds, when we all need to be close to each other."

Isaac pictured it. Lydia and Jack on opposite sides. He and Amalie in the middle. Everyone close to the people they cared for. Able to know they were safe, even in sleep. "I think that's a good idea."

⚜

JACK WOKE UP AGAIN WHEN ISAAC SLIPPED BACK INTO BED. HIS mind was starting to smooth out, and he was pretty sure he'd be able to get back to sleep without crying his eyes out again. He'd decided on something first.

"I want to tell someone," he whispered.

"Okay." Isaac didn't even pause.

"Not everyone. I'm not ready for that. Not yet. Dan probably. I'm sure he's worked it out already. The coven. My sister, maybe. Just a few people, just in case. I feel like there are too many mes in my head some days and—"

Isaac kissed him. This time it was deep and lingered. It warmed him and the feeling settled into his chest where it felt like it always belonged. "You do what you need to do for you, and I will support you. *We* will support you. I'm not going anywhere. None of us are."

This time it was Jack who started the kiss knowing that nothing had ever felt this right and never wanted to lose it again.

ABOUT THE AUTHOR

Ada Maria Soto is a Mexican/American expat living in the South Pacific. She's a veteran of the theatre and film business as well as all the lousy jobs that come with two liberal arts degrees. A psychologist once told her she has a fantasy prone personality, but since she's trying to be a writer that's not a bad thing. She is a fan of rugby, cricket, and baseball, who loves to cook, knit, and poke around her garden.

You can find her online at http://adamariasoto.com/ and on most social media platforms.

To keep updated on current releases and free stories join her mailing list.

Her previous, award winning work, can be found on most online book sellers.

Manufactured by Amazon.ca
Bolton, ON